To: Riya,

Enjoy

# Approaching the Bench

# Approaching the Bench

Shamicka C. Toney

ABSOLUTE AUTHOR PUBLISHING HOUSE

**Publisher:** Absolute Author Publishing House

**Project Editor:** THPeditingServc

US Copyright Case Number: TXu 2-341-244

PAPERBACK ISBN: 978-1-64953-642-6

EBOOK ISBN: 978-1-64953-643-3

PRINTED IN THE UNITED STATES OF AMERICA

# Table of Contents


Praise for Approaching the Bench ........ vii

Special Thanks ........ viii

Chapter 1 In a Word – Sealed ........ 1

Chapter 2 In a Word – Bombshell ........ 10

Chapter 3 In a Word – Sad ........ 18

Chapter 4 In a Word – Meeting ........ 27

Chapter 5 In a Word – Sting ........ 32

Chapter 6 In a Word – Gratitude ........ 38

Chapter 7 In a Word – Imperfect ........ 45

Chapter 8 In a Word – Grooving ........ 54

Chapter 9 In a Word – Unmentionables ........ 59

Chapter 10 In a Word – Reflections ........ 64

Chapter 11 In a Word – Haunted ........ 75

Chapter 12 In a Word – Issues ........ 83

Chapter 13 In a Word – Ambush ........ 90

Chapter 14 In a Word – Distracted ........ 101

Chapter 15 In a Word – Finally ........ 108

Chapter 16 In a Word – Exhales ........ 114

Chapter 17 In a Word – Suspicions ........ 123

Chapter 18 In a Word – Thirty-Six ........ 130

Chapter 19 In a Word – Unexpected ........ 136

Chapter 20 In a Word – Reappeared ........ 141

Chapter 21 In a Word – Chilling ........ 147

Chapter 22 In a Word – Searching .......... 155
Chapter 23 In a Word – Anticipation .......... 159
Chapter 24 In a Word – Disbelief .......... 162
Chapter 25 In a Word – Breakdown .......... 172
Chapter 26 In a Word – Cagey .......... 179
Chapter 27 In a Word – Recount .......... 186
Chapter 28 In a Word – Courage .......... 194
Chapter 29 In a Word – Gathering .......... 202
Chapter 30 In a Word – Emotions .......... 208
Chapter 31 In a Word – Callous .......... 213
Chapter 32 In a Word – Weighty .......... 220
Chapter 33 In a Word – Broken .......... 227
Chapter 34 In a Word – Unwind .......... 233
Chapter 35 In a Word – Reconcile .......... 244
Chapter 36 In a Word – Cupcakes .......... 253
Chapter 37 In a Word – Simmering .......... 262
Chapter 38 In a Word – Connections .......... 269
Chapter 39 In a Word – Coaxed .......... 273
Chapter 40 In a Word – Realizations .......... 280
Chapter 41 In a Word – Torn .......... 287
Chapter 42 In a Word – Breather .......... 297
Chapter 43 In a Word – Exhale .......... 306
Chapter 44 In a Word – Confession .......... 310
Chapter 45 In a Word – Jarring .......... 316
Chapter 46 In a Word – Speechless .......... 322
Chapter 47 In a Word – Partners .......... 330
About the Author .......... 344

# Praise for Approaching the Bench

**Brilliant!** Shamicka has written another beautiful book that is entertaining, engaging, and well worth the read. The story has enough subplots that keep the reader wanting more. The twists and turns were great and to not see things coming was a major plus! I loved finding out new things about the characters and the plot as I read on.

**- Kemone Brown, Tamarind Hill Press, United Kingdom**

**Excellent writer!** Shamicka has a very keen interest in keeping the reader hooked from chapter to chapter. From the beginning, the stakes felt high and really drew me in. This beautiful novel took me on a journey. It was adventurous and fun and I experienced growth. This is exactly what a good manuscript should do! Well done!

**- Jacob Cyrus, South Africa**

**Captivating!** This novel is a sequel to *Discovering the Covering* and is as mesmerizing as the first. It is a great read written in a familiar vernacular that uplifts, educates and makes you laugh out loud. This is a page-turning family drama. Have another book ready, because you will devour this one quickly! This is a story about family, but more about the infusion and abundance of love that makes this family work.

**- Frances W., Harrisburg, PA USA**

# Special Thanks:

**To God:**

THANK YOU FOR my life and the experiences you've allowed – both good and bad. These have provided a perspective, insight, humility and depth that I would not otherwise have. Thank you for giving me these characters and allowing them to be blessings to others. Thank you for allowing me to stay focused and continue writing, no matter how much was going on, and for giving me the strength to hit send when fear of rejection and failure trickled in. I am so excited for the blessings that are sure to come from this story.

**To Meech, Jymil, Tyler, and Deshon:**

THANK YOU, AGAIN for giving me the space and time to develop these amazing characters and to tell their stories. Your sacrifice has allowed me to create something truly special! I love you so much!

**To my parents, siblings, friends and family:**

THANK YOU FOR your unending support and encouragement. Your belief in, and continued excitement about this sequel, helped make this a reality. This is for you!

**To Kingsley Okechukwu**

YOUR TOUGH LOVE and gentle insistence that I write harder and better helped me deliver another amazing story!

# Meet the Characters

## Amia Wilford

Spouse: Darren

Father: Ramon

Mother: Elaine

Younger Brother: Jamari

Younger Brother: Shamir

Younger Sister: Bria

Younger Sister: Jordyn

## Darren Wilford

Spouse: Amia

Father: Marshon

Adoptive Father: Gary

Adoptive Mother: Mable

Younger Sister: Camille

Younger Sister: Adrienne

I pray you enjoy reading my novel as much as I enjoyed writing it.

- Shamicka

# Chapter 1

## *In a Word* – Sealed

"Babe, please don't ask me anymore. I get what you're trying to do, but I'm not interested." With that, he extracted the grey, unopened envelope from her hands, dropping it unceremoniously on the island.

"Darren, you two haven't spoken in almost thirty years. Maybe it's—"

"No," he said flatly, swallowing hard while shaking his head.

"Amia, could you plea—"

"Mom," yelled Daniel, speeding into their spacious, airy kitchen.

“Christina took my baseball cap and she won’t give it baaaack,” he wailed, frustrated that his first two calls for parental intervention had gone unanswered.

“Bean,” Darren called. His voice was a gentle mixture of seriousness and aggravation because they were having to address her touching Daniel’s belongings yet again. Although truth be told, there was an underlying relief in his voice. Darren wanted no part of this conversation that had been recurring more frequently over the last few months.

The twelve-year-old impatiently wrung his hands more and more with every passing second. His behavior told Amia and Darren exactly which one had been touched. The last time Christina took the prized orange striped cap, she cut a hole in it so her baby doll’s puffy ponytail could be pulled through the top. It had taken one of Grandma Mable’s needlepoint miracles to fix it.

“Dad. Make her give me my hat back, please,” he urged while imploring Darren off of the bar stool.

“Alright, Champ. I’ll go talk to her,” he replied, wiping Daniel’s teary face.

As he turned to his lovely wife to let her know he’d be back shortly, their seven-year-old cutie pie skipped into the kitchen happily. Her thick coiled hair was poking out of several slits cut into—an orange-striped baseball cap.

“Christina Renee,” Amia said so loudly that their daughter dropped the other orange striped item she’d been hiding behind her back. The startled youngster immediately burst into tears. Daniel knelt to pick up the dropped article, relieved to find that his prized possession hadn't been the one subjected to the budding fashion designer's latest scissor-inspired idea.

She scooped up their sobbing daughter, kissed her, and apologized for yelling. Moments later, Darren lovingly lifted Christina out of Amia's arms, embracing them both while motioning the irritated big brother to join them.

"So, what do you call this design?" asked Amia.

She slightly lifted her adorable head off of her father's shoulder. Slow, soft descriptions of the newest creation began spilling from her lips.

"Oh no, no, no," Amia countered playfully. "A fashionista must be excited about her creations," she added with a hint of faux French, much to the kids' amusement. Amia continued butchering the world's most romantic language.

"A fashionista wants the entire world to be excited about the magic she has created," she added, now mixing choppy words and overly exaggerated arm movements. "No, Ma'am... This will not do." After a few more moments of accent-destroying mayhem, Amia continued, "Now, Bean... You must tell us all about this majestic creation."

Darren kissed their daughter and tousled their eldest's curly hair. He gestured to Daniel to grab a seat while the now sparkly-eyed youngster explained the inspiration behind her newest piece created from the orange and white cap she'd convinced Pop Ramon and Grandma Elaine to get for her. Darren listened attentively, as he wrapped his arm around Amia's waist and nibbled at her shoulder, still smiling at his wife's playfulness.

The conclusion of Christina's description was greeted by supportive applause. The pair then took the moment to remind their daughter that she is not to touch her big brother's things without his permission.

"Bean," Amia began searching for the words that would be best suited for a second grader. "You know this hat is very special to Danny, that's why you wanted one just like his, right?" The youngster nodded remorsefully, crocodile tears beginning to well.

"You don't have to cry," Amia soothed. "But you have to understand that Danny's heart would hurt for a very long time if anything ever happened to that hat. Remember, he loves it so much, he only wears it on special occasions."

The youngster apologized to her big brother and swore—for the 915$^{th}$ time—to respect his belongings. Darren whispered something to each child who hurriedly exited the modern navy and white kitchen, satisfied that they'd been heard. Amia noted they seemed extra excited upon their departure. The parents high-fived each other, shaking their heads while chuckling.

"What are we gonna do with her?"

"I dunno." Amia shook her head. "But I think she'll finally be leaving Danny's stuff alone thanks to you. 'How would you feel if you were having a show and someone had taken your fabrics?' Babe, that approach was genius."

"I really hope so." He replied, taking his own swing at the French dialect. "After all, she loves her fab breeks."

Amia turned her chair so that she could gaze at her handsome husband whose rugged features always spurred an impromptu biting of her lower lip.

By this point, they'd been together for seventeen years, and he was still everything she'd ever wanted. No matter the occasion, be it owning courtrooms or mastering Saturday morning sibling drama, Amia loved the easy command that defined her husband.

Her loving fingers traced his forearm which was resting on the table. She inched slowly towards him before planting a long, endearing kiss on his full lips. That simple 'I love you' escalated quickly as arms, fingers, and legs began rubbing against chests, lower backs, and glutes.

"Dad, are you ready?"

"Five more minutes," he called back after his tongue reluctantly let go of his wife's. "Fortnight," he said in response to Amia's inquisitive eyes.

"I thought I saw them skipping outta here. You gave them a few minutes to practice?"

"You know it. I'm letting them warm up, 'cause I ain't trying to hear nobody's excuses." He said, helping himself to a handful of her curvaceous backside.

"What's that on your neck?"

"What?" she asked, rubbing her hands along either side, stretching her slender nape in either direction towards him so he could assist in removing the mystery item.

"Where is it?"

"Right there," he replied.

Juicy lips sensuously followed the long finger that traced a streak of peach jam below his wife's ear. Her eyes rolled behind closed eyelids as he fastened down on her sensitive flesh.

Amia gasped. His strong, delicious tongue was masterful, causing her toes to stretch and twist in response. His sturdy, wandering hands traversed along and under his old, overstretched T-shirt which Amia had claimed as her own years ago. The expert hands, fingers, and tongue delivered a trifecta of sensation, coaxing inaudible, involuntary sounds from Amia's throat as her body endured the welcomed onslaught of her husband's well-practiced probing.

"Babe, the kids," Amia whispered hoarsely as she clawed Darren's muscular back, teetering at the edge of mother and womanhood. She'd also been engaging in her own intent exploration of the fine adult male specimen who was responsible for her increased body temperature and impending happy ending.

"Dad?"

The parents groaned, freezing against each other and smiling at their predicament.

"He'll be up in a sec," Amia said, somehow successfully peeling herself away from the most magnetic man she'd ever known. She took a half step back, allowing her husband to will his manhood back to normal. This task was 'harder' than usual since her hands kept gripping and sliding intentionally along his nether regions.

"Don't plan on getting any sleep tonight, Mrs. Wilford," he whispered.

"Sleep's overrated, Mr. Wilford," she cooed softly, allowing one set of short-manicured nails to slide slowly down his bare torso as the other traced the back of his neck. Within moments, both minds returned to the earlier conversation. Their eyes focused again on the gray tattered envelope lying face down on the edge of the spacious marble island.

"Babe, aren't you even a little curious?" she asked. "Don't you at least want to know what's inside?"

"Nope. Not even a little bit interested. As far as I'm concerned, another thirty years can pass by." He paused before adding, "I'm good."

"Ok, then I'll read—"

"Amia. No," he replied firmly, stepping in front of her as she attempted to make her way toward the opposite corner of the kitchen.

"Babe, I need you to promise you won't—"

"Darren, what if I jus—"

"Amia! Please... God, I am begging you. Please just—don't."

His voice wavered. A panic ripped through his being as his hands clasped around hers. That thick vein on his forehead that only showed up while pumping 300 pounds of iron or feverishly cheering on his athletes, was on full display. Amia watched as his eyes drifted to the crown molding, landing on a tiny crack in the corner. She observed beads of sweat surfacing as his jaw clenched.

"Darren? Darren? Hey, Babe, look at me. I won't touch any of the letters," she reassured, wrapping her arms around him, drawing him close.

"I promise."

Amia didn't know what terrors were sealed inside that envelope, but she did know its presence was causing her husband's heart to work way harder than it should for a casual Saturday morning. Darren's deep exhale was followed by one of the tightest squeezes she'd ever received. Amia felt the tension slowly easing in his body as they stood wrapped in that embrace.

She clung onto her husband, quietly fussing at herself for pushing him. In all their years, Amia had never seen him rocked to his core like he was at this moment. Only now did she understand that Darren's reluctance to unseal the envelopes which had recently begun arriving or to engage in this conversation was tied to fear... And pain.

Amia could never truly understand the agony being delivered to her husband via stamp. She didn't know the kind of trauma that would cause words to freeze in midair at the sight of an envelope. The truth is, Amia had never been haunted by a life experience. On the other hand, Darren had, and after thirty years of solace, the ghosts were now returning compliments of the US Postal Service.

She continued her embrace, silently praying for her husband's peace as she waited for the heavy thuds in his chest to return to normal.

"Thank you," he replied softly. With that, he lovingly lifted his wife's head off his chest before planting a tender kiss on her forehead. He then retrieved the envelope, briefly refocusing on that one spot on the molding. A few deep breaths filled his lungs.

“I’m happy, Mia. Our kids are upstairs waiting for me to play video games with them. Our family’s happy… We’re blessed,” he added, tapping the envelope on the counter.

“We have trial next week. I need to focus on that. I can’t be thinking about this right now… or ever again for that matter.”

With that, Amia watched as the long, ominous envelope disappeared into their hallway with her husband. Shortly thereafter, he was making his way up their wrought-iron staircase as the office shredder finished noisily dicing a fourth such unopened parcel and its contents into thousands of tiny squares.

# Chapter 2

## In a Word – Bombshell

"So, I'll ask you to consider the facts...

"First fact: My client is an honor roll student, who has never so much as been to the principal's office.

"Second fact: This young man turned sixteen last week. Can you guess what he wanted for his birthday? His mom and dad, some Oreos, and his assignments. Think about that. This kid has been sitting in jail for a year now, and his birthday wish was for his parents, some cookies, and coursework from his teachers.

"Do you remember when you turned sixteen? Was a history book on your wish list? What about science? Did you want chapters six and seven wrapped up in a bow? No, you didn't, but Trevaris Reynolds did. You see, this quiet young man wanted to preserve his 3.81 GPA.

"One more fact: At the time of these heinous murders, eyewitnesses placed my then *fifteen-year-old* client at Fair Oaks Nursing Home on Ninety-Fifth Street. He is being tried as an adult for a crime that occurred while he was playing cards with his ailing grandmother nine blocks away."

Darren paused, allowing his voice to echo off the dark wood and ivory stucco walls of the well-lit, two-story, century-old courtroom.

"Her only grandchild who'd been glued to her hip since birth, missed her funeral because his parents couldn't afford his bail," he added solemnly. His eyes met those of the older jury members, as he let that last statement sink in.

He only needed one person sitting in the elevated juror's stand to see this kid for who he is—a kid. He needed one of these twelve citizens to look past the cornrows and guarded temperament and remember that he just turned sixteen.

The astute attorney then pressed play on the television, allowing the smiling face of a shapely seventy-six-year-old woman to appear on the screen.

"This is Gertrude Sims, Trevaris Reynolds' grandmother. Look at that inviting smile… I'm told she gave the most amazing hugs."

He took a beat, allowing the jury and onlookers in the upper and lower levels of the stately courtroom to imagine the wonderful cuddles that accompanied a smile of that magnitude.

"Imagine this incredibly warm lady, who Trevaris says made the world's best Seven-up cakes, spending her last few years waiting for Sundays. She lived for that specific day because that's when her honor student grandson would visit, spending all day with her.

"Someone had to tell Me-Ma Gerty that Trevaris wouldn't be playing Yatzi with her anymore. She would no longer be lovingly braiding his hair as he sat on a pillow on the floor of her tiny yellow living room while recapping their week... If you close your eyes, you can see them. You can almost hear the conversations between a loving grandma and her daughter's son.

"Put yourself in Me-Ma Gerty's shoes. Your only grandchild, your pride and joy who comes to hang out with you every Sunday at the lonesome nursing home, is suddenly never coming by again. Not because he did anything wrong. No, it's because someone who looks kinda like Trevaris, but wasn't as thin or even wearing the same clothes and whose DNA doesn't even match, committed an unspeakable crime. Can you imagine the devastation?

"Need I remind you that Trevaris had extra cards in his hands at the time of the murders?"

Darren then held his hands up, mimicking the cherished grandmother playing cards with Trevaris and the youngster picking up the extra cards after having to Go Fish.

"Objection, Your Honor. Go Fish? Really? What's next, Peek-A-Boo? Seriously, is this really going anywhere?"

"Your Honor. I didn't interrupt Mr. Bradley's thirty-minute dissertation about the sun's position in the sky or the number of cars parked along the sidewalk. I also said nothing while he painstakingly described the Valencia oranges and Michigan apples that were in one of the victim's grocery bags. If you'll grant a little latitude, please. I'm getting there," Darren said while looking up at the no-nonsense Caucasian woman peering over her glasses and down at him.

"I'll allow, but move it along Counselor," she urged.

"Thank you, Your Honor. As I was saying, Trevaris was a fifteen-year-old kid who loved playing card games with his grandmother and still watched cartoons when our men and women in uniform cornered and placed him in handcuffs... For good measure, I'll give you another fact: The honor student sitting at the table behind me never left home without a Pokemon and some Yu-Gi-Oh cards in his bookbag.

"Now," Darren began before pressing the button on the remote allowing another image to appear on the screen. "Mr. Bradley would have you believe my client is a hardened criminal. Ladies and gentlemen, this is the booking photo taken following Trevaris' arrest.

"Oddly enough, the very first thing I notice is that he's been crying. They probably got this shot between sobs. In fact, the child in that image cried all the way to the police station. He was bawling his eyes out and begging for his parents while in central booking.

"Look again at this photo," he implored, noting the eighth juror's pained reaction to the teenager's red-eyed, tearladened face. The image appeared to have also struck a nerve with the blonde, thirty-something year old soccer mom.

"Ladies and gentlemen..." Darren stepped towards the twelve jurors, noting moisture in the eyes of a sixty-ish-year-old Hispanic grandfather. He placed his hands on the thick, dark wood railing that divided the jurors from the rest of the citizens in the packed courtroom.

"I'll ask again. Look hard at that screen. Do you really see a hardened criminal? Don't worry if you don't... Nobody does—including Mr. Bradley."

"Objection."

"Sustained."

Darren walked towards the tan metal rolling cart, pointing towards the flat screen perched atop.

"I keep looking at this photo, and I'll be honest—I just don't see anything other than an innocent child, and if I'm being *really* honest, I see nothing more than an innocent child whose face is reflecting the trauma of being kidnapped by Pittsburgh's finest."

"Objection!"

"Counselor!"

"Withdrawn, Your Honor."

"Counselor?" The inquiry came from Judge Emmerson after an unusually long pause in Darren's summation. He had been wrangling with himself since Amia pulled him aside not long after closing arguments began. There was one additional fact he could share, but it was risky. It could result in a mistrial, him being fined, held in contempt, or worse.

"Sorry, Your Honor." He paused again, turning to his young client who'd just wiped the welling tears following Darren's fond remembrance of his beloved Me-Ma and the incredibly accurate depiction of his mental state captured in the photo.

Their eyes locked. For the first time since meeting in a tiny, windowless prison room a year earlier, both sets of eyes were afraid. Trevaris' fear was obvious. His attorney's, not so much.

The usually unflappable counselor bit his lip as his eyes traveled to the back of the courtroom, connecting with Amia's before directing his gaze at the prosecutor. Paul Bradley was impatiently tapping his pen, motioning his counterpart to conclude the theatrics. His thin-cut mustache stretched from side to side as he shifted his lips in irritation.

Though he couldn't have known, Paul's body language, especially his elongated huffs, was instrumental to Darren's reset. There was something about that man's complete disregard for this kid's life that flipped the switch. Darren's nostrils flared with irritation. His fear vanished.

Confident fingers found their way into his dark-brown trouser pockets as Darren briefly studied a long crack along the hundred-year-old, dark hardwood flooring. He smiled at the reminder. No matter how solid the case before him seemed, there was always a crack.

"*Thank you, Lord,*" he whispered silently before turning his attention back to the jury.

"There is one more fact you should consider, ladies and gentlemen. I've mentioned Trevaris was fifteen at the time he was accused of this crime. I've told you he's a good kid, a quiet kid, a kid who's been on the honor roll since third grade. You also know he's a kid who minds his business...

"What I haven't told you is that Trevaris is in love with a sixteen-year-old who will be turning seventeen in a few weeks. She's a lovely girl who just so happens to have given birth to an adorable baby boy almost ten months ago.

"I've shared with you the fact that Trevaris' bail was set exceptionally high. You know from the course of these proceedings that this *teenager's* mom and dad are both productive members of society with full-time jobs. Even still, they've been unable to secure the funds needed to post his bail, so Trevaris has been in custody since his arrest."

Darren's heart began pounding. A hint of fear returned. He swallowed past the dryness in his throat, looking back at Amia, who was still standing behind the seventh pew. His wife nodded slowly, matching his deep breaths.

They both knew what needed to be done and were fully aware that once the next words were muttered, there would be no turning back. Still, they couldn't let this innocent child go to prison. Amia said a silent prayer. Her heart was torn, but a fact was a fact—and there was one more.

Darren returned his attention to the jury, pausing as he glanced at a ray of sunlight filtering into the large courtroom.

Millions of dust particles floated within the beam. He couldn't help but imagine his twenty-year career obliterated and floating amongst the microscopic specs after what he was about to say.

His eyes returned to the twelve Pittsburgh residents honoring their civic duties. All were eagerly anticipating his next words. He made eye contact with the forewoman who'd just lifted her pen off her yellow notepad. Darren scratched his goatee, resigning to let the words fall where they may.

"Ladies and gentlemen, Mr. Bradley's teenage daughter delivered a baby boy about ten months ago. He sees that beautiful baby nightly..."

There was an uncomfortable stirring and clearing of the throat coming from the right side of the regal courtroom.

"The final fact, is that the Prosecutor is actively trying to imprison the father of his grandchild. Isn't that right, Mr. Bradley?"

The courtroom erupted with collective gasps at the stunning revelation. Reporters began buzzing in the background as did the rapid-fire of clicking cameras. Judge Emmerson immediately cleared the courtroom, angrily summoning Darren and his astonished counterpart into her chambers.

# Chapter 3

## *In a Word* – Sad

"What the Hell was that, Darren? Are you trying to get thrown in jail next to your client?" spat the heavy-set brunette as she angrily unzipped her robe, flinging it onto the tall, aged ornamental coat rack.

"No, Your Honor," he replied earnestly. "With respect, I asked for a recess and to see you in chambers ahead of summations in light of this new exculpatory evidence."

"Respectfully, Your Honor," said Amia who'd accompanied the trio to chambers since she was part of Trevaris' legal team. "I tried to share the information which I advised was vital to this proceeding. I told Dar— um, Council Wilford about the evidence earlier today and planned to be here before the end of the lunch break, but I somehow misplaced my keys. I truly apologize, Your Honor. Please know, I meant no disrespect."

The judge scowled, but gave Amia a pass as she'd tried countless cases in her courtroom through the years. Judge Emmerson was a witness to the young attorney's reputation for punctuality.

"Paul?"

"You know, Your Honor?" said Paul Bradley, the apt prosecutor who also had an impeccable reputation—but for winning. He'd successfully dismantled case after case brought by defense attorneys far and wide. The exception was Darren Wilford, one of three partners at the law offices of Worthy, Wilford & Meyers. The clean-cut Paul Bradley was on the verge of breaking his winless streak with his iron-clad case against Trevaris Reynolds. That is until Darren's last-minute hail Mary.

"I'm starting to put this pathetic picture together," Paul said. "Over the past couple of months, every person in this courthouse, including Your Honor and myself, has been treated to desserts and favors, compliments of these two. If I remember correctly, our Jury received desserts with their lunches on Monday.

"Isn't that right?" Paul accused. "And here I was thinking these gestures were out of the goodness of their hearts. Your Honor, it appears, these two have been conspiring to sway Justice for their defendant.

"When that didn't work, they tried this. These two and that unethical firm they represent should be investigated to the fullest extent of the law. This is a completely false allegation and the insinuation is a blatant attack on my character."

At this point, anger was causing Paul's well-built frame to shake. "You're desperate, Darren Wilford, and everybody knows it."

Darren elected not to reply. Instead, he donned the cat-that-ate-the-canary smile. The same one that haunted every foe who dared sit a briefcase down on the opposing table. Paul diverted his eyes as Darren's leer became increasingly unnerving.

What opponents misunderstand about this tactic is that it's less about what Darren actually knows. It's all about the first to blink. This trick was one of the few things Darren learned as a young man growing up with his father. His eyes smiled as, yet again, the other guy blinked.

"Your Honor," Amia began calmly, seeing the questions on the judge's face. "Your confusion is because I specifically excluded you and your staff from the deliveries.

"Worthy, Wilford & Meyers has topped the list of most ethical law firms in the nation for the last fifteen years. Even without that fact, I would have excluded you to avoid subjecting your office to scrutiny." Amia paused as Paul scoffed in the background. "Permission to get back to the facts, Your Honor?" She continued upon receipt of the judge's approval.

"Your Honor. Paul's signature is on each of the invoices. See for yourself." Amia presented copies extracted from her black briefcase.

"It is fascinating to me that this tidbit is just now coming up. I mean, I guess it's possible Paul forgot about all those signoffs. I guess it's also possible Paul's memory is sharp enough to recall the jurors receiving the desserts earlier this week, but not quite good enough to remember they were in the same clear, unmarked packaging that his were in."

That last part is what she wanted to say to the judge, but those words never actually came out. Instead, Amia simply allowed the judge to review each invoice bearing Paul's signature.

"You know what's sad, Paul?" Darren began with evident irritation as the judge handed the receipts back to Amia upon the conclusion of her review. His mind drifted back to the child who'd been sitting in jail for a year—the real reason they were in chambers. He'd had enough of the distractions being thrown against the wall.

The tension in Darren's clenched jaw released just enough to allow him to continue speaking, though he opted not to address the man who was supposed to fairly represent The People. His respect for Paul was gone, with a snowball's chance in Hell of ever returning. He spoke to Judge Emmerson directly.

"What is sad, Your Honor," he began, "is the DNA test results that were pulled from Paul's office trash late last week. And before he denies having knowledge of the documents in his waste bin, forensics confirmed the latent fingerprints found on each page of the results were a match for Paul Bradley.

"And, in the spirit of due diligence, Your Honor, we had the lab test the large glob of spit found on the last page of Trevaris' paternity test."

The Wilfords watched Judge Emmerson's facial expressions move from disbelieving to exasperated to appalled, as her eyes scanned the pages before landing on the confirmation of a familial match between the mucus-laden sample found on Trevaris' discarded DNA report and the swab from baby Bradley's cheeks months earlier.

"Your Honor, we questioned the five-million-dollar bail requested by The People. My client was a fifteen-year-old kid who had never so much as jaywalked. The suspect was taller, thinner, and there is no DNA connecting Trevaris Reynolds to the crime scene. To say the bail request was prejudicial is the understatement of the century.

"Your Honor, Paul's nondisclosure of the possibility that our client could have been the father of his grandchild is the height of malpractice. For him to continue on this case..." Darren paused again, reigning in his temper.

"I'm sure Your Honor can appreciate the magnitude of this conflict of interest. Paul's non-recusal *and continued* prosecution of this child ride the border of criminal... It's also desperate *and sad*," Darren asserted making eye contact with Paul as the last words were muttered.

"And, I submit the fact that the District Attorney tried this in your courtroom shows how little respect he has for Your Honor and the Justice system. This case should be dismissed without prejudice, and Paul should be sanctioned. I don't even want to think about the number of cases that will need to be retri—"

"Thank you, Amia," the judge interjected, fully aware of the gravity of the situation.

"This is preposterous!" exclaimed Paul. "Your Honor, anyone could have lifted my fingerprints and people spit, for the love of God. Come on! WW&M is a supposedly respected law firm. Their half-baked evidence is completely suspect, and circumstantial at best."

Paul, feeling a sense of emboldenment, turned his nearly six-foot fame towards Darren and Amia, "You've got to do better than that."

"How about confirmation from Tori herself? Does that work for you?" Amia asked. "Your Honor, I called Tori Bradley last night after receiving a voice message from her. She told me everything, including the fact that she told her father, Paul Bradley, that Trevaris Reynolds was the father."

"Your Honor, seriously—"

"That's hearsay, Amia. I'm sure you know we cannot allow that. Where is Tori Bradley? I'd like to hear from her."

Amia took a half step forward, presenting the judge with a photo showing Tori in Hawaii with her mother and sister.

"Your Honor, Tori's loving father took the extraordinary step of treating his daughter to a trip to Hawaii for her birthday," Darren started. Amia shared a text exchange between her and Tori in which the youngster confirmed her birthday was coming up in five weeks.

As the judge reviewed the messages, Amia added, "Mind you, Your Honor, the semester ends for most of our area in six weeks. If Paul really wanted to send her to Hawaii for her birthday, he could have actually waited for her birthday."

"Judge, the timing of this trip can't be coincidental," noted Darren.

Judge Emmerson scanned all three well-dressed, fully invested attorneys, resting her eyes keenly on each before moving on to the next and lingering in Paul's direction.

Paul provided counterarguments to each of Amia and Darren's assertions but had nothing to say about the timing of the trip other than that Tori had been stressed out lately and his wife thought it would be good for her to get away.

"Then you go to the Hamptons for the weekend or take her to the Jersey Shore, for Christ's sake. You don't take a teenager out of school for a week, especially when final exams and SAT preps are coming.

"Did you think about the additional stress you've caused? She's a teenager with a baby! For God's sake, that girl has enough on her mind without worrying about flunking out of tenth grade."

That particular response didn't come from a judicial officer. At that moment, the highly esteemed, short-statured jurist was just a fifty-something-year-old grandmother with teenage granddaughters of her own.

Judge Emmerson's tone was soaked in disgust at the ridiculousness of it all. She angrily repositioned the silver-rimmed glasses that she'd snatched off her face when snapping at Paul, before turning back to Amia.

"Before you press play, Counselor," the Judge warned sternly, her thick brows furrowed, "whatever is on that recording better support your allegations."

"Yes, Your Honor."

With that, she confidently pressed play, ignoring the repeated, and seemingly desperate protests of Paul Bradley. The room fell silent as the teenager's bombshell allegations pierced the afternoon air of the off-white office's chambers.

"We had the DNA and forensics run by two separate and unaffiliated offices," Amia added as she stopped the recording, but not before letting the judge hear the girl's tearful pleas for her secret boyfriend of two years.

"Trevaris is the father of Paul's grandchild, Your Honor. According to Tori, Paul has known since she was four months pregnant. That means he was fully aware of the conflict of interest before deciding to prosecute our client. And... if that wasn't enough, Paul has had concrete proof of paternity since last Wednesday." She handed the other folder with the second lab's results to the Judge for review.

"I guess the esteemed prosecutor didn't want a lower-middle-class Black kid showing up at the baby shower or God forbid, the first day of school. I suppose that wouldn't have gone over well at the country club."

Amia wanted to add that last part. In fact, she'd practiced those lines in her mirror prior to her younger sister, Bria's, impromptu visit earlier in the day. She just couldn't bring herself to go there. Instead, she quietly let the judge review the additional pages.

"What happened to you?" asked Darren in disbelief as he recalled a savvy, up-and-coming attorney named Paul Bradley who had gotten his start at WW&M months before Darren was hired.

"What happened to me?" Paul spat. You are singlehandedly flushing WW&M's reputation down the toilet and you have the audacity to ask what happened to me. Take a look in the mirror, Darren."

"Your Honor," Amia interrupted, stepping in between her husband and the district attorney who'd inched uncomfortably close together during the last few exchanges.

"The allegations about council Wilford's football camp's financing are completely baseless, unlike the matter before us."

"Paul Bradley has been attempting to send a teenage boy to prison for the sole crime of getting *his* teenage daughter pregnant. This cannot happen."

"Your Honor," Darren began as he systematically returned folders to his brown leather briefcase. "I move for an immediate dismissal."

# Chapter 4

## *In a Word* – Meeting

"Weeks later, Amia found herself smiling fondly as she scrolled through the first photos of Trevaris Reynolds at home with his baby boy. With no evidence tying him to the murders and the massive civil rights firestorm that had been unleashed, the State had no choice but to release the young man and dismiss the charges.

She noted the young dad's easy comfort with the cute, chubby-cheeked little guy. Her heart swelled as she paused on one particularly beautiful snapshot. In it, the baby's fingers were wrapped around Trevaris' pinky as he bottle-fed wearing a bib that read, 'My dad is way cooler than yours'.

Trevaris' eyes were peering into his son's light brown peepers as the pair engaged in a loving silent conversation. There was another adorable photo of the pair, in matching green and white striped shirts, crawling on all fours in the kitchen.

It hurt thinking of the pain this young man and his family endured at the hands of the justice system. Nothing would ever make up for the abuse he suffered. There was no way to apologize to an honor student for having to repeat the tenth grade. There weren't enough words to offset the pain of missing his baby's entrance to and his beloved Me-Ma's departure from this world.

Amia shook her head in anger, but also smiled, knowing the restitutions heading his way would ensure financial comfort while he worked to regain his footing. She pulled her attention from the phone and began scanning the interior of the familiar bistro, marveling at its eclectic mixture of old instruments, photographs, and nautical artifacts.

She fell in love with its New England atmosphere upon her initial impromptu visit years earlier. Back then, she and her bestie, Janelle, happened upon the hideaway café while on an early-morning jog. As usual, nature called for Janelle around the third mile and because the friends opted to forgo their usual riverfront path, their go-to pitstops were nowhere to be found.

With no restaurants in sight, the pair's normally relaxing run turned into an intensive search for a suitable alleyway. As the minutes became more desperate, finding a safer, more discreet option gave way to just finding a dumpster behind which she could squat.

A waving white cloth just down the street caught Amia's eye. It turned out to be a woman cleaning a window in what appeared to be an abandoned building; except, the large, weathered opening featured a small red and white sign tucked between its old panes.

"Janelle! Wait, come back," yelled Amia as Janelle sped knock-kneed around the corner, willing her bladder to hold on for a few more seconds. "That looks like a store."

"Amia, I'm not gonna make it. You know I have a weak bladder."

"Girl, come on," she yelled, waving her arms at the stocky German woman and dragging Janelle in her direction. Thankfully, Frau Gerry granted the ladies admission even though the dire straits were occurring ten minutes before the doors were set to open.

The pair would be the first-ever patrons of the Coastal Sounds coffee shop as that day happened to be the grand opening. Frau Gerry's only ask in exchange for the facilities was that the pair come back to visit someday soon.

Now, Amia and Janelle visited the Coastal Sounds every other weekend. The ladies parked in front of the store, ran one-and-a-half miles out and since Janelle's bladder was sure to be calling, they'd cap their mileage off with a restroom visit followed by a Coastal 'Rhythm & Infused' smoothie.

That said, today's visit to the cozy Fifteenth Street shop was different. Janelle hadn't partnered with her on this Saturday morning's outing. It hadn't been preceded by the usual three miles of pavement pounding.

Amia found herself fidgeting while tucked into her favorite sun-soaked corner table. She'd arrived twenty minutes early, and while the sun's warmth caressing her skin offered a welcome distraction, the minutes were dragging by with agonizing slowness.

"*Amia, what are you doing*?" she chided herself under her breath as her tension grew. "*This is a terrible idea. You need to leave, right now.*"

"Oh, I'm sorry. I didn't mean to scare you," uttered the young waitress who was just as startled by Amia's response to her quietly sliding a freshly baked pudding bratzel onto the round birch tabletop.

"You're really deep in thought today. Thinking about a big case?"

"I'm sorry, Johanna. I'm planning a surprise and just connecting the dots in my head." Then turning her attention to the glazed aromatic pastry and inhaling deeply, she said, "Thank you so much, Jo. This looks and smells amazing."

Frau Gerry's teenage granddaughter smiled before placing a piping hot cup of coffee on the table.

"You're welcome, Ms. Amia. And I brought your favorite peach jam to go along with the bratzel," she added.

Amia thanked her again and began chatting with Johanna about school and her upcoming prom plans. She was then treated to images of seven gowns which Johanna had narrowed down from twenty-five. With less than two weeks to go before the event, she asked for help eliminating a few.

Amia's response was to immediately scratch the four thigh-high options. She winked at the adorable, exasperated teen just as the bell jingled announcing the arrival of a new patron.

Amia's nerves steeled. Not one to let her fears get the best of her, she managed to add, "Your grandma wouldn't let you out of the house wearing either of them anyways."

Johanna quickly tucked the phone back into her teal apron and greeted the newcomer.

# Chapter 5

## *In a Word* – Sting

"You were right. This is a hidden gem," remarked Andrew as he finished off his Farmer's Breakfast and brotchen.

"I tell you what, you and that husband of yours should consider running for office. The way you took down the District Attorney, you'd be a shoe-in. Sounds like there are a few other folks downtown who should be worried, too.

"I've gotta give it to you, that was ballsy. I mean, I expected something like that from your husband, but not from the sweet-natured, God-fearing Amia Wilford," he added, dabbing his fingers on the white linen napkin. "Have to say, though, I find it very titillating," he added with a grin.

"That child was in jail for a year, and for no reason. He has his life back now... And, I talk to God all the time, Andrew. He's not upset about Trevaris being back at home with his parents and his son."

"You know, some of the most important people in the bible—Paul, Daniel and Joseph, just to name a few—stayed in jail for years. I don't know, Amia. You might have robbed that kid of his legacy.

"Ok, I will change the subject," he said, throwing his hands up in phony defeat after a long, awkward pause. Though her lips never moved, Amia's softly furrowed eyes told the story. She had no intentions of giving the satisfaction of a response.

"One thing's for sure though, everything in here looks amazing." He allowed his eyes to scan the white-paneled interior while the subtle sounds of waves rolling ashore spilled through strategically placed speakers. Andrew paused momentarily. Then, sipping his newly capped-off beverage with eyes aimed squarely at Amia, added, "And I do mean *everything in here* looks amazing."

"You said you had proof about this accusation against Darren. Do you have it?" she countered, squelching her nagging intuition and dismissing his not-so-thinly veiled intentions. She fixated on his eyebrows, refusing to meet his gaze.

"All business, huh? Does your man know you're here?" He smiled wryly as he took an exaggerated sip of his coffee. Andrew clearly wanted to move the conversation to a different level. Amia's eyes drifted towards a mark on his left cheek. She noted that the injury couldn't have been more than a few weeks old. Her curiosity piqued.

"What? This little thing?" he asked, noticing her gaze. At the same time, a solitary finger traced the long, scraggly scratch that ran along his chiseled jaw and disappeared behind his blue and white checkered collar.

"Got chased by a pit bull last weekend. Had to jump a fence and landed in a damn rose bush in my neighbor's yard." Then licking his lips and leaning towards her, he asked, "Wanna see the one on my thigh?"

Amia didn't reply. Instead, she watched as he stirred a fourth brown sugar packet into his coffee then chased scrambled eggs and sausage around his plate with his fork. She noticed that he placed the fork and knife in the exact same spot each time he set them down. This was followed by dabbing the corners of his thin lips with the napkin after each bite.

*This man has been trying to meet with me for weeks now,* she thought to herself. *He doesn't have any proof,* she concluded, watching the silverware placement and lip dabbing ritual repeat itself.

"Oh, these? Thorns from that damn bush," he added, noticing her lingering on two long scratches along his forearm. He then smiled, tracing his straight teeth with his tongue while marveling at her flawless skin and imagining the soft treasures hidden behind the denim shirtdress.

"The proof," Amia asked, faking curiosity. "What do you have?"

"I have a copy of a document for you, but you're gonna have to be a lot nicer to me in order to get the original," he replied, sensing a bit of leverage.

"Tell you what... One second," Amia's train of thought was interrupted by her vibrating phone. She fished it out from under a long, gray envelope tucked deep inside her purse.

"Hey, Babe."

"Hey, Trace and Daryl picked up breakfast. Miguel and Cy are at Starbucks."

"Tell everyone I'll be there in about fifteen minutes. I need to stop by the post office. Love you, too."

"Sounds like you've got plans," Andrew commented, half annoyed that she'd answered a call from her husband during their 'secretly' scheduled meeting. He was equally miffed at the 'Love you, too' at the end of said phone call.

"As I was saying, I brought a copy. Maybe we can figure out some kind of special arrangement, and I might be convinced to give up the original," he added, positioning the comment as if he'd just called 'check' in chess.

"That's an interesting proposition, Andrew," Amia said, her courage now back after speaking to her husband. "Aren't you going to ask me out first," she asked coyly, leaning towards the attractive, olive-skinned salt-and-peppered conman.

His demeanor softened and a smidgeon of hope dashed through his being as her eyes met his solidly for the first time since he'd sat down. A grin stretched across his deep pink lips as bells jingled, signaling a couple of new mid-morning patrons. Amia didn't allow him to answer, opting simply to remind Andrew that her husband was waiting and retrieved her purse which had been hanging off the knob of the wooden rectangular chairback.

"So, it's like that? Maybe it'll only be you running for office. Your husband might be too busy explaining his IRS situation to his cellmates when I'm done. Maybe one or two copies will be featured on the six o'clock news.

"How do you think Darren Wilford will feel about that? Mr. Air Tight, right? At least, that's what that sham article in the City Magazine called him," he said, angry that this attractive woman had conned him into thinking that she would do anything to save her husband's reputation. He'd been envisioning sliding in between the sheets with Amia ever since she finally accepted his breakfast invitation.

"Do whatever you want. Darren has nothing to hide." She turned to walk away, pausing momentarily.

"Oh, when you first sat down, you mentioned Trevaris Reynolds and that you were concerned about his legacy. You should know, that young man's face is the symbol of injustice. There are new laws being drafted in his name as we speak, and Trevaris Reynolds will be appearing on PowerPoints in lecture halls across the world for decades to come. Thanks for your concern, but he and his legacy will be just fine."

All of that would have sounded great if she'd actually said it. Giving people a piece of her mind wasn't Amia's nature. Sometimes though, she wished she had the candor and courage to put others in their place rather than just holding her tongue. It seemed so easy to do. Darren, her mom, her sisters, brother, their best friends—literally everyone else—spoke their minds freely.

Amia groaned inwardly at her silence, but kept walking after her brief pause. She watched Andrew watch her move to the front of the coffee shop and say goodbye to Johanna's uncle, Sven, who had relieved the youngster while she took a break.

As the door began to close, Amia was treated to the sound of the FBI agents who had entered the shop moments earlier, addressing Andrew DeSimeon and reviewing his Miranda rights.

# Chapter 6

## *In a Word* – Gratitude

"She slipped off the trail and slid down into a ravine while we were hiking in the Appalachians two weeks ago," said Jordyn so that her older sister, Bria, wouldn't have to retell the story to yet another curious partygoer.

At twenty-seven and twenty-eight, Amia's younger sisters were respected social media influencers. The pair had chronicled their college lives from scraping by on ramen and tuna fish to turning ten dollars into five-star meals. Jordyn and Bria's *Broke & Eating Good* YouTube channel quickly amassed a loyal following, which got them invited to colleges and universities across the country.

Never one to miss an opportunity to teach others their tricks, the pair started a secondary channel wherein they videoed and documented their experiences while traveling. Soon, the savvy sisters had parlayed sleeping in their VW clunker and taking bird baths in hotel restrooms into staying in the Embassy Suites and lounging in The Conrad bathrobes paid for with coupons, points, and now, sponsors.

Their second endeavor, *Broke with Reservations*, is more popular than their first because it often combines their savory low-budget meals with cool, inexpensive accommodations at the some of the most picturesque locations, one of which they'd just returned from days earlier.

It was this trip to the mountains which was given responsibility for the scrapes, scratches, and blackened eye socket hidden behind Bria's oversized sunglasses.

There was so much interest in the story because while the camera-ready entrepreneurial pair usually filmed every aspect of their travels, neither sister had managed to capture Bria's nasty spill or their painstakingly difficult trek back to the cabin.

"How in the world did the queens of videography manage to miss filming that?" asked the girls' oldest brother, Jamari. "Y'all are glued to your phones," he added, shaking his head incredulously.

"Bria was in the process of starting the recording when she slipped and my phone was dead," replied Jordyn.

"My phone got broken when I fell, so we couldn't have filmed any of it anyways," added Bria. That was quickly followed by a safety lecture from Ramon about the importance of keeping the phones charged and having the proper equipment.

He'd preached this to the kids repeatedly as preparation saved his unit's hide multiple times when the former Special Forces photographer was in dangerous territory overseas. Ramon was truly disappointed that his daughters had not heeded his advice this time.

"Ok," chimed Amia, looking to lighten the subject before the girls, though adults, got fussed at and things got off track, "if y'all are going to be out on trails and stuff, strap one of those hands-free video thingies on your heads when you go out. That way, you're not fooling with the phones and getting distracted while walking."

She paused for a second, throwing a playful side-eye to her father who had more than a few points still lined up to lay on his youngest daughters.

"We're glad you're ok," she added, giving them both another hug.

Everyone had converged onto the Wilford's residence in celebration of Daniel's thirteenth birthday. Amia's parents, Ramon and Elaine, fresh off celebrating their forty-fifth wedding anniversary in Italy, and Darren's parents, Gary and Mable, back from their final missionary trip to Ghana, were clinging their wine glasses. Uncle Marty and Aunt Victoria admired Christina's latest home-spun designs in the meantime.

Jamari and Michele were busily getting the twins settled after just getting in. *Man, it's good to see them,* Amia thought to herself. Her heart nearly exploded as it did every time she saw him with his family. She said a silent prayer of thanks every time she saw Jamari, and not just because he had once been her wayward little brother who'd managed to beat all the odds.

Amia was infinitely grateful for that, but her prayers were because Jamari had endured some painful struggles over the past couple of years and had managed to hold fast onto his faith. Seeing him with those precious jibber-jabbering babies warmed her heart.

Her thoughts were interrupted by the cheers roaring from the grill area. She peeked outside to find her sister-in-law and newly minted PhD recipient, Camille, hip-bumping and jamming with Darren.

It was immediately clear that her husband was outmatched by his younger sister and all her rhythmic command. He quickly surrendered, waving his trademark metal grill tongs—now lovingly bedazzled with pink gems—in the air.

Amia surveyed the entire scene, smiling contently. There was absolutely nothing like family.

"So, are we ever going to meet him?" asked Ramon, helping Bria open her soda, since her right arm would be tucked safely in a blinged-out sling for at least a few more weeks while her hairline fracture healed.

"Dad, I told you. Drew is self-conscious because everyone in our family is successful. He feels like he can't measure up."

"You keep saying that, but I don't understand why, Bree. You know we would never judge him. If he makes you happy, that's all we care about," Amia said.

"Mari was broke when we met and stayed that way for a good… long… eternity after that. Right, Babe?" Michele teased.

"Yeah, I was broke, but eating good," he replied, cleverly referencing his sisters' YouTube channel. With that, he deliberately popped a tortilla chip loaded with Bria's famous grilled watermelon salsa. The whole house laughed at his wit and overexaggerated chomping.

"I just wasn't smart enough to market my broke-tivity, like those two," he added. He turned and scooped out some of Amia's corn pudding.

"Look, Bree, if he's making an honest living and he's working to better himself, that's all that matters." Elaine paused. "It's just that you have been seeing this man for two years and we've never met him."

Bria winced as she stretched her leg. The scabs and scrapes on her knees and thighs were healing, but still painful when bent or straightened.

"Guys, I know you mean well, but could you not keep asking about Drew? He'll come around when he's ready," she added with a dose of snip.

"I'm gonna chalk that up to you being in pain, little lady. I don't care how old you are, you'd better remember who you're talking to," said Elaine, a faint, but distinct twang showing up in her voice.

Darren and Amia, and Jamari and Michele all exchanged silent 'Oh snaps.' The temperature had increased a few notches even though the thermostat still read 71 degrees.

"Babe," Darren nudged, "get your mama befo—"

"And, I'm sorry, I still don't buy it. He can't even stop by to say hi? We've invited him out so many times. He's got an excuse for this. Something came up for that. He's not feeling well. He got the dates mixed up," went Elaine, her arms waving in alternate directions in unison with her statements.

"And you're telling me he couldn't even come up to Ramon's hospital room after his gallbladder surgery last year? I still can't get past that. He stayed in the car while you came up. It just doesn't make any sense to me. Jamari, does it make sense to you?"

At this point, if you hadn't known Elaine, you'd have never known that she left Jamaica when she was in elementary school. Through the years, she'd lost the unmistakable dialect. Now in her sixties, if that accent showed up, someone was about to experience a full-throated tongue-lashing.

Jamari opted not to wade into that choppy water, choosing instead to continue sipping on his lemonade with extended swallows. His stalling worked. Elaine moved on, turning to her youngest daughter. "Jordyn? Even your boyfriend at the time came up and asked how Ramon was doing. You two had only been dating for a few weeks. It just doesn't make sense why the man can't show his face," Elaine added, now hydrating via a glass of Moscato with her pinky finger extended.

Before Jordyn could respond, Amia interjected, "Mom, can we table this for later, please?" Sensing her little sister's frustration and discomfort, also acutely aware of where this was going, she continued attempting to move the conversation, "Matter of fact, did you all try Michele's banana br—"

"Is this one married too, Bria?" asked Elaine flatly.

# Chapter 7

## *In a Word* – Imperfect

Mouths dropped. Widened eyes darted back and forth in disbelief. A palpable discomfort floated in the air amidst the sports-themed helium balloons as stunned family members and guests wrestled with what to say and do next.

Every eye in Amia and Darren's two-story contemporary residence landed in Bria and Elaine's direction. The party music serving as a backdrop to the day's event, now clashed with the mood, especially since the jovial afternoon had screeched to a jarring halt.

"You always figure out how to ruin everything," yelled Bria, completely embarrassed. Her anger was also evident but tempered by the pain wracking her arm and legs due to her sudden attempt to stand and leave.

"I guess I haven't been as good at picking them as the rest of you," she spat. With that, Bria managed to ease herself off of the large white arched barstool before gingerly weaving through guests and storming into the hallway. Away from everyone, she allowed the tears of frustration and shame to drip past her eye rims.

Normally, family and friends spent a few moments in the expansive pinstriped hallway, taking in the smiling faces captured over the decades. It was well-known that Amia routinely switched out the images in the multi-sized frames to feature new memories, keeping it interesting. Even if Bria had felt like lingering, the photos wouldn't have been visible through the never-ending pools of moisture that kept filling her eyes.

"Bree, wait," Amia called after her younger sister, her hands motioning everyone to sit tight. She then shot her mom a look of disappointment. She was torn though, because it was true.

Everyone in America knew those men were married based on Bria's excuses regarding their nonsensical schedules and inability to be there for holidays or other big events. That said, they were years ago and the family had agreed to leave that in the past. They were not supposed to bring those relationships up, even though deep down, everyone suspected Elaine was right—again.

"For the millionth time, I did not know Larry was married until his wife called. I broke up with him right then. Elijah was separated and Marquis told me he was divorced.

"Bree, don't leave," begged Mia as her sister attempted unsuccessfully to navigate the seven steps leading from their brown and white window-walled home to the sidewalk below.

"It's Danny's birthday. He's only seen you once in the last few months because y'all are traveling so much. Besides, you have to do the honors with the cake. He literally waits all year for it. You know it's one of his favorite things in the world."

"Mia, I'm the laughing stock of this family and I'm sick of it. Yeah, I made some mistakes, but I didn't know they were all married."

"Bree... Girl, you know I love you, right?" she asked as she wrapped her arms around her younger sister. Bria nodded, turning to face her older sister. At twenty-eight, Bria had heard that phrase enough to know that her oldest sister was about to hit her with a healthy dose of big sista girl talk.

Amia sat next to her on the hanging swing inside the ebony-stained wooden porch and took her hand before continuing, "Bree, ask yourself if it makes sense that your boyfriend of *two years* has never taken the time to come meet your family.

"He won't even let us pop in to say hi. Think about it. He has never even allowed himself to be seen. Now, unless he's got a third eyeball, a severe case of fleas or is somewhere locked up, you know something doesn't make sense."

"I keep telling you all that he's not comfortable. Everyone in our family is successful. He doesn't have anything close to what this family has and at his age, he feels like a failure because he's not on his feet."

"Bree, you don't believe that any more than I do. Dad had surgery. You needed a shoulder to lean on. Do you think we'd have cared what his occupation was? When Mari and Michele lost Jasper, you were alone at the funeral. Do you think anyone would have been asking Drew about his finances?"

Bria shook her head, pausing for a long moment before responding, "The truth is..."

"Is what, Bree?" She asked after another long pause. Amia could see her sister was struggling to get something off her chest and turned to face her. "You can tell me," she encouraged.

"Bria wanted to confide in her sister, but couldn't. She decided against it, assuming Amia and 'all of her perfection' would never understand.

"The truth is I know something's not right, Mia. But, I'm not you." Amia tilted her head, her confusion evident.

"You're not me? What does th—"

"Give me a break, Amia. You have no flaws," Bria blurted out as the tears began freefalling. "You're beautiful and successful. You're confident and smart. You've got all the plus signs in your column. On top of that, everyone respects you.

"And Jordyn looks like a short supermodel. She's funny and feisty and has a personality that just attracts people. She can have any man she wants. I know it's true, 'cause they're always groveling at her feet.

"I mean, I love you and I love her. She and I are killing it on YouTube. I'm creating amazing dishes and we're always all over the country. That part is wonderful. Mia, men are constantly around, but they don't look at me like they look at her.

"Hell, truth be told, no man really looks at me; not like that. Sure, there's interest in my cooking and the fun we have traveling, but outside of that, if we're out, all men gravitate to Jordyn. She's always trying to introduce guys to me, but it's evident that they'd rather get with her.

"I'm the jolly dark-skinned, kinky-haired fat girl who's just tolerated," she cried.

"Bria," Amia urged. "Please stop calling yourself fat. If you don't like something about yourself, make some changes, but stop doing that. There are women who can't gain weight and would kill for your curves... And that cleavage, Bree. Come on, Sis. You know your girls work magic.

"Mia, please," she continued, her eyes rolling and emotions completely raw.

"I am never seen or even acknowledged, so when a man finally pays me some attention, I'm genuinely excited. If I'm being honest, I sometimes feel like the last dog at the shelter and when a guy is interested in me, it's like I finally get to show someone that I'm pretty cool, too.

"Bree," Amia whispered. Her heart was aching along with her sister's.

"God, Amia," Bria groaned in frustration, cursing her injured state because she couldn't easily remove herself from the situation.

Amia paused, waiting for her tightening throat to make space for air so that she could continue. "You can't honestly believe any of that. Those are lies, and they're all coming straight from the pit of Hell.

"And, I'm not sure where you're getting this idea that I'm so perfect. Have you seen the dried drool on my face first thing in the morning?"

She held her sister's hand.

"There are candles burning in our house right now because, I forgot the eggs were boiling on the stove this morning. Two hours ago, the entire place smelled like burnt farts.

"And, you know I busted my behind walking into court last week, right? I literally tripped over nothing. Broke my heel and ripped a hole in the armpit of my blouse. So, do us both a solid and chunk this whole notion that I'm somehow perfect."

"Geez, Amia. Nobody says do me a solid anymore. Please don't say that around Danny or Chrissy's friends. I'd hate for my babies to have to change schools because their momma is corny."

Amia's jaw dropped for a third time today. The first occurred when she ran into their kitchen after hearing a series of pops, only to find egg shards splattered all over the stainless-steel appliances, walls, ceiling, and floor. The other instance was moments before chasing her sister onto the porch and now, this same sister, the celebrity YouTuber, was sitting here coming for her cool points.

"Seriously though... You couldn't possibly understand, Mia. No matter what, you're still the woman who looks amazing with makeup, but even better when you're not wearing any. You've never had any problems getting guys, but I have.

"Truth is I've allowed myself to be really dumb and believe some incredible lies... You know what," Bria confessed in a mixture of complete embarrassment and self-loathing, "I even pretended not to hear Marquis whisper, 'Love you, too,' before leaving the bathroom to join me in bed.

"So, yeah. Maybe I put up with crap that you or Jordyn or Mom or Michele wouldn't, but I don't get that many chances at relationships. And as bad as it sounds, having twenty-five percent of a man sometimes is better than having a hundred percent of no man all of the time," she resolved, dabbing her cheeks.

"Bria JaKerry Copeland!" exclaimed Elaine in a half whisper. Their mom had silently made her way to the front door and had been listening to her second youngest child's heartbreaking confession. Amia was surprised to find their matriarch standing in the now open doorway. Bria never turned to face her; instead, dropping her head, wishing she'd never bared her soul within earshot.

It wasn't until Elaine joined them sitting down on the blue and green ceramic stool next to the sisters that Bria saw something she'd never seen before. Anguish was on the face of her strong, impossibly unshakable mother.

After a few more moments, the conversation continued. "What about David, Bree?"

"David? You mean David at UPS, Mia? God, he was so corny."

"What about Carl?" asked Elaine.

"Ma, Carl is way too chubby. How would that work? He's fat and I'm fat? No, I don't think so," she added, avoiding Amia's disproving glare while removing the last of the fake eyelashes that had come loose with the tears.

"What do you mean how would that work, Bree?" Elaine asked. "Aunt Terry and Uncle Mike? Suzette and Ernest? Jackson and Shannon? Estelle and Steven? Honey, there ain't nothing wrong with either one of those relationships... You need to open your eyes, young lady.

"A big man might mess around and rock your entire world. Ask Suzette," Elaine continued. "Every time I look up, Ernest has her giggling about something. And you know Estelle stays pregnant, so there ain't nothing wrong in that area either," Elaine added with a smile.

Bria nodded slowly as her mother's wisdom registered. "I guess. I've just never thought about it," she said. "Carl wasn't for me."

"Braedon?"

"That skinny White guy, Amia?"

"Ummm yeah. That same skinny White guy who's been hanging around randomly for months. You know he wants a couple scoops of your thick, juicy Mocha Chocolata."

Bria smiled for only the second time since they'd been outside. She briefly rolled her eyes before adding, "Ummm, no, and before you ask about Ricky, he was only five-two. His head came up to my chin."

"So, the truth is, Bree. This has nothing to do with your weight or your complexion or your hair. And it's not that men aren't paying you attention, it's that you're not giving shots to the ones who are interested in you," said Elaine. "You need to tell the truth about that, and you need to stop being so closed-minded."

Amia held her sister's hand. With the list of men who she and Elaine rattled off, Bria knew she was being shortsighted and began to feel sheepish.

"Bree, maybe you're looking for a certain type. I mean, you're attracted to who you're attracted to. There's nothing wrong with that. But you can't sit here and act like no one's ever interested in you. We just named several and those are just the ones we know about."

"I guess," replied Bria. "It doesn't matter. We'll never know about Drew anyways. Truth is, I haven't heard from him in a couple of weeks."

Amia and Elaine's heads both tilted at that revelation. Bria paused before continuing, "We had a big fight before me and Jordie went to the mountains. I've called him a few times, but he never answered and hasn't called me since," she sighed. "I guess he ghosted me," she added, feeling defeated.

"What was the fight about?"

"Why didn't you say anything," asked Amia and Elaine at the same time. Both women were searching the younger Copeland for anything that would make sense.

"I told him I wanted him to come with me today. He started with excuses. I told him he was coming or it was over... So, here I am, alone and embarrassed... I guess it was easier to pretend I was still dealing with him than to admit he dropped me just like that."

"Well, hallelujah and praise God for His miracles," replied Elaine, patting an unscratched surface of her daughter's leg. "Bria, you listen to me and listen to me good. There ain't no point in fighting to be in a relationship just to end up alone in it."

# Chapter 8

## *In a Word* – Grooving

"Looks like they're wrapping up," Amia announced as she rejoined the partygoers in the backyard about twenty minutes following her earlier departure. She was just in time to hear Gary's account of his and Mable's five-day survival while lost in the Ituri Forest in the northern Congo.

While this adventure was over fifty years old and at the onset of their mission trips, Gary had a way of making it sound like it just happened. Everyone had heard the story of the pair's Jeep breaking down and their decision to walk after waiting for several hours for help that never came.

They were in awe as Mable recounted making a bed out of saplings and shingled tree leaves while surviving on honey and nuts. Gary proudly added that he'd managed to trap a squirrel, but they'd been unable to start a fire, so they couldn't eat it.

Though the seventy-something duo could laugh during this part of the story, it was a bit of a sore spot. After all, Mable asked Gary to bring the fire starter when they'd set out to spread the Good News to the next town, but he intentionally left it, advising they wouldn't need it.

Unfortunately, the alternative—striking rocks together to produce a spark—proved to be unfruitful. Gary was in the midst of animatedly reliving the moment they were awakened by twelve Pygmie men, in full battle markings, each with spears almost the length of their bodies when Elaine, Ramon, and Bria rejoined the family.

"Thank God. We were getting to the part where I peed my pants!"

"Yeah, and the part where she finally found people who she was taller than."

Everyone laughed heartily at the tiny, five-foot-one-inch silver-haired grandmother.

"Hey Dad, lay off my momma," countered Darren as he landed a pretend body shot on his adoptive father.

Mom and dad were treasured monikers as Gary and Mable were never able to have children of their own. Darren, Camille, and Adrienne were literally placed in their lives thirty years earlier.

And here they are today, the proud parents of three incredibly successful children who've so far blessed them with two beautiful grandchildren, one of whom was celebrating his thirteenth birthday today.

"Aunt Bree, you ready?" asked Daniel, excitedly tapping the table in anticipation of the main event.

"Yep, but I'm gonna have Auntie Adree and Auntie Jordie help since I can't lift the cake this time. Jordyn and Adrienne placed the two-tiered Hines Stadium replica gently on the long rectangular white table.

"Alright, y'all ready?"

"Yeah!"

"Nawl, y'all ain't! I said, are y'all ready?"

"Yeahhh!" came the roaring response from everyone, including the giddy birthday boy now sporting his beloved orange and white striped baseball cap which was won by his beloved Uncle Shamir years earlier at Six Flags.

With that, MC Breezy was in the house laying down the bars. No doubt about it, she was a multi-talented young lady with an immense vocabulary thanks to challenging herself to learn ten new words per week.

Bria was expertly weaving in lyrics featuring Daniel's favorite sports and teachers, new braces, and sneakers. She was hitting them with book reports and field trips and fashion designer snippety snips.

Amia couldn't help but wonder how her brilliant sister with so many gifts could have ever formed such a low opinion of herself. *Please touch her, Father God. Let her see herself the way you see her. You made Bria beautifully and wonderfully. Please let her see it. In Jesus name, amen.* Her attention returned to the entertaining show before her.

Jordyn, Adrienne, and Janelle brought the hype, holding their own as backup dancers. One aunt broke into the Running Man while the other resurrected the Cabbage Patch. Aunt Janelle, came through with the Prep. The entire family, including Gary, who'd never so much as swayed to a beat, joined in with some dance variation.

Jamari added the beats as usual. He'd taken his place next to Bria, pounding rhythmically on the table as her lyrics flowed. As with every year, Jamari's beats were supplemented with his unmatched beatboxing.

The birthday rhyme was always a highly anticipated feature that never disappointed. This year, as with all previous years, the hook was, "Cuz it's his birthday. Circled the sun again and it's his birthday."

Because the rap changed each year, the only parts Daniel could really contribute to were the hooks, but man did he take full advantage of them. Grooving to the beats, he was in his full hand motion, collar popping, pose and profiling glory.

Ramon was behind the camera capturing the moments. Marty and Amia turned their iPhone and Galaxy into videography devices capturing all the hands in the air waving like they just didn't care. Though normally a reliable recorder, Darren was too much of a hip-hop head to be trusted with these videos.

They learned that at Daniel's seventh birthday party after everyone became seasick while attempting to watch the playback. Mia jokingly, but seriously, fired her handsome husband on the spot.

The endings of MC Breezy's lyrical renditions were always met with thunderous applause combining adoration for the skills and commitment involved in delivering another memorable performance.

Shortly thereafter, the entire family sang the traditional happy birthday song. Elaine and Mable lit the candles as Jamari winked playfully, turning Daniel's treasured cap backward to avoid the flames (this year).

Within moments, the wish was made, candles were blown, and everyone was partaking in Bria and Jordyn's latest culinary masterpiece, all the while, oohing and awing as Daniel ripped into his presents.

# Chapter 9

## *In a Word* – Unmentionables

"Look on top of the refrigerator," instructed Darren to Adrienne who had been looking for the extra candles.

Though it was Daniel's birthday, the family wanted to take a moment to celebrate one of America's newest neuro psychologists, their very own Dr. Camille Wilford-O'Tannen.

Daniel's cake and ice cream were served and another round of barbequed remnants were licked off fingers before Darren retrieved the blue, yellow, and white cake which featured a photo of the other person of the hour.

Amia cleared the remaining multicolored wrapping papers, tattered card envelopes, and clear plastic plates to make room for Camille's graduation honors. Though a simple task, she was having difficulty completing it due to her husband's wandering hands which were exploring her nooks and attempting to invade her crannies.

"Man, get a room," said Todd as he strolled through the dining room on his way to grab an iced tea. He'd rounded the corner just as Darren helped himself to a handful of Amia's D-cup. To cap his 'disgust,' he covered his eyes, only to part his fingers in jest as he passed by.

"Keep it up, Imma tell ya mammas y'all in here being freaky."

"Who let this Bama back in the house?" asked Darren as he squeezed Amia tightly and nibbled on her neck.

"Hey, Ms. Mable, Ms. Elaine? You need to come get your kids."

Elaine didn't respond as she was outside with Ramon, Marty, and Vicky, stepping to Gregory Porter's *Holding On*. Mable though, was in the vicinity and responded, "What, Todd? I didn't hear you." The sound of her voice told them that she was now heading in their direction.

"You know what?" she whispered as Todd snickered, exiting the paisley wallpapered space while waving a 'shame on you' finger. "I never did like him," she added while brushing Darren's hand away one final time. Mable entered the dining room as the cake was finally positioned in the middle of the table.

"Hun, I didn't hear. What was Todd saying?"

"Nothing, Ma," Darren replied, bending his six-foot-four-inch frame down to kiss her on the cheek.

"Oh, you're misbehaving. That cheek kiss only comes when you've been up to something."

She then squeezed him tightly around the waist and winked at Amia. "If you kids need a few minutes alone in the pantry, I can stall everyone. Oh now, don't you look at me like that," she remarked in response to their surprised faces.

"Sweetheart, your dad and I are old, but we're not dead. What do they call it? Getting your groove on? Well, your dad and I sti—"

"What the? Objection!" Darren interrupted.

"No, Ma'am, we are absolutely not having this conversation."

He motioned the amused Mable and her pink flamingo cardigan to one of the silver and white high back dining room chairs, quickly handing her a clear plastic plate featuring one of Jordyn's cookie treats.

"Eat this, Ma," he insisted, gently coaxing the plate upwards towards her face.

"I don't understand why you're being so uptight, Dear. We have sex every day. It's a normal—"

"Oh my God, Ma. You're killing me right now! Eat a cupcake, please."

"And have some cucumber water," added Mia, quickly handing her the chilled beverage that she'd just extracted from their tall glass canister.

Seeking to change the subject, Darren remembered his sister and her earlier quest.

"Adree, did you find the candles?" he yelled into the kitchen.

"Mia," he whispered under his breath. "Remind me to kick Todd's ass. The one thing I did not need in my life was a visual of those two having... relations. I'm never gonna unhear that," he said as he dutifully pushed Amia's tickled jaw shut.

"Not yet," replied Adrienne. Unable to quite reach the top of the stainless-steel chef's fridge, Adrienne called in Camille for assistance. She was able to locate the candles, which were lying just under a curious packet.

Camille and Adrienne returned to the gift-strewn blue-gray dining room passing so quickly they didn't notice Mable or her chocolate-covered lips in the corner. They surrounded their older brother as Adrienne brandished the correspondence. Amia's heart sank. It was the envelope that Janelle stuck up there during she and Todd's visit to Amia and Darren's a week earlier.

Amia and Janelle were in the kitchen prepping side dishes and talking while Darren and Todd were in the back on the grill. The letter arrived just as Darren and Todd were returning to the kitchen with the last of the grilled pork chops.

She wasn't going to ruin her husband's day by letting him see the letter right then. With no other place to stash it, Mia's eyes darted to the highest obscure surface, which is where Janelle stashed it.

She'd planned to circle back to Darren about the letter later that evening, but between work, the kids' activities, and planning for Daniel's party, Amia hadn't given it any more thought. Now that momentary slip had blown up in her unsuspecting husband's face.

Darren was understandably confused because he'd been systematically destroying the letters within moments of receipt. He couldn't figure out how he'd somehow missed this one. It wasn't until he looked over at his beautiful wife whose remorseful facade told the whole story without her uttering a single word.

"Th- this is a letter from Dad. Errr… Marshon," stammered Adrienne, her voice teeming with a nervous surprise. She'd been only seven years old when everything went down.

"Why is it on top of your fridge?" she asked, flipping the envelope back and forth while trying to process its presence.

"Better question, big brother: Why haven't you mentioned it?" asked Camille sharply. She was eleven when their parents were convicted, and had a vivid memory of the courthouse, her parents' convictions and every conniving transgression their biological father, Marshon Wilford, had subjected Darren to.

# Chapter 10

## *In a Word* – Reflections

Exactly four weeks following Daniel's birthday party, Jamari joined Darren for a Saturday morning chock full of coaching and mentoring. Darren's Will Forward football camp was now in its twenty-second year and was regarded as one of the most elite training programs on the east coast.

Having credited his own collegiate success to Darren and his organization's tutelage, Jamari was uniquely qualified to lend his expertise to the new class of aspiring athletes.

Unfortunately, a knife attack by Amia's biological father while a sophomore at Penn State, left his right hand badly damaged. Two successful surgeries and years of rehabilitation weren't enough to allow Jamari to regain the hand strength required to snatch well-thrown spirals out of midair.

He'd completed less than ten of his famous one-handed Air Jordan-esque catches in his short post-high school career. The attack not only ended his professional aspirations, it also cost the university hundreds of thousands of dollars in marketing materials of the then-number-one recruit. Jamari's fully splayed signature move had been superimposed on the number Thirty-five and branded on everything from ticket stubs to hoodies and banners.

Though he was unable to break the receiving records and dominate at the next level as was the expectation of all the talking heads, he was instrumental to that team's success over the course of his five years at the esteemed university.

Jamari was beyond honored to spend time coaching and mentoring the kids, giving them as much attention as he'd received from Darren. He made sure to call every child's name and make eye contact with each one at some point during the sessions.

Of all the lessons he learned from the years of one-on-one with Darren, looking a person in the eyes when you speak to them was right up at the top. That conversation still vibrates in his core.

"Of course, I hear you," a frustrated Jamari responded after doing his fifteenth wind sprint. "I said, yes. Why do I have to look you in the eyes when I say it?"

"Because, Jamari," Darren replied as he took a seat on the bleacher, peering down at the exhausted teenager who was sitting on the track squeezing Gatorade into his parched throat. "If you asked me a question and I responded without ever looking at you, how would you feel?"

"I'd be cool. I mean, you answered the question. What else is there?"

"What about respect?"

"I don't get it," Jamari replied with obvious confusion. "You're respecting me by answering my question, right?" he added.

"True, I would be answering your question. But without eye contact, I might as well waive my hand and tell you to kick rocks. Look, Mari, if a man doesn't respect you enough to acknowledge your presence when he's speaking to you, you should question his intentions.

"What do you mean, D? I don't have any hidden agenda."

"Alright, let me say it like this... You used to run the streets, right?" He continued after Jamari shrugged his shoulders and nodded, "That would be a yes, right?"

"Yes."

"Always speak, even if you're not proud of what will come out of your mouth. Your voice has power. Use it. Do you understand me?"

"Yes"

"Alright. Back in the streets, even though you couldn't trust many people, you knew who you absolutely could not trust, right? It was those cats who would never look you in the eye 'cause they were up to no good.

"It's the same principle. Granted, it's a different game, but we're still talking about people. You need to make sure the people you talk to know you've got integrity. They need to know you care enough to be present in the conversation. There aren't too many people who will give you a shot if you can't do something as basic as show respect.

"Let me ask you a question. This whole time we've been talking, it's been eye-to-eye, right?" Jamari nodded in agreement. Darren tilted his head and paused.

"I mean, yes," Jamari corrected quickly, realizing that he'd just employed a nonverbal response.

"Good man," smiled Darren. "When you realize how much strength and command are in your voice, you'll never stop using it." He took a few long swallows from his water bottle.

"I'll finish with this: I'm interested in who you are as a person *and* in what you say. You know that because, I'm always physically engaged with you in our conversations." Then, crushing his now empty water bottle and replacing the cap, he added, "Never forget that, Mari. Shake a hand and make eye contact when you're speaking with someone. Let them know you care. Try it, and watch what happens."

Jamari smiled. He fondly remembered all the moments he and Darren shared back then. Looking back on it, he credited every single one of them with shaping him into the man he is today.

Darren was the big brother he'd never had and Jamari was the little brother Darren begged God for year after year growing up. As he laced his green Adidas and stretched the gold whistle's lanyard around his neck, Mari thanked God again for the opportunity.

"Good morning, Coach Copeland," greeted Corey, one of the campers who'd made it his business to be car side as soon as possible whenever he saw Jamari's blue gray Wrangler pull into the parking lot.

"Good morning, Mr. Burroughs," Jamari replied, smiling widely at the bright-eyed seventh grader.

"Thank you, Sir," Mari added as Corey grabbed the ball bag out the trunk. Because Jamari was all about ensuring these kids knew they would one day be grown men, contributing to society, he referred to them as Mr. then last name.

Jamari's theory was that calling them Mr. So-and-so would reduce childish behavior because the coaches expected more from them. In his eight years as assistant coach, the kids, ages thirteen to eighteen, hadn't failed him.

"You're welcome, Coach. I got a B+ on my science test and an A- on my math test," he beamed.

"My man," Jamari replied fist bumping the youngster. The pair continued chatting as they were greeted by more eager teens ready for today's activities.

"Coach Mari, Grayson said you jumped out of a plane last week."

"He said what? Where's Grayson Jennings?" Jamari asked, scanning the curious faces near him. A burly lineman popped his head through the density of shoulder pads. "Right here, Coach," the husky youngster responded.

"You gotta check your sources before you repeat stuff, Mr. Jennings. Where you getting your facts, Bruh?"

"My uncle said he saw you last week," he replied meekly.

"Well, your uncle's wrong, Mr. Jennings... I didn't jump out of a plane last week. I jumped out of two planes last week!"

Helmet grabbing and full-blown calamity ensured as that revelation coursed through the youngsters. Jamari and Grayson shared the team's cool, intricate handshake which always accompanied an extra-amazing play.

Jamari poked Grayson's shoulder, smiling at the youngster who was beyond relieved that his uncle had been right about seeing Jamari suit up at the skydiving center. His confirmation trigged a multitude of replies.

"That's so cool."

"You're crazy, Coach."

"No way could I ever do that."

"Can I go next time?"

"Didn't you ride an elephant too, Coach?

"Can we see pictures?"

Jamari's pearly whites were on full display as he interacted with the youngsters. Because they still had a few minutes, he kneeled allowing the guys to crowd around oohing and awing as he swiped.

"That's your wife, Coach?"

"Yep. Her name is Michele."

"She's in the blue jumpsuit right there," Jamari added swiping again and zooming in on the free-falling pair who were roughly fifteen hundred feet below him at the time of the photo.

"She's really pretty," noted Cameron, the ladies' man of the bunch.

"You checking out my wife, Mr. Jackson? Alright..." Jamari quipped as he pushed himself off the ground. "We're done here," he added, playfully smacking Cameron's helmet.

The entourage walked towards the freshly-lined turf of the impressive football field to join Darren, while the kids intently discussed whether they'd be brave enough to parasail, hike Glacier Bay, ride a camel, or take on the Dragon's Breath zipline like Jamari. One thing was for sure, the kids got to live vicariously through Coach Jamari's love of adventure, which he hoped would rub off.

"What up, Coach D?"

"It's all you, Baby," exclaimed Darren as he and Jamari embraced. "Ready to whip these young men into shape, Coach D?"

"Let's get it."

"Bet... Hey Mikey, lead us in prayer." Everyone bowed their heads as the ginormous ninth grader with a surprisingly soft voice prayed earnestly for an impactful, injury-free day.

Jamari smiled again at God's goodness. Here he was in a position to pour into the lives of these young men, just as had been done years earlier for him. Not only that, he got to do it alongside one of his favorite people on the planet, Darren Wilford.

Every amen Jamari ever said was meant, but todays was uttered with an extra happy heart.

"I-I-I d-d-don't know, C-C-Coach," replied Trevaris after Darren suggested he step into the quarterback position.

"Look at me, Trevaris Reynolds. If I didn't think you could handle it, I wouldn't be putting you into this spot. You're about as accurate as it gets. You scramble well and you've got a high game IQ. Yeah, you're a good receiver, but I think you'd be a better quarterback. You know I've been watching you.

"B-B-But, I-I-I can't."

"Why not? Because you stutter?

"Y-Y-Yes," replied the sophomore weakly.

"So, you're telling me that rather than try to figure out a way to make this happen, you'd let this one thing stop you?"

"N-Nooo," he replied with tears of frustration welling, because Trevaris secretly dreamed of being a QB. To pass the time while unfairly incarcerated, he'd pretend to take snaps, step back and throw.

Trevaris knew he was better than every other kid currently in the spot, but to be really good, he had to be able to communicate effectively, and that's something he could not do. His stuttering kept him from taking the stand in his own defense and here it was again, threatening to take away another opportunity.

"Mr. Reynolds," Darren counseled while putting a hand on either side of the youngster's shoulder pads. "What did I tell you during trial? Trust in the truth, right?" Trevaris nodded. Darren tilted his head to the side.

"I-I-I mean ye-ye-yes."

"Good man... Look, I know you're afraid, and that's ok. Some fear is good. It means you're human, but fear can also steal your blessings. We can get so caught up in being afraid that we miss out on what God has for us. I'm not gonna to let that happen to you, understand? Yeah you stutter, but your voice is still as strong and important as anyone else's.

"Listen, Satan was already mad because God made him back up off you. Now he's mad because you're handling your business as a young dad. I saw the photos you posted with him earlier this week, and that last report card looked pretty slick too if I remember correctly." Trevaris smiled for the first time since the non-stop practice began.

"I mean, truth be told, you might as well piss Satan all the way off by continuing to outlive his lies."

Trevaris kept smiling and began beaming as it sunk in. Darren believed in him. Of course, his parents believed in his abilities, but this was different. Darren Wilford, his attorney who knows how badly he stutters, thinks he can be a great quarterback!

Trevaris' adolescent heart threatened to burst through his scrawny chest. It seemed to grow larger as another dream appeared to be coming true. In his short life, he'd had two constant prayers. The first was to get out of jail. The other was to play the quarterback position. His prayer had been to take one snap. Never did he imagine there was a chance he could actually hold the spot.

Trevaris looked into the stands. He could see his dad standing, trying to decipher their on-field conversation while his mom and Tori played with little Charley. The teen began nodding his head at Darren. His shoulders appeared to sit up higher. His fearful short breaths replaced by long, confident inhales. Trevaris didn't know how it was going to work, but he trusted Darren, who was married to Amia, who seemed to have God on speed dial.

"Now," he said, happy to see this young man willing to rise to the challenge, "how about you get your talented self over there and do the job that we both know you can do," he added with a loving whack on the shoulder pads.

Overhearing the conversation, Jamari blew his whistle, motioning everyone in and giving the stage to Darren who was now deep in thought. The boys stood in silent anticipation awaiting the head coach's comments.

Five one-thousand, six one-thousand, seven one-thousand. Jamari nudged Darren whose gaze had fixated on one of the four dozen dirty jerseys now heaving repeatedly due to the athletes hustling over. Moments later, he addressed the bunch.

"Guys, Trevaris is moving to quarterback. Everybody knows he stutters. Y'all have seen him throw the ball. You know he's got one of the best arms out here, and he can read a defense like nobody's business."

He paused, making eye contact with the scrawny youngster he'd spent over a year bonding with, before continuing intently, "We all have an opportunity to find out exactly what we're made of. Offense, you have to learn another method of communicating.

"How many straight A students do we have? Good, how many AB students? Alight, what about my ABC students? Where are my ABCD students?" he asked, though all hands were already raised.

"Mr. Brewton, we're gonna have that grade situation taken care of by the end of the summer, right?"

The kids erupted in laughter at Chris Brewton's confused facial expression. After all, he and Trevaris were the only ones who'd raised their hands in response to the straight A question.

"All jokes aside," said Jamari, scanning the youngsters intently, "Coach D and I find ourselves surrounded by some pretty incredible critical thinkers this morning. We have no doubt you'll figure something out."

# Chapter 11

## *In a Word* – Haunted

Amia headed down the darkened staircase towards the home office. She'd been making the late-night journey into the workspace far too often for her liking these days, but she knew she'd find her preoccupied husband hard at work.

"*That's weird*," she thought pausing at the hallway entry. Unlike previous wee-hour visits, this night, there were no hints of light peeking from behind the closed barn doors.

"Babe, what are you doing in the dark," asked Amia as she reached for the light switch to illuminate the blackened space.

"Leave the light off, please," he responded tersely. Darren had snuck into the confines of their home office repeatedly in the weeks since his family learned about Marshon's letters.

Though initially angry with his wife for allowing the secret to surface, it had proven to be a small blessing. Darren no longer had to worry about what would happen or what his family would think if they'd found out.

Everyone knew and the only person who wasn't angry at Marshon's intrusion was Adrienne. Darren's little sister hadn't experienced their parents in the same manner. As the baby, she'd only seen the givers of teddy bears and lollipops. Adrienne never got to meet the ruthless, cold-blooded killers.

In addition, Gary and Mable never spoke ill of their parents. They would only say Marshon and Desiree made mistakes that got them in trouble with the law. It wasn't until Darren, in a fit of rage, blurted out their crimes after Adrienne's second full week of crying endlessly for their parents. In the years since, Mable and Gary nursed her, Camille and Darren's hearts back to health.

"Babe, tell me what's wrong. I'm scared."

"Mia, I'm good. I got it. Go back to bed, please," he added, taking a swig of White Hennessey.

"You're drinking in the dark," she uttered incredulously. "Darren Jamison, I'm going to ask you one more time, and I swear, you better not tell me nothing." She was now really worried, but it was manifesting as anger.

"Oh snap... Whipped out the middle name on a brotha," he replied, swirling the liquid half drunkenly.

Amia pulled up a chair next to him in the corner. Soft lighting filled the space with a gentle tap at the base of the elaborate white rattan floor lamp. Only then could she see the pain being concealed by the darkness.

"C'mon, Babe," he winced. The light highlighted a solitary trail of moisture that had made its way from his eyelid to his rigid jawline. She hadn't seen a tear leave his eyes since their precious Christina Renee was placed in their arms at the hospital years earlier.

This lonely, salt-laden streak; however, was not the result of joy or heartfelt happiness. Amia pulled his head into her chest, holding her man tightly.

"Babe, let me in, please. Tell me what's been going on."

Darren inhaled his wife's essence, feeling her loving spirit and desire to lift this load from him. He leaned into her embrace, resting his head on her chest, listening as the breath filled and exited her lungs. The rhythmic thumping of her heart filled his ears.

Darren's powerful arms snaked around Amia's curves tightly, pulling her out of the white leather armchair and onto his lap.

"I need you," Darren whispered hoarsely, as he tugged at the tie holding the folds of her robe together. He kissed her fiercely upon finding her completely naked underneath.

"Where's the nightgown?" he asked, distinctly remembering her clad in a faded green and white gown when he slipped out of their bed.

"I thought you might like this outfit better."

Though Amia had fallen asleep clothed, upon waking and finding herself alone in their king-sized bed for the fourth night straight, she slipped out of the sleeper, dawning the thick teal terry cloth garment and headed towards the office.

"My gown's on your side of the bed," she replied with a sultry smile.

Darren's side of the bed is where any garment he removed from her body always landed. She traced his jawline with her lips. All other nights, Darren was able to convince her to go back to bed before following up soon after. Tonight though, she had no intentions of leaving the cozy office without a very satisfied husband in tow.

Their tongues tangled as she freed her love's love from his tweed pajamas, immediately sliding onto his hot, firm strength.

The passion intensified as she rocked fiercely against him in the high-backed leather chair. They eventually found their way into the corner behind his desk. Darren growled in appreciation of Amia's new-found flexibility, thanks to her and Janelle's last five months of Bikram Yoga. She was on her tiptoes, holding onto his neck and back for dear life. The two connecting walls offered support as they engaged in the oldest rhythm known to man.

The pair ended up thoroughly enjoying themselves atop the thick marble desk, before collapsing in a sweaty, exhausted heap on the floor in front of the gas fireplace.

Darren retrieved Mable's quilted blanket from a drawer within the large white wall unit, as she pulled a few napkins from a frosted glass tissue box. The fire roared to life with the simple flip of a switch.

"Thank you," she said happily, after taking a sip of ginger ale that he'd extracted from the built-in's mini fridge.

They sat silently basking in the warmth of the fire and each other while watching the flames wrap around the realistic brown ceramic logs. Amia knew her husband enough to know that some good lovin' was always enough to get him to open up. She waited patiently as he traced tiny circles along her outstretched forearm.

Moments later, Darren left Mia's side to retrieve a gray parcel from his top drawer. As he slid back down, he lovingly nibbled her earlobe before handing her the unopened envelope.

"I know I told you I didn't open any of the letters, but I did read the first two. I know, I'm sorry," he raised his hands apologetically as Amia's eyes widened.

"Marshon somehow heard that I was a defense attorney. He wants me to look into his case. Supposedly, he thinks he was tried unfairly and had the nerve to say that there was no case without me. He's claiming parent/child privilege, citing a Nevada case from 2003 as a reason to throw out my testimony.

"He actually said he forgave me for lying because he knew the government made me testify against him... "Darren paused to control the source of his earlier sadness. Amia shifted her still-naked body so that one of her long slender legs slipped between his. She pecked his shoulder, encouraging him to continue.

"Babe, it's embarrassing and I can't believe I'm saying this out loud, but thirty years later, I can still hear him yelling that I'd never amount to anything right there in the middle of the courtroom.

"He told me I was dead to him. Now, suddenly, I have something of value and I'm alive again. I don't know why I care still, Amia. I mean, it's stupid, but sometimes... "Darren paused, staring into the fire.

"Sometimes what, Babe?"

"It's stupid. I don't know why I still care." He shifted, shaking his head in frustration.

"Babe, it's not stupid. It hurts. It has to. I'm so sorry you're dealing with this."

"You know what's ironic," he added while kissing her knee and stroking her thigh. "Today, I pushed Trevaris to move to the quarterback position. He's petrified, but I'm pushing him to do it, because I know he'll excel." He paused for a half-hearted chuckle before continuing, "I had the nerve to tell him not to let fear stop him.

"Truth is, I'm a hypocrite, Amia. I'm afraid. That's why I haven't opened any more letters. I'm scared to find out he doesn't really care about me and probably never did. Babe, all my life, I've fought to be somebody. I've grinded so hard to be successful because I still hear those words... I wanted to prove him wrong.

"What if it was all for nothing?" he paused, clearing the building lump in his throat, dabbing his eyes. He kissed Amia's knee again, before continuing.

"Then there's the other half of me that wants him to catch the next flight straight to Hell. In neither letter did he offer one apology. Not one 'I'm sorry for letting you sit in juvie for a year.' Not a single, 'I heard you were doing well.' Not one 'I'm proud of you.' Not a question about my life or a 'How are Camille and Adrienne?' I'm forty-seven-years old... Cards on the table?"

"Of course, Babe."

"Remember my summation at Trevaris' trial before we went into chambers? Remember when I put his photo on the screen and told the jury that he'd cried all the way to the station and bawled in central booking?"

"Yes," she replied softly.

Another round of tears left his eyes. This time, he didn't dab or blink them away. "I was talking about me," he confessed. "When Marshon framed me, I cried in the squad car. I was crying so hard in central booking that I couldn't breathe, and my mugshot was taken right after I blew my nose for the tenth time... My hand had barely moved away from my face when he took the picture. Truth be told, he had to. That was his only chance to get it."

Amia cupped Darren's taut jaw gently before running her fingers across his salt and pepper goatee. She turned her handsome husband's face towards hers, planting a loving kiss on his full lips and moist cheeks.

She started to respond to the outpouring of the heart, but was cut short by his soft lips and probing tongue. His strong fingers traced her long neck before tangling fiercely in the coils of her hair.

Amia's goal in life was to never see her man upset or anxious, but deep down, she enjoyed the intensity of these moments. The spiritual connection that always emerged as their bodies literally collided was unmatched. It actually felt like the heavens and Earth moved differently during these impassioned encounters.

She had Darren pause his focused ravishment of her body long enough to grab the lone envelope and toss it into the fire. They watched in silence as its unopened contents were consumed by orange and white flickers.

He wasn't sure how it was even possible but, in that moment, Darren fell hopelessly in love with his wife all over again. Oh, how he thanked God for sending her his way. There, in those waning early morning hours, he made it his mission to let her mind and all five feet ten inches of her beautiful caramel physique know it.

# Chapter 12

## *In a Word* – Issues

"Weeks later, Jamari exited the beautiful Pittsburgh Field Clubhouse, carefully balancing two tall glasses in one hand while extending a frothy pint of golden goodness to Todd with the other. The trio just finished the first nine holes of the brilliantly landscaped course. Todd and Jamari each garnered their usual sixty-two, but interestingly, the Ace, Darren had managed to shoot a measly fifty-three.

Darren hadn't shot above forty-five since the Sunday after Amia's breakfast meeting with Andrew DeSimeon months earlier.

"Dude, what gives?" asked Jamari as he watched Darren interlock his hands behind his head. His eyes focused on two bald eagles circling over a nearby patch of woods. Todd gently tapped his shoe against Darren's, getting his attention.

"My bad. We've got the Bear Heart fundraiser coming up. I'm tying up loose ends with that, and I've got a huge case tha—"

"Wrong answer," interrupted Todd, his arms crossed making an X.

"You love that event, and honestly, you weren't this distracted the first time you ever tried a case. If I remember correctly, you were in the bathroom puking your guts out ten minutes before that trial began. Come on, Bruh. We've been Boyz way too long. You gotta to come better than that."

"D, it's us. We keep it real, right? Ok, so what's up?" added Jamari after Darren muttered a soft 'yeah' under his breath.

Darren scratched his goatee which made both men take notice. They knew that any conversation which began with his fingers on the chin was going to be deep.

"Marshon is dying. He wants me to come see him."

"How do..." Jamari's voice trailed off as Darren extracted two folded pieces of paper from the back pocket of his green checkered trousers.

Jamari studied Darren's poker face as Todd angrily snatched the sheets from his best friend's outstretched hand. Todd was always the guy who got along with anyone and never held grudges, but with all of the pain inflicted on Darren in his youth, Todd could easily push Marshon off a cliff and not think twice about it.

*I don't know why you haven't responded to my letters. Maybe everyone has turned you against me. I'm innocent and have asked you to look at my case several times. I don't understand why you would let me rot in prison.*

*I'm your father and I did nothing but love you.*

Todd stopped short of ripping the letter to shreds.

"Man, forget Marshon," Todd curved his fury and his volume as a father and his young son appeared suddenly, excusing themselves as they quickly crossed to the large, adjacent cobblestone patio. He stood holding the now crumpled college-ruled pages.

Jamari slowly pried the contents from Todd's fists. He'd only heard of Marshon Wilford a few times in his life and each had been during a discussion of Darren's courage and perseverance. Now, the former drug lord was front and center.

*I have prostate cancer and the doctors say I have about twelve months, but what do they know. Maybe you can get off your high horse long enough to come see about your dad.*

The last few words were spoken at just above a whisper as Jamari could not believe the audacity emanating through the squiggly black ink.

*"If this kind of arrogance can jump off of a page, I can only imagine how pompous this man must be in person,"* Jamari thought to himself, feeling just a mere fraction of the complex emotions that Darren had been experiencing.

Darren chased the salty tortilla chips and guacamole with a small sip of his Carib Lager. His fingers fidgeted nervously on the glass flute.

"He's something else, right? This man planted two kilograms of coke in my bookbag when I was fourteen and then tried to frame me for murder, but we're just gonna breeze by all that." Darren popped another dip-filled chip.

"All these years, all I've ever wanted was for him to apologize and say he's proud of me. Now, he's dying, and I'm probably never gonna hear any of those words from him."

Darren took a full gulp for the first time since easing down into the heavy red Adirondack chair.

"You know what's crazy? I imagined him trying to call on my birthdays and hating he wasn't there to help me with my tie for the homecoming dances. I dreamed about him cheering me on and bragging to other inmates about being my father during our televised games at Temple."

"Dawg, you've got kids. You know what a real father is and what it means. Marshon was a hustler who made a name for himself in the drug game. The fact that he helped create you doesn't change who he was. He was a gangster, not a father. Period.

"That fool looked out for Marshon and I hate to say it, but based on what's in that letter, he's still looking out for Marshon," noted Todd between crunches on his pretzels.

"Look, D, that father figure you spent years conjuring up doesn't exist. He never did," Jamari said.

"Remember when I first went to live with Mia, and I was mad about my mom and dad? I was telling you what I wished they would have done and how I wish they would have acted. Remember what you told me?"

Darren elected not to answer; instead, returning his focus to the sky and the now tiny black specks swirling at the edge of the heavens. Undaunted, Jamari repeated Darren's wise words which he's even repeated to campers a few times over the years, "The most successful people see a shark as a shark. They know it's a shark and behave accordingly. The ones who struggle are those who see a shark, know it's a shark, but act like it's a dolphin. The point is ignoring reality can be bad for your health."

"Dawg, I know that you know that I know you know Marshon ain't no damn dolphin," Todd added, taking a swig of his brew.

Darren and Jamari each shook their heads in response to Todd's timely Kevin Hart impression.

"Seriously though," Todd smiled while rubbing the mustard sauce from his hands onto the black cloth napkin,

"Besides our opinion, Gary and God's are the only ones that should ever matter to you." Todd winked at Darren then stood up pulling his best friend since college in for an embrace.

"Shake that fool off. If you want to see him, go see him, but don't let him guilt you into anything. I wish he would brag to someone about you being his son. Dying or not, I'll choke slam that brotha and send him off yonder myself," he added.

Darren and Jamari each paused at the visual of Todd in all of his WWE glory choke slamming Marshon.

"What? Why y'all looking at me like that? I mean, I'm saved... Just not delivered," Todd added as Darren and Jamari laughed again at his craziness and the return of Kevin Hart.

"I'm just saying. He's been busy delivering me from all my other stuff. I mean, I got this cussing thing. You know I like my Black Jack tables way too much. And real talk, I'm still learning the difference between thee and thou.

"I mean, you two need to relax your freakin' expectations a little. I'm just now learning how to pray more than three sentences at a time. Like seriously, y'all gots ta give a brotha a couple more minutes. I mean, my boys Matthew, Mark, Luke and John had me on a conference call just last week talking 'bout Jesus put me on a performance plan."

Two-thirds of the trio were no longer reclined in their chairs, instead, Darren and Jamari were each leaning forward in laughter. Their overpriced beverages had long since assumed residence atop the all-weather glass-top end tables. This positioning ensured the tickled friends would take in the next nine holes without wet clothing or the smell of hops announcing their presence.

"Dude, what is wrong with you?" Jamari managed, stretching out the cramp he'd caught in his side before cracking up once more.

By the time the trio regained their composure, Amia was on the line, fully agreeing with the world's need to cover Todd in extra special prayer.

Ten minutes later, Darren thanked his circle for their friendship and wisdom, advising that he'd give some thought to visiting Marshon, but was pretty sure the timing would be closer to twelve months from now. With the cold beverages gone and snack plates squeaky clean, the forever bonded trio was back in their carts, rounding the second nine.

# Chapter 13

## *In a Word* – Ambush

"Let's go, Marty! Let's go, Darren! Come on, Mike!" The WW&M staff chanted while waving signs as their firm's three partners gritted out the last 400 meters of the endurance run.

Scores of fans cheered on all the finishers as they increased the pace, throwing every last ounce of energy into crossing the line. The WW&M cheering squad sported custom blue and orange T-shirts.

Twenty minutes after crossing the finish line, the partners regained enough stamina to head back to the finish line and wait for additional finishers.

"Let's go, 'Nel. Come on babe! You got this," Todd yelled, beaming with pride at his wife for taking on this challenge. Everyone excitedly crowded near the foot-long finish line again to root on Janelle, the only female of their entourage, who signed up for today's marathon.

"Where is she?" asked Amia, unable to reconcile her bestie's features with the distressed faces and physiques of the passing competitors as they pushed through the last leg.

"Excuse me, Mr. Wilford. I mean, Darren," came a familiar voice from behind. A microphone and camera met the group as they turned.

"Darren... I'd love to ask you a few questions."

"There she is! Asley Tesleep from WBEA TV," he said with a friendly warmth. "How've you been? How's the family and your new Labradoodle pup?"

"Everyone is fine," she replied. "And the puppy. Oh goodness, he is full of energy. Thanks for asking. If it's ok, I'd like to ask you a few questions about—"

"Today's event?" replied Darren.

"I wasn't planning on speaking with the media today. I mean, I'm drenched. I know I smell, and I'm exhausted. I'll probably be blabbering. Not sure I'd be the best subject."

"Oh, come on, Darren. Please, it'll be quick. I just have a couple of questions," she countered.

"I'd be happy to answer questions about today's Bear Heart event—but *only* questions about today's event."

"Darren, I've left several messages and I'm really trying to get your side of the stor—"

"The story about our Bear Heart event?" he cut in again. This time, the dimples and winning smile were replaced by a taut jaw and a piercing glare.

"Look, I've always respected your hustle, so I'll give you an interview, but I'm only discussing the fundraiser."

Asley reluctantly agreed to interviewing Darren about today's activities. She knew from years of interviewing the partners at WW&M that they would eventually give her a scoop. After checking the connection and lighting, the brief live chat was underway."

"Well, Asley, this is the sixth year of The Bear's Heart, our blood and organ donation awareness event in honor of Steven O'Tannen, my brother-in-law and Shamir Copeland, Amia's youngest brother. As you know, Shamir and his coach, Steven, tragically drowned along with fifteen teammates while boating in the Chesapeake Bay."

"Yes, we remember that. If I recall, the weekend excursion was a gift from the University's Athletic Director for winning the Division I Championship two years in a row," added Asley. "It was an engine fire that caused the yacht to capsize, right? So tragic. We are all so sorry for your loss."

"Thank you," he said as he pulled Amia into the shot, kissing her forehead.

"Good morning," Asley said, extending her slim silver microphone in Amia's direction. "You're the primary organizer of today's event. Can you tell us more about why events like this were so important to your younger brother?"

"Sure, Asley. Shamir had been a staunch advocate for organ, blood and plasma donations since the infamous shooting at Weeboy Manor which occurred when he was a junior in high school."

"Yes, I remember that. Our viewers might recall you and Darren, your husband, were critically wounded during the incident."

"That's right, we received a total of fourteen life-saving blood transfusions. We owe our lives to God and the generous blood donors. Shamir recognized that and urged his classmates to donate blood. The endeavor was so successful that he continued organizing blood drives and awareness events twice a year, every year until his death.

"My brother was a registered organ donor, but of the fifteen passengers, he was one of the seven whose bodies were never found," she added with strained courage.

"We decided to channel the pain of losing Shamir, into motion. Though we couldn't honor his wishes to be an organ donor, we could honor his memory by continuing his cause. With that, the blood drives and organ donation registrations continued. Each year, it has grown. We added the marathon to this year's event because Shamir loved running and would have turned twenty six this October."

"And Steven, my sister's husband," added Darren, "was a lifelong distance runner and advocated for more Black athletes to compete in those events. As a coach, he was responsible for the tremendous growth of Morgan State's incredible distance program and Shamir's success. Steven was a gift and is truly missed.

"That's wonderful. I applaud you for keeping your brother and brother-in-law's memories alive and for promoting such an incredible cause."

"Thank you, Asley," replied Amia and Darren in unison.

"Just one more question. Darren, would you like to comment on the rumors surrounding the illegal financing of your Will Forward Football Camp?"

Acutely aware of the audience peering through the other end of the camera, Darren offered, "Asley, there's nothing I can do about rumors. I can tell you that in life and in business, I have never made any illegal or unethical moves." The last two words were carefully chosen and aimed directly at Asley for this ambush on live television.

"Asley," Amia interrupted as Darren excused himself, returning to the finish line. "I'd like to remind everyone that we will be here for a couple more hours registering donors and saving lives."

She then shared the location with the viewers and urged those at home to consider blood and organ donations.

The irritated WW&M staff also returned their attention to the finish line. Asley threw it back to the studio and signed off as Amia confronted her.

"I'm not about to go off on you right here, but please believe I got you."

"Careful, Amia. I would hate to think you're threatening me," replied Ashley with a warm smile, giving the impression that this was a friendly conversation.

"No, you know that's not who I am. But since you're in the mood for questions, I have one for you. Does Terrence know that baby might not be his?"

Asley's faux smile cracked.

"Oh yeah, Sis. I know. I'm on Fifteenth Street regularly. There's this really cute Bed & Breakfast that I've watched you creep in and out of with your other boo for months now.

"And before you say it's not you, I'll just add that whoever is messing around with Terrence's cousin pulls up in a white chromed-out BMW with a two-toned tan interior. She also carries a white Dooney in the fold of her arm.

Remarkably, it looks exactly like the one tucked into your wing right now."

Asley swallowed hard, her poker face failing. "So what? You're resorting to blackmail?"

"Again, that's not who I am."

If Amia's thoughts had been attached to sound, this is how the conversation could have actually happened. She could have easily let the words fly because it was true. She'd seen Asley exit that white Mercedes and head into the Bed & Breakfast for over a year. Sometimes, she'd arrive before the bodybuilder. Though, most often, he'd be waiting in his black Navigator, hopping out just after her arrival.

Amia thought of it as an interesting coincidence the first few times she saw them. It all changed the moment she watched him pretend to drop his keys and kiss her belly on the way back up as they left that February morning's rendezvous. Back then, there was no bump poking through the body-hugging neon leggings. Aside from those two, and maybe Terrence, Amia was the first to learn of the pregnancy.

Even still, she couldn't bring herself to go there. Instead, Amia just employed the facts.

"Asley, there are three news stations here today. Each of them has approached Darren. Did you know he agreed to one interview and one interview only? You literally just locked yourself out of every future exclusive—and not just from our firm, but WW&M Pro Bono, Reyes & Reyes, Steepleton & Green, and The Hopsteds. Those are just the ones off the top of my head... And for what?"

"Amia, Darren volunteered the story about how his camp got started when I interviewed him for last quarter's City Magazine," she retorted. "I'm getting calls that contradict his claims and just need him to correct the record."

"Calls from who exactly, Asley? Oh, right," she added, "you can't reveal your sources.

"Asley, Darren gave you your first job. He's been a built-in reference for any and everything related to your career goals. There's nothing to correct, and you know it, Hun," she said with the soothing tone of a big sister.

"My source is credible, Amia. If it wasn't, I wouldn't be asking... No... demanding that Darren respond. And yes, Will

Forward paid for my books and some of my tuition. That doesn't mean I'm gonna torpedo my career by not following this through. If Darren had nothing to hide, he'd have taken my calls and I wouldn't have had to do what I did today," she replied boldly.

*This would be a good time to get her straight,* Amia thought to herself. A moment later, the sounds of cheering in the background were on-time reminders that she needed to remain cool. After all, they were still at the Bear Heart event.

Amia's plan was to avoid a spectacle that would have surely overshadowed the entire event. Even with Asley hitting a nerve, that goal hadn't changed. She drew a deep breath, turning her head to the heavens, allowing the sun to shine on her skin.

"Listen, Asley, you're not too much older than my sisters and you've got a world of living ahead of you, so I'll tell you like I tell them; you've gotta keep your eye on the big picture. Always think bigger and smarter."

"Think smarter?" Asley repeated as if insulted. She nonchalantly flipped her wavy brownish-blonde hair over her shoulder.

"Your husband better be 'thinking smarter.' If he doesn't address these rumors, he might be heading towards an IRS investigation." She paused before continuing. "You're telling me to think smarter? You need to be giving him that advice," she scoffed.

*Oh no, she didn't,* Amia gritted her teeth. Her nostrils flared as her blood boiled in her veins. *Amia, put this two-timing, arrogant, ungrateful woman on blast! If anyone deserves to get told off, it's her.*

"*Woo, Jesus,*" Amia said to herself, again lifting her face skyward and allowing the soft breeze and sun to penetrate her senses. There was something about taking a breath that allowed enough space to reduce the temperature.

"*Not today, Satan,*" she murmured, resolving that he was not moving her off her rock. Amia could have easily returned to the finish line, but this was Asley Tesleep. She'd known this young lady for years. Amia wanted to reach her. She wanted to give her truly heartfelt advice.

"Asley, I'm not sure why you've chosen this path. I get you're trying to make a mark and a name for yourself, but listen, Honey, if you're planning to build your career by cutting throats, no one will be there to help you when yours gets cut." Amia paused, praying her words were being absorbed, though she figured the young woman was too interested in saving face to acknowledge the smart life advice.

She could hear a new round of cheering in the distance, reminding her to get back and cheer on the rest of the finishers. Amia began backing away as Asley hoisted her white Dooney to her shoulder, turning her pregnant frame back towards her white eClass with the chrome package.

"Amia?" Asley called softly after turning back towards her. Hoping she'd been heard, Amia turned eagerly back to the younger woman.

"Keep your unsolicited and unnecessary advice to yourself. What you need to do with those breaths is tell your husband to answer the phone the next time I call. I really don't want to be the one to ask the IRS to investigate Darren, but if you play with my career, I will." She turned back towards her vehicle.

*Tell her off, Amia!"* screamed a voice from deep within.

*Ugggh!* she thought to herself. As bad as she wanted to, the words wouldn't emerge. She growled again at her inability to go there.

Asley was completely oblivious to Amia's internal struggle, though she never expected a response. She knew what everyone else knew. Amia was way too nice to trade shots. It hadn't happened in the years since she'd known Amia and Asley was willing to bet the farm that it wasn't happening today either. Amia was the person who never lost her cool, which is why Asley felt comfortable firing the shots.

Amia was completely frustrated, but as with her years arguing in chambers, she leaned on rule number one: never let them see you sweat. She never got in the mud while arguing cases. She never had to. Amia's expert positioning of the facts and truth was more than enough, but sometimes...

Amia inhaled again, refocusing. They were still at the Bear Heart event. It was their first marathon. There were more sponsors than the last three years combined, and they were saving lives. That was the name of today's game. Amia would not be giving Asley Tesleep the drama she was itching for.

"Hey, Asley," Amia called back as they were about fifteen meters apart, surprising her with a friendly, earnest tone.

"You should really consider being a blood and organ donor. Bring your husband and have him sign up too. Matter of fact." She paused. *You should bring his cousin, too. No, Amia. You can't say that,* she scolded herself. "You should bring your whole family," she said instead. "I haven't seen most of them since your wedding a couple of years ago. I would love to see your mom and sister. Yeah, bring them by, and let's make it a happy family event."

With that, Amia rejoined her husband, the WW&M family, and Todd at the finish line, just in time to see Janelle emerge from the forest path and head into the home stretch.

"Go, Janelle," she screamed excitedly as her best friend crossed the finish line, even as the heat of frustration was still rising from her scalp.

# Chapter 14

## *In a Word* – Distracted

An ever-growing pile of discards littered the large brown defense attorney's desk inside of the spacious, Maplewood courtroom. Less than three minutes later, another crumpled, scribbled-laden eight by eleven sheet of paper joined the grouping. Amia's aggravation at her inability to weave the right words together in defense of her latest defendant was evident.

"I still think you need to speak to them in Martina's language."

Amia turned towards her brother who'd spent the last thirty minutes listening to her attempts at a closing summation.

Jamari, a psychology professor at Tulane, often lent an opining ear in these crucial moments.

"Listen, she's not the ideal client. She's abrasive, blunt and really not that friendly. Amia, you've got to remember, none of those jurors are gonna hang out with this lady when this is over. Stop trying to make them like her. Lay out the facts. That's it."

Amia tried again, getting a quarter way through before once again growling in frustration.

"Admittedly," Jamari started, "the cards are stacked against this lady. She's an all-around, unpleasant person. Martina's probably borderline narcissistic. That's my professional opinion, but of course, that's without me examining her," he added with a winking smile and his hands up before him.

Amia smiled back at her brother while giving him a phony eye roll. They'd done this dozens of times over the past few years, and even though he knew it was completely unnecessary, Jamari never resisted a chance to throw out the disclaimer to his sister when giving her his professional point of view.

"Any whooo, Professor Copeland," she added with humored disdain.

"You and your professional opinion get on my last nerve, you know that," Amia responded with a small smile in the corner of her mouth. She added one more overly dramatic eye roll and air quotes, emphasizing the words.

"You're really distracted. What gives?"

"Cards on the table?"

"Of course, Sis."

"Part of me wouldn't mind losing this one, because Martina's such a piece of work, but she's innocent." Amia paused before adding, "Besides, I can't do that to the inmates who she'd be joining."

Jamari chuckled.

"She's just so friggin' obnoxious." Amia paused to confirm that she'd landed on a proper middle-ground word. "Yeah, let's go with that."

The difficulty with representing Martina was that she was such a mean-spirited, nasty soul. Amia had to constantly put on a nice face and dismiss the downright ignorant comments Martina would point in her direction. There were countless times she wanted to fire back, but never did, and all that tongue biting was taking a toll.

"Ugggh!"

"Mia? Hey? Come here," Jamari said, stretching his arms out for the second hug since his arrival. "Don't let Martina's spit change your shine."

He squeezed her tightly.

"You've got this, Sis..."

Amia sighed, leaning into his embrace and absorbing her younger brother's wisdom. "You're right," she said before taking a seat next to Jamari on the bannister. The pair scanned the courtroom's high-gloss maple finishes and oversized windows.

"Anything else bugging you?"

"No," she replied.

"Man, Amia. I still can't believe Asley Tesleep. What was she thinking about coming at Darren like that last week? It's hard to believe she's the same sweet little Asley who used to intern at the camp. She is outta control."

"Mar, God knows I wanted to get her for that, but it was our Bear Heart event and our first marathon. Do you know how many cameras were there, Jamari?" Amia groaned again at the thought of the annual event's highlight being a viral video of two Black women, one of whom was heavily pregnant, arguing in the middle of the day with kids around.

"I don't even want to think about that nonsense or the rumors that would have swirled from it. Do you know how embarrassing that would have been for Bean and Danny? For Darren? For you guys? For WW&M?" Amia sighed again, leaning her head on her brother's strong shoulder.

Amia chuckled to herself. "Mar, could you imagine my conversation with God after the videos came out? Talk about awkward," she said, shaking her head.

"Like, I can hear the Lord now, 'Amia, I know you heard Me tell you to keep your mouth shut.' Then, I'd try to respond and He'd ask me to hold on so He could turn down the audio from the videos."

"I don't know how you do it, Sis. You still have the patience of Job."

She slowly leaned herself away from Jamari's shoulder to face him.

"I actually wanted to tell her all the way off, Mar. Truth is, I want to give people a piece of my mind sometimes, I just don't do it. The crazy thing is that I know something about Asley that I could have hit her with, but I swallowed it. And if I'm being honest, Mar, always biting my tongue just to keep the peace is frustrating."

She turned her focus away from her brother. "God, I understand that You fight my battles, but sometimes, I wish... I wish I had the courage to fight on my own," Amia said with her head upturned to the ceiling.

"Mar, just once, I'd like to have the same strength that Janelle and Mom and Darren... And you, Mr. Professor, have. You can just say exactly what's on your mind... I can't."

"Amia, are you serious right now?" Jamari was beyond surprised at his big sister's revelation. He'd spent years watching her effortlessly take down one ignoramus after the other gracefully–without so much as a flinch.

"Sis, that's why everyone loves and respects you so much. The truth is, we all wish we could have as much discipline as you. Seriously, we talk about that all the time," he added as Amia immediately upturned her head, shaking in disbelief.

"Mom and I were on the phone last week. She's still kicking herself for how she handled Bree's situation at Danny's party, especially after finding out about Bree's low self-esteem. Don't get me wrong. She's not apologizing, because she feels it needed to be said. She just wishes she'd sprinkled some of that Amia-flavored seasoning into her delivery," he winked, nudging her with his elbow.

"Speaking of which, you talk to Bree lately?"

"Yeah, and I'm catching up with her and Jordie this weekend. Have you talked to her?"

"Yeah, we had lunch yesterday. Imma keep talking to her," he added.

"Yeah, me too."

"Cool... Now getting back to you, Sis. You feel that not speaking your mind is a lack of courage. I hear what you're saying, but can I give you another perspective, and not because I'm your brother?

"If there's a sticky or uncomfortable situation, everyone is relieved when you come in the room. We all take out our notebooks to watch a master class on how to handle it. Amia, you've been perfecting that since college when you were a youth counselor.

"I can't tell you how many times I watched you handle ignorance with honey. I remember wanting to throw fists with a lot of them, but you'd even sweettalk my hands back into my pockets. Real talk, you're the reason I'm still employed as a professor at Tulane."

Amia tilted her head trying to understand that statement.

"Do you know how many students question their grades and either try to go off on me or have their wealthy, well-connected parents write in to the dean? Do you know how many adjunct professors have come in, instantly thinking I'm beneath them?

"You know the stories I've told you through the years. In each of those instances, I'm like, 'WWAD (what would Amia do)?' Now, being completely honest, early on in my career, it was more like, 'WWAHD (what would Amia have done)?' That's because most times, I ain't handle it *exactly* the way you would have.

"Seriously though. Do you know how many people were watching that interview with Asley and literally saying that you're a better person than them because they would have snapped off on her? Like, literally, we would be watching videos of someone going off on her right now, Amia.

"Listen, Sis. You obviously don't know, so I'm gonna try to make it plain. You have a gift. No matter what you try to call it, it's still a gift. You've never so much as raised your voice. I mean, not for nothing but, Jesus lost his cool and flipped the tables in the Temple. Now, I'm not comparing you to the Lord, because he was dealing with some heathens, but I'm saying… Amia, that thing that comes so easily to you, is something we all want. Keep doing you, Sis. You're making us all better," he finished, all the pearlies in full view.

"You know what, Professor Jamari," Amia began, wrapping her arms around her younger brother.

"I sorta like you," she added softly as she was swallowed up by his return embrace.

He smiled back, holding her firmly. "I kinda like you too, Sis."

# Chapter 15

## *In a Word* – Finally

"Hey, beautiful."

*Must be Michele,* Amia thought to herself as the world's biggest smile stretched across Jamari's face even before lifting the phone to his ear. Her mood instantly lifted, listening to her handsome brother gush at the news of his baby girl letting go of the coffee table and standing on her own for the first time.

That was the perfect reset. Here she was, aggravated at pointlessness—rumors about Darren's camp's financing and her 'lack of bravery.' All the while, things like this—meaningful events that actually deserved attention—were happening.

Leave it to God to put things in perspective. Amia decided no more of her precious energy would be devoted to nonsense. She knew the right words for Martina's defense would come eventually. They always did. She also knew there was nothing to the swirling insinuations that caused Asley's ambush.

That said, there was one other thing that had been on her mind quite a bit these days and had crossed her mind again this afternoon, but Amia brushed it aside, choosing instead to focus her attention on her brother and the exciting news about her only niece.

With their busy schedules and lives, the siblings had to get creative in their quality time. They decided these were the perfect opportunities to strengthen their already impossibly close bond. They'd catch up as Amia worked on her summations as Jamari provided juror psychoanalysis.

Amia playfully eavesdropped on the conversation chatting with Michele and goading her brother as they ended the call.

"Sooo? What are you getting her, Jamari?"

He knew the question was bound to resurface. He was just surprised it wasn't the first question out of her mouth when he walked into the impressive courtroom.

Jamari directed his eyes to the ceiling and Amia watched a peculiar smile stretch across his face. It was the same one she'd seen numerous times while raising him. This particular grin was gleaming with the pride resulting from a pretty huge accomplishment.

Amia's jaw dropped as she shrieked. "You didn't! Jamari, are you serious?" she asked with excitement, almost unable to contain herself.

"Speak man," she urged as his silence caused her to almost shake him from his lean against the banister. Although seemingly impossible, Jamari's smile appeared to get bigger as laughter at his sister's uncontrollable happy feet erupted from his throat.

"Yeah, I'm getting it."

At this point, Amia was absolutely giddy. Now, it was Jamari playfully rolling his eyes, telling Amia how she gets on his nerves.

"She finally broke you down, huh?" nudged Amia teasingly.

"I'm still not 100% sold, but I guess it'll grow on me," he resigned with a disbelieving smile. Jamari then retrieved his phone for a photo of the long-awaited birthday gift. Amia studied his face as he scrolled through the images, pausing to show her a few of the latest family photos and his and Michelle's recent gold-panning expedition.

*He's excited. He just doesn't want to let on,* she told herself knowingly. That coy expression currently residing on his face had also appeared countless times through the years.

"Alright, here it is," he smiled, shaking his head as he turned the phone, giving her a glimpse. Amia's second shriek was accompanied by more giddy dancing feet as she happily jumped and hugged her brother.

"Calm down, Sis." He laughed. "I still don't know how I'm gonna feel about walking this teeny, tiny thing."

"Oh my goodness, Jamari. She's gonna flip all the way out! Michele has been talking about that dog since y'all were in college," Amia said while still ogling the cute Poodle puppy on the screen.

"You know I know," he added.

"So, Mister 'I'm never getting a dog, but if I do, it'll be a manly dog' is getting a cutsie, curly fur ball?"

"I mean, a dog is supposed to have some umph, Amia. Some meat on his bones, you know? It's supposed to be like a protector." Jamari paused again looking at the photo shaking his head. "What's this little fuzzball gonna protect?"

Amia turned facing her brother, "Umm hmm," Amia challenged after a few moments. "You like that little fuzzball." She paused, scanning his features more intently. "Yeah you do, just admit it. I can see it all over your face," she added as both attorney and her inner pseudo-mom made reappearances.

"And don't even try to deny it, Jamari Copeland. I bet you even have a name picked out. Don't ya?" Amia prodded, leaning in pretending to search his eyes for a confession.

"Any whooo. Get offa me, woman," Jamari replied, playfully pushing his doting sister away. He loved Amia dearly, but would rather the sun fall out the sky than admit she was right about him fan girling over this tiny ball of fur. Oscar and his cute little black nose already had Jamari wrapped around his tiny brown and white paws.

In fact, the breed's intelligence alone had his inner psychologist pretty excited about the possibilities. Oscar's purple collar and blinged out name tag, picked from Michele's "Poodle" Pinterest board, were already in Jamari's office drawer just waiting for his arrival.

Just then, Amia's phone buzzed. As fun as these shenanigans were, she did need to get back to work. After all, it was her turn to pick the kids up from practice and that alarm meant she only had thirty minutes before steering into the evening traffic. The siblings wrapped up and chatted about the incoming weather on the way to their vehicles.

"Good night, Poodle Dad!" Amia yelled lovingly as she pulled up to his vehicle in the five-story parking garage. "Love you, drive safely."

"Hey, Sis. You do remember I lived with you for nine years, right?" He didn't give Amia a chance to respond. "Just saying. When I asked you earlier if there was anything else bothering you, you said no... I'm your brother. I know there's something else. And I kinda do this for a living. See that little eye shift you did right there? That proves I'm right," he added with a wink.

"You don't have to tell me what's really on your mind. Just know that I know there's something." With that, he slid his all-weather bookbag into the passenger seat next to his gold whistle and clipboard.

Jamari then stretched his long, jet-black locs, which had been in a neat ball behind his head before tucking the thick strands into a tie behind his back. "You drive safely, too. Love ya," he added.

"Yep, still getting on that last nerve," she smiled mumbling under her breath as she blew him a kiss, then rolled her window back up as they parted ways.

# Chapter 16

## In a Word – Exhales

While still early, the morning sun had heated Amia's favorite corner spot so much that sweat began glistening on her skin. She was enjoying the company as she took in the roaring ocean waves compliments of the Coastal Kitchen.

This morning's Bikram yoga with Janelle had been swapped for breakfast with her sisters and Amia was reveling in the range of conversations. The sisters covered everything from Bria and Jordyn's latest Broke with Reservations adventures to Daniel's first crush on the girl next door.

Amia was patiently awaiting a chance to reconnect in-depth with Bria, but because her younger sisters were heading to Canada for a few weeks, she opted to enjoy just hanging out for the moment.

She thought about sharing Jamari's puppy surprise, but Bria's inability to hold water was a well-documented fact. Some way, somehow, Michele would have known about Oscar before the butter melted on their bread. Nope, as bad as she wanted to say something, Amia Wilford would not be an accomplice to that secret's leakage.

"Thanks, Frau," the ladies chimed in happy unison as multicolored smoothies and appetizing German Krapfen pastries were placed before them. The trio listened intently as Frau Gerry explained the new recipe that was created in honor of her son, Ian, who was tragically killed by a hit-and-run driver weeks before the grand opening.

The teenager hugged her grandmother as the Frau described Johanna's father, Ian's, insatiable desire for an extra helping of the sweet orange fruit on everything. Both smiled in response to Amia, Bria, and Jordyn's adoration of their new, savory masterpiece. The ladies left the sisters to continue enjoying their goodies.

"Mia, like I said when we spoke last Saturday, we'll handle Asley Tesleep," Bria said frankly, squeezing a lemon into her iced tea.

"Yeah, and don't worry about your prints showing up on anything," noted Jordyn. "There won't be any," she added licking the strawberry jam off her butter knife.

"You know what," Amia said. Her eyebrow arched at Jordyn's metaphor as she ensured all traces of jelly disappeared from the knife before wiping it extra clean with her white linen napkin.

"Yeah, I'm not about to have the two of you on the run. I can see it now, *Broke with Reservations is being brought to you live from a secure, underground cave in Podunk, Arkansas. And tonight's dinner edition of Broke & Eating Good features flame-roasted skunk with a side of skewered wild mushrooms, and lukewarm grass-infused water,*" Amia added.

"I mean, that does sound good, though. Jordie, we need to write that down," Bria said.

"Already on it," replied Jordyn, her sparkly pink phone out, pretending to type those menu items into it.

Amia just shook her head at her younger sisters.

"I went by Drew's house earlier this week," Bria announced out of the blue, to the shock of both sisters.

"Bree, why on Earth would you go back over to Drew's?" asked Jordyn almost angrily. Amia noted something else in her voice, but couldn't quite pin it down.

"I just wanted to know why," Bria replied. "I wanted him to tell me why he stopped talking to me. His phone has been going straight to voice mail. I... I just don't understand what I did that was so bad," she said meekly.

"*What you did*? Are you frigging kidding me right now, Bria?" exclaimed Jordyn, clearly annoyed.

"What am I missing, here?" asked Amia. Her eyes darted from sister to sister. Bria and Jordyn's eyes were locked. Neither sister said anything, but Amia could hear a silent conversation occurring. She just couldn't quite make out the words.

"OK, let me try it differently. Ladies, what am I missing here?" asked Amia, intentionally going with the same question because it was posed perfectly the first time.

"Nothing. Just that he's clearly not interested," Jordyn paused before adding, "Bree, you've gotten him out of your life. Could you just leave him there, please?" she begged.

That little something was in Jordyn's voice again.

"Jordie, the way you asked Bree what she did. What did you mean by that?" Amia pressed.

"Just that Bree has always gone out of her way for him. She constantly bent over backwards to please him and never got anything in return... Like ever! Bree finally stands up for herself and he ghosts her. I'm just over it, and I hope to God he never comes back."

"Bree," Amia began softly.

"You said your last fight was because you insisted Drew come to Danny's birthday party, and that's when he stopped talking to you, right? Have you given any thought to Drew maybe having another life?

"With his phone going straight to voicemail, is it possible he used that just to call you and had another one for his other life?" Amia delicately positioned the questions, being careful to avoid saying 'other family'.

"I've been to his house and spent the night several times. There weren't any pictures, no women's clothes in his closets or drawers. No perfumes or hair products in the bathroom... I don't think he had another woman in his life, if that's what you're asking."

She didn't give her a chance to respond.

"Besides, he wasn't home, and it didn't look like anyone had been there in a while. There was dust and spiderwebs everywhere; across the garage door, front door, and on the porch. He just... He just up and left," Bria added with sadness.

"Oh, for the love of God," snapped Jordyn. "Nobody cares, Bree! Drew is an idiot. Always has been, always will be. This is just one more example. Like seriously, you wasted two years of your life on that loser, and now he's gone and you're still wasting your life crying over him.

"He's a loser, Bree. Get it through your head. Get over him," Jordyn's formerly animated hands were now angrily snatching up her fork and napkin which had been accidentally knocked off the table.

"Pause, please," Amia said running interference as Bria was preparing her comeback to Jordyn's last statements. She'd placed a loving hand on each sister's wrist.

"Take a breath. Take a sip, and take a bite. That's what we're all gonna do right now."

Amia saw Bria's self-esteem issues beginning to resurface. She knew that was going to make Bria's reply to Jordyn extra harsh, and unfortunately, neither of her sisters subscribed to the WWAD channel.

Amia could have cared less if they argued when she wasn't around, but there was no way she was going to let her sisters go there on each other in her presence. Amia hated conflict, which is an uncanny characteristic for a defense attorney, especially one as successful as Amia. On top of that, the beloved, popular influencers were out in public.

Unlike the youngest Copelands, Amia fully understood the media's presence and willingness to plaster negativity. As their big sister, she was going to do her best to ensure that if the sisters were going to squabble, it was not going to be out in the open.

"So, Toronto? Let's talk about that," Amia said with a wink. "Who invited you? Where are you staying? What are you cooking? Come on. Give me the scoop."

Amia listened intently as their faces lit back up, the scowls disappearing with each passing second. She watched as the dynamic duo began finishing each other's sentences again and bouncing in their chairs with excitement. Amia saw the partnership and genuine adoration the sisters had for each other.

She noted besides their talent, this fun, unrehearsed banter was why their followings were increasing exponentially. What she was witnessing was what she'd seen from them growing up. These were the sisters everyone knew and loved.

Amia noted their body language, too. It was more relaxed and actually friendly, but there was still something about this Drew situation that her sisters weren't sharing. Amia felt that deep within her spirit. Before she got to probe, Bria changed the subject again.

"Hey, Mia. Let's hit up that 'All About Me' spa when it opens. Maybe I'll try the Brazilian wax this time," Bria said unconvincingly.

"What?" she asked in response to Amia's 'yeah right'.

"Yo, the way you were hollarin'... No, Ma'am. I could not bring myself to put Ms. Kitty through that."

"Bree, it was your idea! How you gonna convince me to get my vajay jay literally snatched and then chicken out at the last minute? You are wrong on so many levels," added Amia with a laugh.

"Couldn't have been too bad though, you're still going in for it," said Bria.

"I keep telling you to try it," Jordyn interjected. "The first time I did it, it was a little rough because, I didn't know what to expect. By the fourth rip though, you're in a better place mentally."

"Actually," said Amia, "they should have this soundtrack playing in there. The waves are so relaxing... Yeah, these waves and that jasmine incense..."

Amia's closed eyes were envisioning herself on the table, utterly relaxed and without a care in the world.

"Uh hello, Earth to Amia," said Jordyn, snapping her fingers while Bria shook her head at their older sister.

"Yeah, I'm gonna leave that whole snatching thing to you two," concluded Bria, dismissing her sister's fiftieth invitation for waxing.

With bellies now satisfied and both sisters fully cooled off thanks to Amia's distraction and the delicious, chilled smoothies, they continued chatting about the forecast. Amia shared that Janelle, Todd, and their kids would be riding out the impending hurricane at her and Darren's. Janelle and Todd lived near the dam and with the amount of rain expected, they decided it would be safer to brave the storm from higher up on the mountain.

While they were pretty far inland, this week's projected storm was supposed to make land as a Category 5. The local meteorologists, though normally jovial, were broadcasting dire warnings around the clock to the residents of Allegheny County.

As they were talking, the bell jingled at the front of the café. Moments later, Johanna brought a manila envelope to the table and began opening it before the sisters. "What are you doing, Jo?" quizzed Amia.

"A courier gave me $50 to ensure you received this."

The trio exchanged confused glances, turning to scan the store, then quickly looking outside to see if they could find the messenger. So engrossed in her sisters' descriptions of the outfits they'd packed and content they planned to shoot while in Toronto, Amia hadn't bothered to look up at the new patron.

Though completely engaged, Amia was able to note the unusual closeness of the bell's entry and exit jingles. It registered in her subconscious because everyone entering the Coastal Kitchen stayed a couple minutes, at least. Even the regulars picking up takeout lingered, because there were always fresh samples which were rarely declined.

"Was it a man or a woman?  What did she look like, Jo? Did she say anything else? Which way did she go?" Amia asked in rapid-fire succession.

Johanna answered each question as best she could before extracting an immediately recognizable gray envelope. Amia felt her pulse beating in her throat. Who could have known that she would be here? She cautiously opened the first of two sticky notes which had been taped to the back.

"Thank you, Jo," said Bria recognizing the concerned teenager was virtually frozen near the edge of their table. Bria patted her hand, easing her back into motion. "Jo, could you please grab our check?"

"Yes, of course," she muttered as she nervously hurried away. She'd unknowingly been a party to something that had shaken Amia, something she'd never seen in their years of interactions. Johanna was acutely aware of the major atmospheric shift. The joyful vibes she'd been used to catching from that cozy corner had completely vanished.

The waves that were rolling softly ashore moments earlier, were now crashing through the speakers as she scanned the first note. *Make sure your husband responds to this letter,* Amia read. *There is a price to pay if he does not.*

# Chapter 17

## In a Word – Suspicions

Gary's normally cheery disposition had been replaced by a presence that few people had ever seen. His smile lines disappeared as soon as he read the first sentence of the letter.

Amia called Darren immediately upon exiting the Coastal Sounds and explained what happened. They then called Camille and Adrienne who all agreed to meet at Gary and Mable's the following day.

The envelope had been left unopened until being placed in Gary's hands as was instructed in the second sticky note. Regardless of the directive, Darren would have brought this letter to Gary. After all, he really needed his Dad's support in dealing with his father.

Darren was fairly confident that if anyone would take the inscriptions with a grain of salt, it would be Gary the missionary, so he had no objections when Gary opted to read the letter silently before sharing it out loud.

Mable removed the pages as his shade moved from rosy to pale to beet red twice before remaining on the flaming side. Darren retrieved the letter back from Mable, instantly regretting his decision to allow Gary to be a buffer.

He realized that even his parents had limitations. Gary and Mable, though missionaries, were in no shape to be reading what had been scribbled on the lines or hinted in between.

Still, Darren had no interest in reading the letter himself. He'd just as soon fed it to the goats before heading over to the penitentiary in Florence, Colorado where he would drop his own form of penmanship on Marshon Wilford.

His nostrils flared and anger surged in recognition that he could have easily set his dad up for a heart attack by exposing him to Marshon's cruelty.

With the almost visceral reactions from the normally easygoing Gary and Mable, Camille decided that she too wanted no part of the communication. She instead began looking for contact information for USP Thomson's Warden, vowing to put a stop to the menacing.

In the meantime, Adrienne and Darren busied themselves with getting cold water and monitoring blood pressure. Adrienne, a registered nurse, always traveled with immediate care essentials. Once certain that Gary, Mable, and her husband were fine, Amia began quietly perusing the parcel's contents.

*My son is ignoring me. I'm assuming this is because of you and your wife. Let me be clear. You are kidnappers and imposters. You are not his father, and she is not his mother. I'm sitting in this prison because of you.*

*You convinced my son to testify against me and then stole him. He knows I'm dying and could have been gotten me out of here. I now have about nine months left according to the doctors. I want my son to contact me. Do you hear me? Since you have so much control over him, make him look into my case.*

*As an added incentive, let him know that I might know something about that boating accident a few years back. There is an interesting new guy on my block who has shared some details that Darren's wife and my ungrateful daughter might find interesting.*

*Speaking of Camille, tell my disrespectful daughter that I gave her life, and I will always be her father. I'm not impressed by her degrees. She can have ten of them and thirty initials behind her name and she will still be my daughter. Kiss my beautiful Adrienne for me.*

The letter closed with, *I need to hear from Darren soon or you'll all be sorry.*

While everyone's minds immediately recalled the devastating demise of the Honey Bear, the pristine white yacht with its orange and blue stripes, Darren and Amia looked at each other.

"What kind of game is Marshon running? How did that letter make it out of the penitentiary's mailroom? We have both defended enough inmates to know that only certain conversations were eligible for mailing to the outside world. This letter definitely does not meet even the minimum standards," Darren said to Amia.

"What else is there to know? The ship capsized due to an engine fire. Everyone was lost at sea. There has been no news in six years. Marshon's reaching, trying to get a response," Camille spat angrily.

Darren asked barely above a whisper, "Why the accident, though? If he wanted my attention, there are questions about the camp. That's now in the national news, thanks to Asley. Why not mention that? Why spew venom towards Camille but not mention Adrienne?"

"That's because I wrote to him after Danny's party..." Camille began, her finger was pointing in the letter's direction, using its presence to yell at her father. "... and told him in no uncertain terms that he is to never call me his daughter again. I also told that no good mut—" Remembering Gary and Mable's presence, she paused. "Sorry Mom and Dad... I told Marshon that he forfeited his rights to call me his daughter."

As the family pondered the validity of Marshon's words, Amia said the quiet part out loud, "What if the fire wasn't an accident?" She paused wanting to tread lightly due to the difficulty of the topic and the audience. Carefully, she pressed on, "I have never understood how a yacht that was less than a year old and so well maintained could have had an engine fire.

"According to Pierre Meadows, their Athletic Director, the Honey Bear had been inspected prior to the trip. Steven insisted on it. Camille, you know your husband was meticulous," Darren said.

There were no issues with the Honey Bear's maintenance, but as the Men's Track Coach who considered those young men as his own, Steven O'Tannen wanted to be 100% certain of the yacht's seaworthiness before agreeing to take the athletes out into the bay.

Darren was always struck by his and Amia's like-mindedness. He never bought the accident story, but if it allowed the family to move on with their lives, he wasn't going to create waves. After all, there had been a two-week recovery effort which did not turn up Shamir or Steven or the five other young men, and in the six years since, there had been no new news.

He figured there was no point in stirring the waters and subjecting the family to his suspicions, especially since it wouldn't have brought Shamir or Steven back. His eyes locked with his wife's who immediately knew they were on the same page.

"I looked into the accident for months and wasn't able to find anything. There was nothing suspicious or out of order. No unaccounted boats or vessels that day," Darren said.

Mia looked at her husband lovingly before confessing that she'd also spent months pouring over the files, occasionally checking in to see if there were any new leads.

"I didn't want to hurt anyone by chasing ghosts, but it never made sense to me that there were so many able-bodied men onboard that day and not one of them was able to call for help." Amia wiped the tear that found its way down her cheek.

"I guess I just believed the authorities' theory that the fire made it impossible for them to reach the radio. Steven never had a signal on his phone when they were out on the ocean, so I knew the phones didn't work," whispered Camille.

"Do you really think someone killed my husband and those boys?"

"Only God knows what really happened, Sis," Darren replied solemnly, reaching for her trembling hand.

"According to the divers, only four life jackets were still in the storage compartments of the Honey Bear," said Amia. "I have asked myself several times how the ones they found all drowned—"

"When they were wearing life jackets," Darren said in unison with Amia.

"I know a storm rolled in before Pierre alerted the authorities about being unable to reach the Honey Bear, but it never made sense to me either."

The pair locked eyes for the second time in as many minutes.

"One thing's for sure," added Gary, breaking the building tension.

"We have the right people on it now. I don't know anyone else who has found more needles in the haystack than Amia and son, you don't understand what it means to quit. I just pray God's guidance and wisdom upon you."

Mable pulled Camille, whose tears were now in freefall, into her bosom. "I just pray for God's grace and healing," she began while holding onto her oldest daughter, "whether there's something there or not."

"Let's get through this storm first," suggested Amia.

"Yeah, I'll head to Colorado after the hurricane hits. I want to hear about this man Marshon is talking about and find out what he knows."

# Chapter 18

## *In a Word* – Thirty-Six

"Heads' up!" warned Darren as a black and white multi-hexagon sphere whizzed through the warm Saturday morning air towards Todd's head. Darren's thick muscular hands blocked the ball which would have surely left an impression on the side of Todd's face.

"Hey! Keep that ball on the field," Todd shouted while pointing at each of the kids. "Especially you, number ten. I've got my eye on you."

"Sorry, Uncle Todd," replied Christina.

"Hey, Coach! Control the game," Todd yelled.

"The fans will be respectful of the coaches, Uncle Todd," replied Daniel. He was an unofficial coach of his sister's team today. The older kids completed their soccer game earlier and since he had to stay for Christina's games, he asked if he could take a spot on the bench to sharpen his skills.

"Crap!"

"What's up?" asked Todd.

"I told Amia I'd pick up a few groceries and, I forgot to see what we need. Do you mind keeping an eye on them while I run back home?"

"I got you. How 'bout you add a slab of ribs to that list for me while you're at it. We'll fire that grill up after this storm hits," he added with air quotes. Todd wasn't completely sold on the predictions, especially since they were so far inland.

Darren smiled at his friend. "You still don't believe fat meat's greasy, huh?" He laughed.

"Is it really greasy, though?" Todd asked sarcastically. Darren just laughed. "You crazy, Dawg. Thanks though. I'll be back."

"Nah, do you. Go ahead and pick up the groceries. I'll bring them home. Maybe I'll grab a flashlight or two," he teased.

"Thanks, Bruh." With that, Darren quickly headed home. His mind drifted back to his and Amia's conversation the day after they returned from Gary and Mable's.

"Babe, you're not getting fat," Darren consoled for the tenth time. "So, the jeans are a little tight. I like that," he added with a grin.

"Darren, seriously. The weight gain isn't bad now, but what happens if I gain fifty pounds? Are you still gonna like that." The air quotes amplified her frustration.

"Listen, Babe," he replied, grabbing her hand and pulling her towards him on the bed.

"I'll love you when your hair turns gray and... I'll still want you if you gain a little weight and..."

Amia laughed at her hilarious husband as he belted out Music Soulchild's sultry lyrics. Her Boo was a lot of things, but a singer was not one of them. He knew it, too, but continued undaunted.

"The way I feel for you will always stay the same, just as long as your love don't change." He wrapped his arms around her waist as he continued his off-pitch serenade.

"Babe, you are everything I begged God for and seventeen years later, you are still everything I've ever wanted. If you gain some weight, there'll be more of you to love. Trust me, I won't be mad at that. Do you think I married you because of that fine booty?" He couldn't resist helping himself to a handful of her derrière.

"I love everything about your body. You know that. Even those little stretch marks are sexy." Darren lovingly traced one of the thin fine indentations along her lower belly before planting a soft kiss on it.

"The way your body is set up, them pounds are going to layer out perfectly and," then drawing her closer, "I'm gonna love loving every single inch."

"I know, the most important thing is my health and being here for the kids and with you. I know I have to be careful with this arrhythmia. But I already miss running with Janelle and working out as hard as I used to and this is only my first week... Uggh, I can just feel the extra pounds coming now," she sighed as she flopped down on the bed next to Darren.

"We can't risk you passing out on a trail in the middle of nowhere and unfortunately, you only like swimming when no one's at the pool. We can't have that either." He pecked one of the slender hands that was rubbing her forehead in frustration.

"Amia, you will be sexy in my eyes no matter what size you are... I promise." Darren lovingly kissed her semi-exposed forehead.

"Hey Babe. What'cha doing?"

"Nothing. Talking to Mom," Amia replied. "How are the games going?"

"They're good. Danny went off today! Scored four goals and had three assists. He's coaching Bean's team right now. The Bandits forfeited, so the girls are scrimmaging each other... Everything good with your mom and dad?" Darren asked.

"Yeah. I was just telling her that I hit a wall in digging into WW&M's payroll history. Of course, the first two vendors are no longer in business, and The City only has your incorporation papers. Unfortunately, City Hall only keeps records for twenty years, so we're two years too late.

"Babe, I'm not worried. I know what I did and didn't do. I am kicking myself, though. Remember, I shredded that cancelled check years ago after Vicky took over the accounting? I'd been keeping that thing in the file at the front office. She damn near hopped down my throat for having a check with the camp's account number in an unlocked file cabinet."

"Yeah, I still can't believe you did that. I mean, I get it. There really wasn't any reason to keep the check and you didn't have it secured," Amia replied. "Honestly, it was a shot in the dark. No one keeps records that long. I'm just trying to make these nonsense rumors and speculations go away."

"You know your mom's still on hold, right?"

"Oh Lord," Amia laughed. "Hang on a sec."

Darren smiled as the light turned green and he continued his Saturday morning drive.

"Ok, I'm back." She was making sure we were all set for the storm and seeing if Mari and Michele were riding it out with us. I told her we're good and that Mari and the crew will be in Michigan surprising Michele with the new puppy. Mom and dad are gonna be with Kerry and Tom up in New Hampshire. She's actually still on the other line. I'm filling her in on the fur ball."

"Wait, where are you going?" Amia inquired as she heard the Audi's blinkers clicking.

"Well, Babe. Imma be pulling into the driveway in about thirty seconds. That gives you roughly forty-five seconds to get naked."

Mia's whole body tingled. "Umm. Babe, I've gotta freshen up and get Mom off the line. She's excited to hear about the new 'grandchild.'"

"Forty. Thirty-nine. Thirty-Eight. Thirty-Seven."

Click.

He smiled as he parked the gray Ontario next to Mia's navy Volvo. He tossed his cap on top of the grocery list that he'd made while the kids were finishing breakfast and gathering their cleats. "Game time, baby." He smiled in anticipation as the garage door closed behind him.

# Chapter 19

## *In a Word* – Unexpected

The Wilfords huddled in their cozy family room as the winds howled, its speed driving the pouring rain in rapid sheets against the large windows. The hurricane hit the mainland as a category four storm, just a shade weaker than the monster category five as predicted. While spared triple-digit gusts this far inland, the city was weathering sixty and seventy mile an hour bursts.

Christina was terrified, evident by the shrieks with every leaf and projectile that bumped loudly against their home. The shivering youngster was completely glued to Darren, her Superman, who in her mind was going to personally talk to God and get the storm to go away.

"I'm going to go turn on the generator," said Darren as the lights at 438 Teeton Dr. blinked for the fourth time. "Looks like we're going to lose power soon."

"Danny. Go with your dad," ordered Amia as she extracted a squealing Christina from Darren's arms.

"Bean, we'll be right back. I need you to be brave so Mom doesn't get scared while I'm downstairs. You can do that, right? That's my girl," he said as the youngster nodded, still hugging her mother's neck.

Amia had been putting on a brave face, but the truth was, she was nervous, too. She really wished Janelle and Todd had ridden out the storm with them because some comedy could definitely help pass the time and Christina would be playing with their daughter, Kennedy, rather than choking the life out of her right now. Todd's mother was rushed into emergency surgery the day before the storm hit, so the Hinton crew made a last-minute bee line towards Ohio.

Thankfully, the surgery was successful. She was resting comfortably and the two new stents were placed without incident. The pair exhaled in relief after getting the update from Todd hours earlier, just before the outer bands began dampening the eerily quiet streets.

While they'd seen their share of bad storms, no one recalled seeing anything quite like this in recent memory. *"Father God, please protect us and all of your children. Let the damage be minimal and repairable. Please let everyone be able to stay in their homes and protect those who are on the roads. Please keep them safe and allow them to make it to their destinations safely. Amen."*

Just then, the power went out. Amia managed to loosen Christina's death grip around her neck before the frightened youngster actually cut off her blood flow.

She stepped cautiously towards the window. While there was no view due to the driving rain, they were able to make out the glimmers of candlelight and flashlights twinkling in windows throughout their neighborhood. Mia helplessly looked out at her mighty Pittsburgh below. For only the second time in her life, her precious Steel City was in total darkness.

Darren and Daniel made their way in the flashlight guided darkness. He stopped midway down the basement stairs as the gales they'd been hearing were now pushing past them. He noted that a window must have been hit by flying debris and had Daniel stay put.

At the bottom of the stairs, Darren was greeted by driving water and strewn furnishings. The part he was wrong about was the source of the wind. A window hadn't been blown out. Instead, the decorative siding door of their walkout had been shattered, apparently by the large branch still lodged in the glass.

He remembered the piece of plywood which he'd kept in the basement from a previous project and turned the corner to grab it. The wind-blown flashlight illuminated the figure of a man half hiding in the corner.

A shockwave tore through Darren's being. A stranger was in their home. How did he get in? How long had he been here? Why was he here? Dread pierced his core as he heard Daniel descending the steps after hearing his dad's huff just above the whirling.

"Dad?"

"Stay there!" he yelled. That command was partially targeted at Daniel, partially at the slim, soaking wet stranger, but mostly at the near paralyzing fear that was threatening to overtake him. At that moment, Darren really missed not having Todd here because Daniel would have been upstairs with TJ, not down here, perilously close to danger.

"What's wrong, Dad?" asked Daniel. The young teen's voice cracking from the fear of feeling strong winds rushing by him inside their home's blackened stairwell compounded by the noisy violence of the storm. Also, his dad's voice had a tone that he'd never heard before.

"Darren?"

"Daddy?"

Darren's heart found its way into his throat as Amia and Christina's voices notified the intruder that there were others in the home. Darren's nostrils flared and nerves steeled as he gripped the green flashlight tighter. At that moment, he realized the nightstick with its thick military grade cylinder was about to become Exhibit A at his murder trial.

Up to that point, the stranger had been attempting to block the blinding light from his eyes while looking unsuccessfully for a way past the six-foot four-inch former All-American football star. Suddenly, his attention turned towards the direction of Amia and Christina's voices.

*Darren,* he thought to himself. *Your son is on the stairwell. Your wife is coming down with your daughter. It's now or never.*

He swallowed hard. He had defended countless clients claiming self-defense and often wondered what must have been going through their minds upon realizing there were no other non-violent alternatives. He now fully understood as he hoisted the flashlight above his head fully intending to protect his family from this intruder by any means necessary when he stopped short.

“It can’t be…” he whispered in disbelief, cautiously stepping closer while angling the beam to search the man before him.

“Oh my God!” he cried. “Shamir?”

# Chapter 20

## *In a Word* – Reappeared

"What do you mean we can't let anyone know you're alive, Shamir? We buried you for God's sake." Amia's heart ached thinking one of the saddest days of her life thus far—his memorial service. The pain of having to say goodbye to her youngest brother without a body was unbearable.

"Mir, we have all missed you more than you could ever know."

They'd spent years holding out hope that he had somehow survived, but to save their sanity, they'd finally resigned to the fact that he was gone and let him go. Now, he was standing in their living room begging them not to mention his presence.

"Shamir, I need to know how you got here," said Darren cautiously. "You've been gone for six years and out of the blue, in the middle of a hurricane, you appear. Make it make sense, please."

"Ok, but I'm really hungry. Do you have anything to eat? Maybe a PB&J."

Amia inhaled sharply thinking of the number of years she'd gone without hearing him ask for his favorite sandwich. She wanted to fix the gaunt twenty-six-year-old a million sandwiches, but based on his condition, wanted to be sure he could stomach just one.

"Shamir, we should at least get you checked out at the hospital. You are so thin," she noted with extreme concern.

"No, Amia. I'm fine. I haven't eaten much in the last year, since Simon left. No one brought food. The garden was all the food we got."

"Simon? Simon who?" asked Amia and Darren in unison. "Garden? We?" Those were just four of a hundred thousand more questions to come. Just then, Daniel returned from his room with a pair of sweats and a T-shirt for Shamir to change into as his clothes were soaking wet.

Darren left his wife's side briefly to retrieve the garments, ensuring Daniel and Christina stayed outside of arm's length. While grateful for Shamir's existence, Darren was on high alert. After all, this miracle in the storm made no sense.

She sensed this from her husband and fully understood. That said, this was her brother. Though he certainly looked like he'd been through hell, the Shamir she knew and loved could never harm them. She prayed that guy was still in there. Knowing the kids were secure, Amia returned her attention to her youngest brother.

"I would really like to take a shower. It's been a while." His scent was pungent, but that was the last of their concerns. They'd have learned to live with the smell of homelessness if it meant Shamir was safe.

"I don't think you should shower. You could have evidence on your body that will help us locate where you've been held. I think we should take you to the hospital and then to the poli—"

"NO, Amia. No police. No hospitals. No one can know I'm here. They'll find me and take me back," he said in near panic. His breathing was frantic. "Please, I don't wanna leave, but I will. They can't know..."

"Shamir, Shamir, shhhhh. Calm down, Bruh. We've got you. You're safe. We won't say anything." With that, Darren joined his wife in hugging the trembling young man tightly.

The Wilfords weighed the options. While Shamir could have had evidence on him at some point, based on his brief account, he'd been out in the storm for almost two hours. The driving rain and winds would have surely erased any traces.

There was no cell service. Amia confirmed this while Darren was calling for her and leading Shamir up the stairs. They had the long-lost brother's clothes and sneakers which would be dropped into a dry-cleaning bag and sealed until they got him to the police.

There were still massive gusts of wind and driving rains that were forecasted to last several more hours. No one was going anywhere anytime soon. There would be no blue and red lights coming to escort him to the hospital and police station. Acknowledging this, the pair conceded.

Certain that Shamir was unarmed after a thorough pat down in the basement, Darren showed him to the restroom so that he could shower and change. Once the realization that he was actually talking to Shamir set in, Darren's wariness kicked in.

He needed to affix the plywood to the broken door, but could not afford to devote his attention to drilling without ensuring that Shamir posed no immediate danger to the family.

The lights flickered as Shamir exited the earthy, nature-inspired bath, but didn't actually come back on. Darren met Shamir in the hall to escort him to the kitchen where his sister sat, anxiously awaiting his reappearance. He hugged Amia tightly and for an extended period upon seeing two PB&Js and apple juice sitting in the empty spot which would soon be filled by his presence.

The starving youngster almost inhaled the first sandwich, quickly washing it down with his favorite beverage. Amia refilled the now empty glass as Shamir split and began consuming the second sandwich.

Darren sat quietly studying Shamir's features as he continued eating, though at a much more relaxed pace now that the food was hitting the bottom of his stomach. Amia took the opportunity to give the kids snacks before tucking them in bed amidst a barrage of questions.

"Me too. I can't wait to find out. Me neither," Amia agreed. These were her replies to most of the kids' endless questions.

"We'll know more tomorrow. Right now, you need to get some sleep and we're going to let Shamir rest tonight." This was the first night in years that Amia said goodnight to them at the same time.

Christina asked to sleep in Daniel's room and surprisingly, he agreed. Daniel gave Christina his full-sized lower bunk while climbing the ladder and hopping into the twin-sized top bunk.

Though thirteen now, Daniel was still young enough that he would happily have his little sister sleep in his room from time to time. Besides, her presence spared him from having to admit he was too scared to sleep by himself. Today's events were unnerving and he really didn't want to endure the embarrassment of creeping into his parents' room because he was afraid.

Moments later, Amia rejoined Darren and Shamir who had moved into the living room. Darren was filling him in on the sports world and its superstars. Clearly, Shamir hadn't had the privilege of Sports Center or ESPN as the sports enthusiast was just learning that some of his favorite players were now playing for different organizations or had retired.

She indulged the conversation for a few moments more before joining Shamir on the oversized sectional. She listened intently as the gusts tested their home's wood siding.

"Can we start from the beginning? There were fifteen of you on that yacht. Only four were found. What happened to everyone else?"

"Before that," interrupted Darren softly. His eyes apologizing for cutting off his wife. "Shamir, who is Simon?"

"I don't know, but he definitely knows you."

# Chapter 21

## *In a Word* – Chilling

Shamir walked around the Wilford's impressive home, taking in the architecture, and well-positioned furnishings thanks to a high-powered lantern. The winds had proven too strong for Darren to safely operate the generator. Plan B was to utilize flashlights and candles until he remembered the fishing and camping supplies.

After a few additional moments of exploring the beautiful spaces, Shamir exhaled a deep sigh of despair. "I don't have any money, but I will pay for the damage. I promise."

He then looked at Darren's confused gaze before averting his eyes and confessing that he, not the wind, had driven the large branch into their sliding door.

Once the pair assured him that the damage was a non-issue, Shamir continued, "I think his name is Simon Drew. Coach knew him as Simon, so that's what we called him."

Shamir's shivering began easing as he reclaimed the corner spot on the sectional sofa, tucked under an oversized cream Sherpa throw. Amia handed him a cup of hot chamomile tea to get the final shakes under control.

"He said your address all the time, especially when he was angry. To keep me in check, he would say he'd pay a little visit to 438 Teeton Dr. and kill everyone. He even described the house and the black front gate. That's how I knew I was at your home."

Shamir's sunken eyes focused on the warm tea. He began describing his capturer as a taller, decent looking middle-aged guy who was seemingly bipolar. The mystery man had a surprisingly friendly and charming demeanor but possessed unexplained cruelty and downright nastiness when angry.

"Simon was on the water that day. He was in a ten-foot boat and flagged down the yacht saying that he was having engine trouble. Coach O'Tannen recognized him and pulled alongside... "Shamir's voice trailed off.

"Thank you for letting me come aboard, Steven. I've been out here stranded for about two days. Danged engine's dead," Simon told Steven O'Tannen, the head track coach.

"The anchor's the only reason I'm not thirty miles out to sea. I've been trying to waive down boats since Thursday. They were all just too far away. My horn's not working either, so I've literally been sitting here praying for a miracle."

"God is good, Brother," Steven replied.

"You remember Pierre Meadows, our athletic director?"

"Yeah," Simon answered. "We've met once or twice."

"Pierre recommended this spot, and good thing he did," Steven said.

"We would have been all the way on the other side of the bay if it wasn't for him. We wanted to be in a less traveled area to avoid a lot of wake from other boats. I also wanted a spot where the guys could cut loose and just be loud without anyone complaining. Steven beamed like a proud father as he looked back at the young men who were having the time of their lives, soaking up the warm, inviting sun.

"These guys have busted their behinds all year and have earned a couple days out here on the water. Simon, you know you're looking at the two-time MEAC conference champs, right here? We had multiple personal records, a couple school records shattered, and six of these guys are headed on to Nationals."

"Is that right? Congratulations young bucks! Great job, and great job to you too, Coach."

"I'm just happy to be in their corner. They did put in the work. I just designed the workouts."

"Still too humble to take the roses, huh Steven? Well, I tell ya. Thank God you all showed up."

"Hey, I see what your issue with the radio is. Looks like the positive charge spring is broken."

Steven turned the defective radio's battery opening towards Simon to show him his findings.

"You need to return that if you've still got the receipt, and I'd be complaining to any and everyone who would listen. How can they sell a product like that? People rely on these things." Steven was actually bothered. All he could think of was one of his young men trusting their safety to equipment that should have never passed a basic quality check.

"Here, have some Gatorade, Simon. Hey, Shamir? You and Devin hook Simon's boat up so we can tow him in. Bugg, Quinton, Travis, do me a favor."

"Whatcha need, Coach?" Steven smiled. No matter how many times he'd tried to get Bugg to say, "What do you," those three words never rolled out of his mouth in that order. For the tall, slender distance runner, it was whatcha or bust.

"You three go below deck in Simon's skiff and get his bags, please."

"Aye-Aye, Captain," replied Quinton. This was his first time ever on a boat and he'd been employing all of the lingo since walking the gangway to board their vessel. Steven shook his head at the boys who tossed up peace signs as they hopped off the Honey Bear and onto Simon's crippled white and green dinghy.

Shamir pulled the blanket up around his neck. His shallow breathing quickened.

"When I got back from tying Simon's boat to ours, Simon was acting like he was gonna pass out. He said something about being overcome with relief. Coach helped him to a bench and sent Darius and Trent below our deck to get a cold towel and some ice.

"Next thing I know, there's a lot of coughing. Most of us ran to the edge of the Honey Bear to see what was going on. Bugg was screaming, gasping for air, and trying to get back up the stairs of the hull. Quinten and Travis never resurfaced. When we turned back around, Simon had a gun pointed at Coach and another pointed at the back of Mason's head."

Though the home was toasty due to the power outage, you'd have never known that by looking at Shamir. His entire body was trembling—even under the throw's warmth.

"Mason tried to elbow Simon and got shot."

He struggled to share more of the day that started off as the most incredible time he'd had in his life.

Everything was perfect; at least it was until their attention was caught by a bull horn and frantically waving orange towel.

The calm, rippled water which had offered the guys endless games of name that fin, began rushing before them as Steven quickly steered the sixty-footer in the direction of distress.

The bluest sky most of them had ever seen served as backdrop to a sociopath's well-planned ploy. While Simon told Steven that he'd only met Pierre Meadows, the athletic director, once or twice, that wasn't true. Simon and Pierre had been long-time members of the Harbor's Boat Club.

Simon knew the Honey Bear's course. Pierre had been discussing the planned excursion for months, recently telling fellow members about Steven's, an accomplished sailor, desire to be slightly isolated.

Because of Pierre, Simon knew when Steven was casting off and how long they'd be out. He'd gotten to that spot earlier that morning and waited for the remarkable vessel's arrival. He'd been listening to Steven provide maritime updates over his boat's radio before breaking the spring of his back up radio when they were about a half mile away.

Shamir buried his face behind six years of mangled, uncut hair. He rocked back and forth as his mind relived the unspeakable horrors of the death of his roommate, Trent. Amia gathered him into her chest, shushing his fears, using her warmth to counter a new onslaught of shivers.

"I couldn't look, Mia… I just couldn't… I covered my ears. I tried to block it out, but I couldn't." Shamir's previously bent knees were now drawn up to his chest. The petrified emptiness that Darren saw when he found Shamir in the basement returned to his eyes.

Darren kneeled next to them on the lounger, extending a comforting hand to his youngest brother-in-law's shoulder.

"Shamir," Darren whispered, wrapping his strong arms around the young man. Shamir surprised Darren by clinging onto his torso tightly. The reality that this kid hadn't felt his family's touch in six years weighed on him. Shamir's sniffles and his unwillingness to release his grip tugged at Darren's soul.

Amia slid over on the spacious couch, allowing her husband to hold onto her frightened youngest brother. While the softness of her embrace and smoothness of her voice offered the comfort Shamir had been longing for, Amia understood that Darren's strength and dominating presence provided the protection Shamir needed.

Darren allowed a few moments more to crawl by after Shamir assured him that he was fine. Only then did he revisit the nagging question.

"Shamir, you said this Simon guy knows me. Did he ever say how he knew me?"

"Not just you, both of you. He asked all of us our names, first and last. Trying to scare him, I told him my name, that I was related to you, and that you were both attorneys in Pittsburgh. He asked me my name again and then asked what your names were.

"I told him again, thinking that would scare him. Coach, hoping to add pressure and make him leave, reminded Simon that he was your brother-in-law," he added while looking at Darren.

"'Defense attorneys, huh? Darren Wilford, your brother-in-law, is a partner at a law firm? In Pittsburgh, you said? Is that right?'" Shamir's voice mocked Simon's as he repeated the chilling exchange.

"Yo, the way he smiled at us... was crazy..." Shamir went silent. Without warning, he began attempting to free himself from the deep comfy grey furniture and the heavy cream covering.

"I shouldn't be here. When he finds out I'm gone, he's gonna come here. I can't let him find me with you. He'll kill you."

"Shamir, nothing is going to happen to you or to us. Do you understand?" Darren's voice was stern and matter-of-fact. A dark coolness crept into his spirit. It was the kill-or-be-killed mentality that defined Darren's father.

Until preparing to kill a stranger in his basement, he had only experienced that feeling once before and that was years earlier. Back then, Amia was pregnant with Daniel and some thugs from Jamari, her younger brother's, past threatened the family late one evening.

Darren was feeling the same indescribable rage at the thought of this beautiful soul being held hostage for all of these years and learning that that same someone had the audacity to threaten his family. Amia almost felt that other-worldly presence creeping up on her husband. She tried to counter it by covering his hand and pressing her head against Darren's.

"Why us, Shamir? Did he ever say why he would want to hurt us?" she probed.

"Just something about y'all sending his sister, the only person he had in life, to prison."

# Chapter 22

## *In a Word* – Searching

To see Darren's corner office at WW&M in such disarray, you would never know that its normal state was nearly as pristine as the archives in the Library of Congress. Everything had a place in the well-designed twelve-by-fifteen space.

Now, at 2:00 a.m., the office resembled that of a mad mastermind. Folders upon folders stacked ten deep covered his oak desk, brown carpeted floor, and the large window's ledge. Equally out of character were the half-empty cabinets and drawers that were left open in the law room of WW&M.

While he made wee hour pitstops to WW&M, they had been rare and only prior to a large trial. Today though, there weren't any pending court proceedings which required last-minute polishing.

Instead, this early morning mess was attributed to Shamir's revelation nights earlier that murders and his subsequent captivity were at the hands of someone exacting revenge on him and Amia. But who? He could not wait for the downed trees, debris, and power lines to be removed so that he could get back into the office.

*"A defense attorney defends. We don't send people to prison. It has to be someone related to a case that we lost, but whose?"*

There had been less than a dozen female defendants for whom a loss resulted in imprisonment. Their files were contained somewhere within the massive piles occupying his space. Though all case files within the last ten years were electronic, older cases were stored in the WW&M archives which happened to be across the hall from Darren's office.

"Hey, Todd," he managed after almost missing the call. His phone had gotten buried amongst the myriad of stacks.

"You find out anything? Ok, 'preciate it... No, I haven't found anything yet. I've spent the last couple hours going through the cases that I lost and cases Amia lost. I've even pulled all the case that we sat second chair on, but I don't see a connection.

"Anyone you chose not to represent?" asked Todd.

"That's a good idea. Let me shake those trees."

"Holla back if you need anything, no matter how small."

"Thanks, man. How's Ms. Regina?"

After learning that Todd's mom was on the mend and would be back to baking her famous cherry-berry pies in no time, Darren took an additional moment to reflect.

In the midst of the literal and figurative chaos, two miracles had emerged since the hurricane winds slammed into their beloved city. Shamir showed up alive and his third mother, Regina, had survived what could have easily been a fatal heart attack.

"I don't know why this just popped up in my mind, but do you remember when I was completely against approaching Amia because we were coworkers? You kept pushing me to holla at her and now, look. I'm sitting in this office at the butt-crack of dawn, rifling through files."

"Tell you what," Todd's smile traveled through the phone, "give me that rib rub recipe and we're square. Seriously, I'm glad Shamir's home. We're gonna figure all this out. How is he anyway? Have you told Elaine and Ramon yet?"

"We plan to tell them this afternoon. Dawg, Shamir is crazy skittish and worried the family will somehow be hurt. Sven's security team has a detail outside of our house. He has seen them, so he's relaxed a little bit."

"Have you told Camille?"

Darren's soul sank as he perched on the edge of his completely covered desk. How was he supposed to tell his sister that her husband had survived the boat fire years ago only to die a slow death in captivity.

"I haven't figured out how to yet, but it will have to be today or tomorrow."

"Alright... Hey, you need me to fly to Colorado and holla at ya boy?

"Yeah, ok." Darren laughed at his very overprotective friend. "I'd prefer that you not become an inmate while visiting one.

"Just saying... Love you, Bruh. Holla at you later."

Though Shamir begged them not to say anything, Amia and Darren contacted Sven the night he arrived. If Shamir's warnings were right, they needed added security.

Todd was the next call as his investigative firm's expertise was second to none. Whenever ghosts needed to be found, he and the private investigators of Hinton Tracking would deliver. Darren continued sifting through the mountains of files, trying to find something—anything.

# Chapter 23

## *In a Word* – Anticipation

"Hey, Michele. Welcome back," Amia screamed happily into the phone. She was thrilled to hear the news. Jamari's wife had been teaching overseas for the past few weeks and returned the day before her birthday.

Michele shared Jamari's latest venture in trickery, explaining that he'd suggested she fly into Michigan to spend a little time with her family. Secretly, Jamari timed Oscar's pick up with her arrival. The breeder was an old college friend who happened to live two towns over from Michele's family.

Michele went on to describe her confusion as Jamari met her at the airport with a large white welcome home sign. As she got closer, he lowered the cardboard, revealing a tiny, wiggly light brown slice of heaven. Michele went on to tell Amia that her husband's sudden interest in her Pinterest boards made absolute sense.

Jamari momentarily interrupted the oohs and awws to inform Amia that they were on the way back to Pittsburgh.

"Hey, let me know when y'all are settled and we'll visit," Amia advised.

"If y'all aren't doing anything this weekend, we'll stop by. It's been a while and I'd love to see you guys," Michele said.

Darren, who had been in another room, joined Amia in their kitchen after hearing her squeal in excitement. Their breath caught in their throats when Michele's suggestion hit them.

They wanted nothing more than to see the Copelands and meet their new, wet-nosed nephew, but they hadn't revealed the news about Shamir. *Do we say something now or wait to spring it on them when they arrive?* she pondered.

Amia would have to decide soon. One thing's for sure, it was a must to lay eyes on Michele whenever she returned from her business trips. While deliberating about how to tell her brother that his only brother was actually alive, Amia's mind drifted back to almost two years earlier when Michele left the country for a business trip and was gone for almost five months. They learned upon her 'return' that the entire thing had been a ruse.

Waving hands and the mouthing of "hello" caught Amia's attention bringing her back to the current phone call. Her heart was smiling at the remembrance of that time in their lives.

Darren's facial expression was one of confusion as he was still in the seriousness of the moment. He was searching his wife's amazing almond eyes trying to figure out where the smile was coming from. Her contagious grin coaxed Darren's pearlies out from behind his parting lips.

"We'll see you soon, guys," she said, fully aware that she would be seeing the young Copeland family later today or tomorrow morning because Elaine and Ramon would be laying eyes on Shamir this afternoon.

# Chapter 24

## *In a Word* – Disbelief

"Grandma! Grandpa!" screamed Daniel and Christina excitedly as they flew out of the door and into Elaine and Ramon's arms. They were extra excited to see the grandparents as it had been a couple weeks since their last visit.

"What did you say?" asked a stunned Ramon.

"Oh God," whispered Amia. The one thing she and Darren said to the kids repeatedly was not to say anything to Grandma and Grandpa about Shamir. Amia had to go pee one last time and unfortunately, Elaine had proven yet again that she was still terrible at estimating how far they were away from anywhere.

So, here Amia was on the toilet cursing herself for having that second cup of coffee because this stream proved to be never-ending. All she could do was helplessly peer through the bathroom window as Christina whispered a secret into Ramon's ear.

Darren was upstairs in the game room with Shamir watching a college basketball game on their oversized television while partaking in New York style pizza and wings. The television was on concert mode with extra-loud surround sound.

While he was enjoying the game and spending time with Shamir, this was the only way Darren knew to ensure the sports fanatic wouldn't be walking around their home potentially catching a glimpse of his parents pulling up.

Darren nor Shamir could hear the squealing children. Mia, on the other hand was feverishly trying to force the last drops out so that she could meet her parents, one of whom was now grilling Daniel while they were both hurrying the kids into the house.

"Oh God," Amia said while bouncing on the toilet, somehow convinced that action would move things along quicker. She was in the half bath, and while small, the towels were too far away from her perched position for her to grab and tuck into her panties to absorb the flow.

"Oh, come on," Amia growled, fussing at mother nature. These few seconds now felt like minutes, moving along as slowly as the drops leaving her body.

*Hurry up, Amia! God, please don't let them go upstairs. Please keep us safe. This is going to be a huge shock,* she acknowledged. Tears were beginning to pool as she became more desperate.

She finally finished what felt like a Guinness World record-breaking urination. At the same time, the fastest prayers she'd ever uttered were flying out of her mouth.

"*Please let Mom and Dad and Shamir be mentally and physically okay.*" Amia quickly patted her damp hands on the hand towel. "Protect their hearts and bodies from any danger. Let them absorb this news without harm."

Footsteps were now briskly heading into the family room.

"*Please Lord, Amen.*"

With that, she snatched the bathroom door open just in time to catch Ramon as his hand met the stairway banister.

"Hey Da—"

Elaine cut in, stopping her cold.

"Amia, what is this Christina is saying about Shamir being here?"

The Jamaican accent trembled through her cracking voice. Jingling filled the air due to Elaine's new long, bulky necklace clanging against itself as her nervous fingers fumbled with the jewelry. She'd been unconsciously clutching the large silver loops since overhearing Christina whisper, "Shamir's upstairs."

Elaine felt heavy. Sweat was beading on her upper lip and brow. Her lungs throbbed. She realized it was due to holding her breath awaiting Amia's reply.

"What is this she's saying, Amia?"

Elaine's voice was desperate.

"Bean misunderstood something, right?"

"Amia, answer the question, please," Ramon urged as his body shook. His trembling hand began stroking his mouth and chin in anticipation of her response.

He felt lightheaded and unsteady. Like Elaine, Ramon's breaths weren't coming as often as they should and hadn't since the words, "Shamir's upstairs," made their way into his ear.

The angst in the stairway was profound. Amia could almost feel her parents' hearts thumping in their chests. Daniel was side-eying his little sister who was now half hiding behind Ramon while tightly hugging his shaking leg.

At seven, Christina was too young to understand the full gravity of the situation but old enough to know that she should have obeyed her mama and not said anything.

"Amia," repeated Elaine.

Amia watched almost in slow motion as Elaine joined Ramon at the base of the stairs. Her eyes followed their quivering hands as they unconsciously found each other.

It was interesting. Suddenly, the woman who always lent the right words to every situation was having difficulty with one of the simplest ones in the English language. Amia wanted to force the easy one syllable reply past her lips, but the air kept getting caught in her windpipe.

Daniel was completely surprised by Amia's silence. This is something he'd never seen in his thirteen years on Earth.

Instinctively, he joined Amia's side, squeezing and patting her hand in the same manner of encouragement she'd done for him countless times through the years.

Amia pulled her son tight with one hand while the other covered her parents' still joined hands on the bannister. The tension was thick. She again said a quick inward prayer for her parents' protection before answering.

"Yes," she whispered, nodding her head in response to their understandable confusion and disbelief.

"Shamir is here - he's alive."

Elaine's emotion-laden gasp was almost identical to the one that escaped her throat six years earlier when they learned of the Honey Bear's demise and that Shamir was missing.

Amia prayed she'd never hear that shriek of horrified anguish again, but it was back. This time, though, the sound was a mixture of fear, disbelief and cautious elation. Amia helped Elaine ease her vibrating body down onto the stairs.

The sledgehammer that hit Ramon following the confirmation that his youngest was still alive, caused his legs to buckle. "Where is he, Amia?"

"I'm not saying another word until you drink some more," insisted Amia again, extending the water bottle back in Ramon's direction. Elaine finished her first bottle, downing with it an ibuprofen to counter the slight throbbing in her knee caused by Ramon's half-collapsing onto her.

"When did you get so stubborn?" asked Ramon, seeking to lighten the atmosphere.

"I just got a little light headed because I didn't eat this morning. I wanted to have enough room for your Mama's lasagna. That paired with this news was just a bit much, but I'm fine, Amia... I promise."

Elaine, having regained her bearings, guided peeled clementine slices to Ramon's lips while Amia checked his blood pressure and heart rate, using the home health kit which Adrienne and Mable, the family's medical professionals, insisted everyone keep in their home.

Shamir actually reminded them of the kit's existence. He recalled the gift Adrienne and Mable gave everyone for Christmas the year Darren and Amia were critically injured at Weeboy Manor. At the realization that there were no medical kits on hand at the sprawling residence, both RNs made it their mission to ensure every home had one.

It took a bit of searching, but Darren was able to find it in the back of a closet. This allowed Shamir to stave off their insistence on medical intervention. After all, he'd been using a similar kit for years while caring for Steven and was quite familiar with the interworking's of the equipment.

A quick Google search assured Amia that Ramon's blood pressure and heart rates were within the normal range for a man his age. *Thank you, Lord,* Amia prayed silently. She was truly worried about her parents' health and its ability to handle the news.

"That's enough fussing over me, Amia. I'm fine. Shamir!" she yelled.

"Grandma! Shhhh," responded Daniel and Christina immediately, though politely. Each had an index finger pressed firmly against their lips.

"Grandma, Shamir doesn't like it when people yell," Daniel explained. His voice was nervous.

"Yeah, he hid over there when Daddy fussed at Danny yesterday," Christina added, pointing her finger towards the thick floor-to-ceiling curtains. "Shamir was shaking and crying, too," she added. The corners of her lips turned downward slightly.

"Oh, baby. Grammy didn't know. I'm just so happy and really want to see Shamir. It's been a really long time, Bean. Grammy won't yell again," Elaine replied as she pulled her granddaughter towards her. "Why was Daddy fussing at Danny?" she asked while winking at Daniel who'd taken a seat next to Ramon.

"Because Danny ate his cheesecake and only left a little bit in the box," she giggled as Daniel looked around pretending to look for the other Danny who'd eaten the salted caramel slice of heaven that his dad had been waiting all day to devour.

"I'd have probably eaten it, too Grandson," Ramon said laughing at the youngster.

"Alright, I think you two can stop fanning Grandma and Grandpa now," Amia said to the kids who'd been waiving paper plates in their grandparent's direction since Ramon's episode of lightheadedness. She breathed a sigh of relief because, her concerns about her parents' physical reactions to the news had not come to fruition. She instructed the duo to return the paper plates to the kitchen so that she could begin prepping her parents for what they were about to see.

Sure, Shamir Copeland was back, but the smiley, happy-go-lucky twenty-year-old who they'd all known—hadn't made it home yet. The multi-sport athlete was present, but his frail frame said otherwise. Amia described a wary, traumatized young man now living in the body previously occupied by Shamir's trusting, carefree spirit.

"You're gonna see marks and burns on Shamir's neck," she said, her voice lowered to avoid being overheard by the children.

"Most are old, but there are a few that are more recent..." Amia placed her hand on top of her parents' joined hands. "This is gonna be hard to hear, and I'm so sorry, but the scars from a shock collar that he and Steven had to wear. Apparently, the property had an electric fence so they couldn't escape. They tried a couple times over the years. Shamir has a few deep scars, which make me think the voltage was extra high. Also, y'all. He's really skinny. I mean, really skinny."

Just then, roaring erupted from the Wilford's spacious upstairs bonus room.

"Get some!"

That shout from Darren told the family that there had just been an incredibly nasty slam dunk.

“I’m sure that one will be on the highlight films for months to come,” said Amia. She also knew her husband well enough to know that the emphasis of the words ‘get some’ meant the unlucky opponent who got dunked on ended up with a face full of shorts.

“Ooh, ooh, ooh. Go Pitt, go!” was the next phase that excitedly flew through the halls and down the stairs.”

“Sounds like Pitt is winning,” offered Amia, smiling reverently.

“Nah,” replied Ramon, allowing his son’s unmistakable catch phrase to dance in his ears. “They were in the fourth quarter when we drove up.”

“Yeah boy! That’s what I’m talking ’bout!” Ramon closed his eyes, absorbing another signature expression for the first time in six years, before wiping a happy tear. He began trembling again. This time, the nerves were vibrating from sweet anticipation.

“Pitt won.” That was all Ramon could muster as he held Christina, allowing his relief to freefall in the form of tears. The youngster hopped into her Pop-Pop’s lap to console him after seeing the first tear fall.

“We did too,” Amia exhaled deeply.

“I’ve waited long enough. Can’t do it anymore. I’m going up there,” Elaine announced, promptly lifting herself off the stairs and groaning as her knee responded to the swift motion.

“No, Ma and please keep your voice down. I know that TV is blaring, but I cannot stress it enough; Shamir is really scared. He’s literally likely to jump out a window if he hears any voices or sees anyone coming down the hallway other than me, Dan, or Bean. You and Dad come and have a seat at the table."

Then, scooping up one of the two Krispy Kreme boxes that the parents picked up, Mia asked Daniel to let Darren and Shamir know the donuts were here. That was Amia and Darren's secret phrase to set the meeting in motion.

Daniel skipped back down the stairs excitedly. The message had been delivered. The family sat in nervous anticipation as Darren and Shamir's voices giddily recapped the last fifteen seconds of the nail biter, growing louder as they closed in on the kitchen.

# Chapter 25

## In a Word – Breakdown

Shamir's post-game high vanished instantly as he rounded the corner. Darren positioned himself in the entryway to prevent any possible escape. Shamir stood paralyzed. His throat went dry as his pulse quadrupled. There were additional bodies in the home.

He felt an immediate sense of betrayal as his brain attempted to comprehend how strangers had invaded his safe space. The family witnessed Shamir's metamorphosis in real time as the newcomers' features registered.

Shamir's breath began coming in short bursts. "Mom?" His eyes traveled to Amia and Darren, silently asking if this was really happening. While he could see them, he almost needed their assurance that the quivering figures standing in disbelief before him were in fact his parents.

Though the tear-laden head nods came quickly from the Wilfords, neither Elaine nor Ramon waited for their replies. They swarmed their Shamir, arms wide open. Amia and Darren held their children tightly as the scene unfolded before them.

"Oh my God," Shamir wailed, throwing his skinny arms around Ramon's body. "Dad!" Sobs wracked his frame. "Momma." That was the only other word he could muster as he pulled Elaine's weeping body into his.

At some point, Shamir's hands traced his parents' wet faces as theirs did the same to his, almost imprinting each other's existence. A glimmer of the old Shamir returned as the long-awaited embraces turned into lengthy, happy squeezes. The gratefulness. The relief. The disbelief. The rotation of feelings.

"The one thing I hoped for more than anything all those years was to see the two of you just one more time, and here you are." By now, Shamir's voice was nothing more than a raspy whisper.

Prior to and even during his years in captivity, Shamir hadn't been a religious man. In fact, his time under Simon's control had convinced him that the God Amia and Darren trusted in so much never actually existed.

That said, he did make it to the safety of Amia and Darren's home in the midst of a hurricane and was now back in the loving arms of his parents. The anguished youngster did manage to whisper a thank you to God for making it possible.

"You have no idea, Son." Ramon's normally strong, smooth voice was strained. Words competed with breath as his parched throat prioritized releasing oxygen for speech while retaining enough to maintain consciousness.

While the entire family was relieved at Shamir's return, Ramon's thankfulness was wrapped around remorse. After all, he'd missed three years of Shamir's childhood while on tour with a military unit in Kuwait.

Ramon's life-long dream of becoming world-renown photographer had been put on hold when Amia arrived several years before he and Elaine had planned on having children. Twenty years later, the overwhelming desire led Ramon to accept an offer to become an embedded photographer with the Special Forces. He willingly left his family to pursue a career, and Shamir's disappearance and untimely death hit him harder than anyone else due to the three years he'd lost. Having the gift of his son in his arms again caused a flood of emotions.

Once there was a semblance of composure, the family gathered around the table. As expected, the questions began raining down in rapid succession. There were a ton of 'I don't knows,' but Shamir did have answers to several questions, which of course, led to more questions.

"I just know she was a great cook," Shamir said of Simon's girlfriend. "These Krispy Kreme donuts don't hold a candle to hers.

"No, I never saw her," he responded, answering the next obvious question. "I only heard her voice now and then, but it was muffled through the ceiling above. I truly hated being there, but her visits gave us something to look forward to. We knew the food was guaranteed to be amazing for the next several days."

Shamir noted that it was crazy how captivity changed priorities. He'd been affectionately known as the sneaker snob of the family, because he had a pair of color-coordinated kicks to match every outfit. Shamir wouldn't have been caught dead in a pair that didn't match what he was wearing, even during practice.

"Steven and I had one constant wish. It was that Simon would get company because, in addition to the good food, he was a tad nicer when she left."

Amia's heart hurt again, as it had with each revelation she'd learned since Shamir's arrival a few days earlier. She could see the scars peppered across his body and those sitting deep behind his eyes, but actually hearing that he prayed for his captor to have a visit so he was spared some wrath and could enjoy a meal, hit different.

"It's funny," Shamir began. "His girlfriend called him Drew." The family became concerned about the smile stretching across Shamir's face. He noticed their worry, and explained. "Steven and I created stories about Simon to pass the time. We did it a lot when his girlfriend visited.

"One of our ongoing tales was that Simon was from another country. We even made up countries and fictional towns. This was all based on the way the girlfriend elongated his name. She always called him 'Drewww,' so Steven and I would call him Simon Drew from Drubeckistan." He finished with a smile.

Amia was proud of Shamir for finding the silver lining, even in those dark days. That was something her care-free baby brother was well-known for prior to his disappearance. It's why as a teenager, he started the blood drive following the incident at Weeboy Manor. Rather than do nothing, he found a way to make the situation better. He did it then and even now.

"You need to go to the hospital." That was more of a command than an observation. Before the sentence was fully out of her mouth, Elaine had retrieved her purse from the granite countertop and hoisted it upon her shoulder.

"No, Mom. I can't go to the hospital," he replied desperately. Elaine and Ramon got to see the terror that Amia described first hand. Shamir tensed and began pacing as he restated his reasons for being unable to leave. Darren instinctively made his way back into the opening of the connected rooms while Ramon took his spot covering the entrance at the opposite end of the kitchen. Shamir was quick, but there was no way he was getting past either of them should his fight or flight have set in.

"I'm calling an ambulance," said Elaine, witnessing his sheer terror and withdrawal. Shamir's first reaction was nothing compared to his response to Elaine's suggestion of an ambulance.

He immediately darted from his chair, clambering atop the wooden table, looking for an escape. The young man they'd just been reunited with was gone, replaced by a seemingly feral human being. It took Daniel's sprinting back into the kitchen wearing his prized orange and white baseball cap to coax his favorite uncle from the ledge.

"Uncle Mir, look!"

Darren and Ramon helped Shamir down from off the countertop which he'd scaled once it was clear there was no escape.

Daniel extended his favorite possession which brought tears to Shamir's eyes.

"Remember when you won this for me at Six Flags?"

"I can't believe you still have this." Shamir wiped his eyes, allowing that memory to win the moment. "I think I lost ten dollars trying to shoot that dern duck. That was a lot for a broke college kid," he managed.

"You gave me a dollar, right?" Shamir asked as he lovingly felt its flat brim before setting the striped hat back atop his nephew's curly head.

"Yep. We were getting ready to leave. Remember, Dad and Pop were yelling at you to come on. You really wanted that hat, Uncle Mir. I gave you four quarters and you won it," Daniel beamed.

"You gave the hat to me when we got back to the car."

"That's right," Shamir exclaimed, his fist over his mouth.

"I left Six Flags and headed right back to campus... I still can't believe you kept it."

"It was the last time I saw you," Daniel replied. Tears were again breaching all dams.

Shamir exhaled slowly, drawing his nephew in close. They'd been inseparable up until that fateful day on the bay. Whenever Shamir was home, if you saw him, you'd see Daniel.

When the Wilfords visited him on campus, Daniel was guaranteed to be riding piggy back or sitting on his shoulders touring the sites.

"God, I missed you, Dan," he whispered, kissing the thirteen-year-old's head.

"I'll go to the hospital," Shamir conceded, "but not in an ambulance. They could be working with Simon and take me back. Also, don't leave me alone... Promise?"

"Son, listen to me. I'm not leaving you... ever again. You hear me?"

That response from Ramon was delivered with one hand resting firmly on either side of Shamir's thin face.

"Lighten the pressure of that squeeze there, Dad," Elaine quipped to her husband, noting the tightness of the embrace that followed Ramon's promise. "Don't want you to mess around and break a rib."

With that, the kids hit the restroom as instructed. Key fobs and car keys jingled. Feet made their ways into soles as the family headed for the exits.

# Chapter 26

## *In a Word* – Cagey

Three more warm blankets were brought into the small tan and white room within the emergency department. Elaine politely extracted the toasty linens from the nurse, offering to spread them across Shamir's shivering frame.

She was acutely aware of his increasing wariness of the new faces constantly popping in and out. Beeping from vital machines increased with each screech of the curtains being pushed and pulled as new medical professionals appeared and exited Shamir's room.

"Why do they keep asking my name? Why are there so many people?" Shamir was no longer able to stay in the bed as directed by the Emergency Room physicians and nurses. Panic was again setting in.

"What's happening, Dad?" Though he asked the question, Shamir couldn't hear Ramon's explanations over the thumping in his ears. He was now too busy protecting himself, which included screaming for help and throwing whatever he could get his hands on.

That sense of betrayal creeped back in. This time, it was because his parents seemed to be siding with the strangers. A crippling fear caused Shamir's lashing out at the very people who were there to help him.

"The tape is too tight." With that, Shamir began pulling at the IV. His parents stopped him.

"I can't breathe. This thing is too tight," Shamir said, beginning to hyperventilate. Elaine and Ramon watched helplessly as his fingers attempted to loosen and remove a shock collar that was no longer there.

Orderlies responded to the Code Grey that echoed through the halls of the Emergency Department. Within seconds, Shamir was subdued, a long silver needle ushered calm into the tan and white room. The parents took a breath as they watched their youngest son fight a losing battle with the clear fluid's effects.

"Get me out of here, please," came his weakened begs. His eyes, once wild with fear, were now having trouble staying open. Shamir's panic attack was so real that even in his drugged state, he was still weakly tugging at the restraints.

“They’re calling Simon. Please… That’s why they keep coming and going. Don’t let him take me. Dad… Please… You promised…” Shamir’s mutterings ceased as the sedation won.

Meanwhile, in the colorful waiting room, the Wilford children were saying goodbye to Darren and Amia as their best friends, Todd and Janelle, came to collect them. The kids had been leaning against each other playing on their respective electronic devices with volumes slightly higher than normally allowed. This afternoon’s exception was to reduce the chances of them hearing the agonizing groans and aches of patients waiting to be seen.

Under normal circumstances, the parents would have been comfortable with Daniel’s ability to handle some agony since the thirteen-year-old had been playing soccer for nine years. He’d certainly heard his share of injury-spurred cries.

That said, their oldest was still not protesting his kid sister’s requests to sleep in his room. This told the parents that the normally ultra-independent teenager who loved his little sister, but was still an actual teenager, remained rattled by the events of the last few days. Spending time with TJ and Kennedy at Uncle Todd and Aunt Janelle’s offered the perfect distraction.

The pair thanked the rays of sunshine named Janelle and Todd, ensuring them that they’d fill in as many details as allowed as soon as possible.

"Apparently, things took a turn for the worst when all the doctors and nurses were cycling in and out asking for his name. Shamir is convinced they're somehow working with Simon.

"It was all too overwhelming for him. The doctor said he was in the midst of a full-on panic attack, which is why he was screaming and throwing things," Amia recounted the story as she spoke with her sisters who were still in Toronto, but now making plans to return.

"I know it was heartbreaking to watch. I honestly can't imagine," Amia added, fighting the tightening in her soul. She shared the latest with her sisters after Shamir was asleep. Only then would Elaine leave his side, though Ramon was firmly planted.

"Mom said the doctors and nurses tried to get them to leave while they were getting Shamir under control. You know how calm Dad is, right?" Amia continued after her sisters who had her on speaker replied.

"Mom said Dad told the security guard in no uncertain terms that he needed to contact the President and request the National Guard for backup, because he was absolutely not leaving... I know, right?" Amia exclaimed in response to the 'wows' that came from the other end of the line.

"I could actually hear Mom all the way out here when they asked her to leave. She reminded all of them that Shamir had been declared dead six years ago. Then she told them point blank that she wasn't leaving.

"Thankfully, the ER Physician, Dr. Hassan, is letting them stay in his room in light of the situation. I'm glad he did because honestly, it would have gotten really ugly up in here today.

"Yeah, Shamir's being admitted. We're just waiting for a room... Alright, I'll tell them that you'll be in tomorrow. Love you, Bree. Love you, Jordie. Y'all be safe."

Amia and Darren embraced for the umpteenth time, sighing into each other's arms. Non-stop intensity had defined the past several days. A miracle, straight from God Himself, blew in with a once-in-a-lifetime storm. Marshon Wilford, whose name hadn't been uttered in well over a decade, was now a recurring irritation.

"How are you doing?"

Amia wrapped her loving arms around her husband's strong waist. She'd heard him on the phone with Camille while Elaine came out to provide the update. Because Darren had already started the shocking revelation moments before Elaine came out, he had to stay on the line with his sister.

"I had to tell Camille over the phone that Steven survived, only to die in a basement earlier this year."

He held her tightly, kissing the top of her head.

"She's in Connecticut still, but I had to tell her, Amia. I needed to tell her before she saw it on the news."

Darren gritted his teeth. His eyes closed as he described Camille's disbelief, anger and anguish.

"Larry is on his way to Connecticut now," he advised.

Darren's sister came to grips with Steven's death years ago. She and Larry, a successful jeweler and former college teammate of Darren's, had been dating since Darren introduced the pair almost two years ago.

The pair held onto each other.

"I'm hungry. I'm gonna run to the café. You wanna come?" asked Amia.

"Nah, I'll sit."

"Do you want anything?" she asked, fishing through her purse for her slim wallet.

"Yeah, can you bring me two breasts and a couple of thighs?"

"Yep," she replied, finally extracting the wallet.

"Two breasts, and a couple of thighs. Anything else," she asked, zipping the tote back together and sliding it down beside Darren who'd just taken a seat.

"Yeah, let me get a thick, juicy pair of legs with that."

Amia smiled, suddenly realizing her husband was not referring to nor in the mood for chicken.

"They don't have any of that in this café, but there's this one spot on Teeton Drive. Trust me, all of the meat served up in there is juicy and amazing. I've left several five-star reviews."

"It's a good thing we'll be heading that way later today. Can I preorder? I'm absolutely ravished."

There was something about the way that man licked his lips that drove Amia wild. She bit her lip, exhaling slowly as she waited for the elevator, eyeing her sexy man. It wasn't long before the bell dinged, letting both of them onto the elevator.

Amia knew he'd be heading towards her in no time. Her thumb 'accidentally' traced his lower lip a few times while she played with his goatee.

The silent sexual tension fueled by lip biting and fingers rubbing against each other suggestively was a welcome brain break. It allowed the couple to get away from the seriousness of the moment and reconnect.

Once back in the waiting room, the Wilfords again took their seats, leaning against each other with fingers interlocked as an ever-growing alphabet soup of law enforcement officials filed in.

Shortly thereafter, a thoroughly perplexed Jamari and Michele squeezed past the barrage of media who had turned the emergency room foyer into their staging area. The same level of disbelief wracked their being as heads nodded to the unasked question about Shamir's survival.

# Chapter 27

## *In a Word* – Recount

Five days later, Jamari sat in an armchair next to his younger brother, encouraging him on. The investigators were patiently, but urgently, trying to piece together the story so they could find his captor, the home he was held in, locate Steven's body, and uncover exactly why the Honey Bear had been targeted that fateful afternoon.

"Do you need a break?" asked Elaine. The tone of the question ensured the officers knew she could care less about their agenda. Without question, it was important to get to the bottom of this, but Shamir was just released from the hospital. She was not about to compromise his already fragile mental health.

The agony of saying goodbye to and burying her son was indescribable, matched nearly by witnessing that same son in the midst of a near psychotic break. As far as Elaine was concerned, Darren's best friend, Todd, and his private investigators or Sven and his covert operations teams could take over the investigation and this group of uncaring officials could kick rocks.

"No, I'm good, Mom," Shamir assured.

"So," said the lead detective. His tone was a little softer after having taken the hint. "You were telling us about Devin and Darius throwing Mason overboard after Simon shot him repeatedly. You said Corey and Trent jumped into the bay and were attacked by sharks. Quinton, Bugg, and Travis were deceased by that time, right?"

"Yeah," replied Shamir, his heart aching.

"He made the remaining guys tie Coach O and me to the rails before hitting them each on the back of their head or in their throats. He was just pure evil. While they were disoriented and choking..."

His face distorted as images of his teammates flashed before him. He shook his head, blinking the images away as he continued, "...Simon held their heads down in the water tank or poured buckets of water in their faces, eventually drowning them one by one."

This time, Shamir's head and upturned eyes went to the ceiling. He breathed through the flashbacks of his teammates thrashing while being drowned.

"That's right. Keep breathing," coached Jamari.

"You're doing great, Mir. You still see that spot on the ceiling, right? Good. Keep looking at it and breathe. We're not in a rush. We'll wait 'til you're ready," Jamari said.

"So, none of you drowned due to the storm?" asked the officer after receiving an approving nod from Shamir advising him to continue the line of questioning.

"This Simon person... He killed all of those young men?" The anger building within Darren seeped into each word of his question.

"Yeah. I don't know how long it took him to finish with everyone, but eventually, Simon came back to untie us. He put the gun to my head and walked us back to his boat. We were given gas masks and..."

Shamir's eyes locked on his big brother's. He and Jamari, the licensed psychologist and professor, breathed through this latest flashback together.

"The gas was so strong... We put them on and went into the hull of Simon's boat. Quinton, Bugg, and Travis were... dead."

His leg began a rapid, involuntary bounce. He slinked down into his seat, covering his eyes. Some variation of 'let's take a break' rang out from multiple voices in unison. The sentiment came from all corners of the living room, including from the officers.

"No," Shamir insisted, still bouncing his leg and writhing. His head was now buried in his lap. Jamari was on his knees in front of his younger brother reminding him to breathe; reminding him what day it was. He reminded him that he was no longer on the bay in that skiff. Jamari assured him that whatever happened wasn't his fault.

"He made us remove their life jackets and throw all three of them overboard," Shamir confessed, now despondent. Shamir and Bugg had been peas and carrots since elementary school. He's who convinced Shamir to run track and, in return, Shamir convinced Bugg to turn down the scholarship at North Carolina A&T and join him in Baltimore.

Jamari and Elaine's waving hands signified the mashing of the pause button, despite Shamir's brave claims that he could continue. Elaine pulled her baby boy into her arms, allowing him to weep. While holding Shamir tightly with one hand, she cupped Jamari's face gently with the other. Her heart rang with pride. Elaine pulled her oldest son in close, wrapping him in her other arm.

There were no words to describe that powerful moment. Well, maybe one—healing. Logically, Elaine knew she'd made the right decision to send Jamari to live with Amia when he was a wayward teen. Twenty years later though, the mother's heart still wrestled with it. Today, it was confirmed. She knew in her soul that she'd made the right decision. Back then, Jamari was too far down the wrong path and a drastic change was the only way he'd have gotten off.

Jamari experienced an equal amount of reconciliation. In that moment, his inner thirteen-year-old exhaled with the knowledge that his life went exactly the way it was supposed to.

Had Elaine not threatened the juvenile detention, Amia would have never known how off track he had gotten. She wouldn't have known to intervene. It was Jamari's desperate call to his big sister, once learning Elaine had called his parole officer, that changed his life.

Without Elaine and Ramon's decision to send him to juvenile detention to prevent the then small-time drug dealer from ending up dead or in prison, Jamari would not have leaned into his life. He wouldn't have had a slew of mentors pouring into him constantly.

The soft hug he returned when Elaine pulled him towards her initially, tightened as the realization took hold. "I love you, Mom," he exhaled deeply. "So much," Jamari said, placing long kisses on her cheek and forehead.

After ensuring Shamir was in a good space, he left their side to find his father. Ramon went into the kitchen in search of apple juice, hoping a tall glass could somehow quench Shamir's scorched soul.

"Let me get those," Jamari said, carefully extracting both glasses from Ramon's hands and setting them down onto the white corium countertop. The next action was him pulling Ramon in for a long, heartfelt hug.

"Thank you, Dad. Thank you for everything."

Ramon hadn't been privy to Jamari's inner thoughts, but didn't need to be. That long hug told him everything he needed to know. Ramon kissed his son's cheek as he, too, felt a breakthrough.

The father and son had been good as the years ticked by, going on fishing trips, camping in the Andes mountains, and enjoying the occasional Cuban cigar. That said, there was always something there. It was invisible and nameless, but it was there.

Ramon and Elaine's actions offered Jamari a chance to see life differently and to become the person everyone saw inside of him. The psychology major and clinical therapy minors were chosen as a way to give back. After all, both subjects had huge impacts on his life.

It was Amia's insistence on talking about his day and expressing his feelings. It was Darren's endless one-on-ones that featured peeling his onions of anger. It was the brothers at church who encouraged him to write his visions, making them plain, and the partners at Worthy Wilford & Meyers who taught him how to properly position his words.

Truth is, Jamari's entire trajectory changed because everyone God placed in his path insisted on tackling life by embracing difficult conversations. With that, Jamari wanted to be for others what everyone else was for him.

He wanted to be a voice of solace, helping people work through their demons. None of that would have been possible without Elaine and Ramon's strength in making that life-altering decision.

On this day, Jamari knew for sure that every step, every leg of his life had been ordered by the Lord. Because of their actions, the formerly wayward teen was now a trained clinician who spent his days teaching future mental health professionals how to help others steer through life—just as he was helping his little brother navigate the unspeakable.

"He made us handcuff ourselves to each other and then to the rails of his boat. I remember thinking he was going to sink his skiff with us on it and take off in the Honey Bear because he left us on his boat for a long time.

Shamir finished his second glass of apple juice. Though not nearly as parched as when he downed the first glass, a satisfied 'ahhh' escaped his throat before he continued, "He came back, untied the skiff from the yacht and, we were on our way back to the shore." Shamir paused, incredulously looking at the lead detective.

"There was never anything wrong with his motor. Coach and I just looked at each other when the boat cranked right up. We didn't understand what was happening or why, but we knew it was planned.

"Not even a minute later, we could see smoke and flames coming out of the Honey Bear's hull. We watched the fire as long as we could before he headed west back into the harbor."

"All these years, we thought everyone drowned when the boat capsized… Steven lived," whispered Ramon in sad disbelief.

"What happened to Steven, Shamir?" asked Jamari.

"Simon killed him."

"You saw him kill—"

"No," he replied blankly, drawing a deep pained breath while again finding that spot on the ceiling.

"One day, he took Coach to the hospital." He framed the last word with nonchalant air quotes.

"Simon returned alone a few hours later saying they admitted him.

"I didn't believe it, and honestly, Coach knew he wasn't going to any hospital when he left. I mean, what was Simon going to say? This guy who I've kept locked up in my basement for six years has been really sick for the last year? Could you help him and just ignore everything he says?"

Shamir paused, leaning into the corner of the seat, his knees drawn up into his chest. Jamari rested his warm hand atop his brother's.

"Do you know what was wrong with Steven?" asked the lead detective.

"Something with his stomach," he replied while rubbing his freshly cut hair. The matted locks disappeared the day after returning home to his parents. They were by far the easiest traces of prolonged captivity to erase.

"Coach vomited blood for a long time, like a year at least. Simon was giving him medicine to help, but he kept going downhill. He was always slim, like me. But before he left, Coach was skin and bones. He couldn't keep anything down... He was suffering, ya know? He wanted it to end."

Shamir covered his face with his hands, instantly regretting the loss of his tangled strands, as they allowed him to literally hide his emotions.

"I just hope Simon showed some mercy and didn't make him suffer any longer," he cried. The anguish ripped through his lungs, quickly tearing into the room.

# Chapter 28

## *In a Word* – Courage

"You guys alright? I understand if anyone needs more time before going back in. It won't be held against you," ensured the lead detective as he took a second, deep pull from his newly lit Newport before exhaling slowly.

The team was wrapping a long-overdue mental break. It was positioned as another fifteen-minute intermission for Shamir, but the truth was, everyone needed it.

The four team members who'd traveled to Lancaster for the questioning stood in utter silence in Elaine and Ramon's furnished outdoor space listening to the birds chirping in the distance. Though seasoned officers, having worked their shares of missing persons, human trafficking, and kidnappings, solemn head nods were all they could muster as a response. Exhausted, misty eyes traveled from steaming coffee mugs to the respective smoky exhales of their colleagues.

The officers were processing the depths of unfettered, calculated evil laid out before them. They grappled with connecting the dots while watching the cigarette streams effortlessly intertwine before dissipating into the early morning air.

"Did that young man really say this Simon guy shot the kid, Mason, in the back of the head and made the other kids hold his body over the rail before shooting him a few more times, just to chum the water?" one agent remarked, shaking his head.

"That poor kid in there," another detective began pointing towards Ramon and Elaine's living room, "has a long road ahead. Good thing his brother is a psychologist. He's gonna need a lot of help to get past this."

"The way Shamir described the kids being killed by sharks after jumping overboard and how this Simon guy made each of the others choose their type of death..." The third detective, a twenty-five-year veteran, stopped short before continuing, "You can tell he still hears those screams at night. You also know he remembers the very last breath taken by each of his teammates... It's times like this that make you wonder if there really is a God."

"Oh, God's real," responded the FBI agent who'd joined the officers for the questioning.

"We've all seen our share of depravity, just as we've all seen unexplained goodness. I didn't need Shamir Copeland returning from the dead to know that God is very much real. And neither do you," she concluded before turning her five-foot, seven-inch frame towards the lieutenant, making firm eye contact.

"Jim, thank you for this much-needed mental break, but we need to get back in there. This Simon guy isn't bringing himself to justice. That's what we came here to do."

Within a few moments, the conversation resumed. Shamir shared his survival on fruits and vegetables gleaned from the garden they'd planted at Simon's insistence. The single man needed another food source to avoid tipping off the locals with a sudden uptick in food purchases.

Amia rejoined everyone in the living room, taking her place next to Darren. She'd stepped out to help Michele with restless babies who were now fed and changed.

"Shamir, can you tell us about the day Simon left and never returned? Was there anything unusual? Did he say anything?"

"No, and he was actually in a good mood that morning. Said he was about to dip into some extra fine Honey. I just remember him saying he would tell me all about it when he got back."

"That's so strange. Why would he keep you there all those years just to leave like that?" wondered Amia.

"Maybe a car accident," guessed Darren, the lieutenant, and agent simultaneously.

"A few months after he left, the power got cut off. The steel door that kept us locked in the basement unlocked about a week before the hurricane. I was so afraid it was Simon setting a trap for me that I stayed in the basement for a few more days.

"The day before the hurricane, I went upstairs. There'd been no noise in months and it had been extra quiet the past few days without power. Coach was gone. I never wanted to be there, but certainly didn't want to be there any longer without him, so I decided to risk it.

"I told myself if it was a trick and Simon was there, it was fine. I was gonna fight to the death.

"You know, I'd thought of touching that grey latch on the door for years. When I finally did, my entire body went ice cold... I remember thinking today's the day and if Simon's out there, he's gonna have to blow my brains out. I didn't know what was gonna happen, but I did know I wasn't going back in that basement alive.

"The door at the top of the steps opened to a small, dark room. There was light at the bottom of the closed door in front of me. If I'm being honest, I felt like throwing up... Not gonna lie, I actually feel like throwing up right now just thinking about it."

"Breathe, Baby. Breathe through it," said Elaine.

"Find that spot on the ceiling," coached Ramon. Amia and Darren smiled warmly at the parents using the tools Jamari provided.

"I was so afraid to turn the knob. I mean, my hand wasn't shaking. It was wobbling.

"One one-thousand, two one-thousand, three one-thousand…" Jamari whispered gently. He and Shamir counted to eight before the fright subsided.

"That second door opened into the kitchen. I was expecting Simon to pop up, so I stood in the doorway for a little bit, scanning the rooms between where I was and the front door. There wasn't any movement. He wasn't there.

"You know what's crazy? All those years, I expected the house to be a mess, because it would have to be, right?"

He paused, trying to understand how someone who was surely mentally deranged could have such a clean, spotless home. He explained that everything was neat and in its place.

"It happens, Shamir," assured Jamari. "It's possible for someone who seems very put together to be a hoarder. It's just as possible for this man who needed so much control to require that everything around him be in order."

"Can you recall any other details? What did you do next?" asked the FBI agent.

"Just that the basement entry was the backside of the kitchen's pantry. While I was scanning the house looking for Simon, I also looked behind me. That's when I noticed food and stuff on the shelves. I guess that's why we could sometimes hear the girlfriend's voice clearer than others. It was always muffled, though.

"I also remember the house felt old, like the old-timey movies. There were long, rectangular wooden arches at the windows. You know, like the ones in Grannie Netta's house back in Maryland," Shamir added, turning to Ramon as he described the faded pink window dressings of Ramon's childhood home.

"Wooden valances. Good job, Shamir," replied the youngest of the detectives.

"How'd you get to your sister and brother-in-law's home?"

"I found a couple hundred dollars on the kitchen counter. I wanted to come here. I wanted to come home," he added.

His voice was pained as he connected eyes with Elaine and Ramon before continuing, "Simon told me you moved last October. He said he was out in Lancaster and saw a young family living at the house. So, I decided to go to Amia and Darren's, since I had their address."

"Last October?" asked Amia.

"Why would he be in Lancaster?" added Darren. "How would he know where we lived?" asked Ramon. These questions were asked almost simultaneously.

"Each year, you held a vigil on my birthday. Simon would attend. Then he'd drive by the house. He always brought back pictures, mostly to taunt me, but also to remind us that he knew where our families lived."

A kaleidoscope of emotions broke free. The audacity of this lunatic! He attended every year and even pretended to be concerned about Shamir!

"No, that's good," stated the FBI agent, attempting to quell the uprising.

"If Simon has photos, someone else does too. Someone in the public has a picture of him. Maybe a partial, maybe even a video."

"We'll contact neighbors to see if they can remember anything. Maybe someone has him on a home security video. Shamir, this is really helpful," added the lieutenant.

"Last October? Last October?" Jamari repeated, trying to understand why that timeframe was relevant. "Wait... Dad had his gallbladder surgery the day before Shamir's birthday. Mom stayed at the hospital with him."

"Mari and I stayed here with the twins," Michele said. "It rained that entire week. I bet Simon saw us going in and out of the house with their car seats."

"Do you know where you were being held?" asked Amia.

"Not exactly. I just know it was an older white house with big columns and huge trees in the front yard. There was a lot of land. It's near water because we always saw seagulls and smelled salt in the air.

"When I left, I wanted to stay off the road, so I wouldn't be spotted, so I mostly ran along the wood line for miles—" His face went ashen.

"Simon knows this house. He knows where you live. What if he finds out I'm here? What if he comes back for me or tries to hurt—"

"Shamir," Jamari asserted, "no one is coming after you. Do you hear me?"

"Listen, Son," consoled the lead detective. "You see all these people?" he asked, making eye contact with his partners as well as Darren, Jamari, Ramon, and the rest of the family.

"I can assure you, the one thing you will never need to worry about ever again is this Simon guy.

"We are going to find him and he's going away for the rest of his life," added the FBI agent. "He knows we're looking for him. Showing up here is the last thing he'll do. He's not dumb."

"But he said—"

"Simon was going to say whatever he needed to in order to keep you under control," Darren interrupted with a calming, unmistakable authority. The cool iciness that had visited him multiple times in the recent weeks was back. "Please God," he prayed silently. "Let us find him, but please don't let me find him first."

# Chapter 29

## *In a Word* – Gathering

"Chrissy," called Amia. Her usual easy-going tone was underlined with a bit of urgency. "Everyone is waiting on you, young lady. You were supposed to start two minutes ago."

"Ok, Momma, I'm ready now," she replied from the hallway with excitement. Amia nodded to Darren who promptly hit the beat and 'Christina Bean's' inaugural fashion show was underway.

The twins who were just starting to walk, were lovingly sauntered down the red strip of carpeting which served as the night's runway. Jamari and Michele twisted the cute tykes left and right to allow the audience a view of their tiny outfits.

They were followed by a few of Christina and Daniel's friends, Johanna, as well as the grandparents who modeled scarves and bracelets created by the gleeful fashionista.

The family enjoyed this first activity with Shamir. Because it was wrapped around Christina's show and a barbeque cookoff between Darren, Todd and Jamari, there was no pressure for Shamir. The attention would be elsewhere and he could just enjoy being part of the family and catching up on years that were stolen.

Christina wrapped the show with the designer's walk which featured her in a purple feathered boa that matched Oscar's purple puff. The overly spoiled pooch's white tail had been carefully colored for the occasion.

After the show, it was time for the blind taste tests and as usual, Darren's rubbed ribs were the crowd favorite. In keeping with previous years, Jamari and Todd were each $50 lighter and on grill cleanup duty following their fourth straight loss.

Elaine and Ramon wrapped their arms around Shamir as he soaked in the spectacle of trash talking and cheating allegations. It pained them that he'd been locked in a basement, cut off from the world, and missing out on all of this.

They fought off the guilt of moving on after years went by with no signs of life. She squeezed him tighter as she recalled releasing blue and orange balloons into the sky on the agonizing day of his funeral. Ramon clutched them both in never-ending gratitude for this moment.

Shortly after Todd and Jamari officially conceded defeat, everyone gathered outside. The kids and Oscar, all with floaties, played in the pool as the family and friends chatted. A clink filled the air as Darren and Sven's beer bottles connected while they kicked back. It was the first time the pair had gotten to catch up in a while.

They were careful to stay away from anything related to Shamir's ordeal as he was still recovering and they wanted to keep it light, though Shamir was now completely at ease due to Sven's presence. Much to Mia's chagrin, Sven revisited her run-in with Andrew DeSimeon months earlier.

Though time had passed, Darren was still unsettled with how it went down. His nostrils still flared at the thought of his wife putting herself in harm's way by meeting with him alone. Amia cupped her husband's hands and began apologizing again for worrying him.

Since Sven brought it up and because there were a few folks who hadn't heard the story, Amia started from the beginning; actually, from the moment she realized the sting was in jeopardy due to Tim, the lead agent's, team being held up by the train.

Mia stole a seat on the outdoor chaise next to her sexier-than-sexy man who was even more delicious looking with that hint of worry. His fingers locked above his dark chocolatey bald head.

*Lord, Jesus. Why is so fine?* Amia thought to herself. She briefly contemplated throwing everyone out, so that she could get ahold of him.

"*Focus girl*," she scolded herself before jumping back into the story, checking again to ensure the kids weren't anywhere around.

Amia began by reminding everyone that Federal Agent, Tim, and Sven had been friends since meeting decades earlier. Sven was an accomplished combat instructor who just happened to be Frau Gerry's son. Tim arranged the controlled meet at the Coastal Sounds, Frau Gerry's restaurant.

Because Sven was at the café that morning as planned, Mia knew she had backup, even though Tim's team had been held up by the slow-moving cargo train.

Sven chimed in to add that though she was on shift that morning, he sent his niece, Johanna, to the grocery for eggs as soon as Andrew arrived and while Andrew was walking towards Amia, he quickly flipped the store's open sign to closed.

Amia explained to the thoroughly intrigued crowd that she was worried because the backup wasn't in place as planned, but she did take some comfort in Sven's presence and precautions.

Since she was facing the front of the restaurant, she saw the sign flip. Sven added his talking up the Farmer's Breakfast when waiting on Amia and Andrew because he'd already made it and had it sitting under the warmer.

To ensure Andrew took it, Sven offered the meal on the house, using his first visit as an excuse. With that, Sven explained that he really never left her alone in the bistro's dining area with Andrew for more than a minute.

Amia reminded her sexy boo that less than ten minutes later, he was calling with the code phrases, "Picking up breakfast," and "At Starbucks," confirming that Tim and his agents were ready to move in.

"So, that's the story," cooed Mia thoroughly pleased and even more impressed with herself after retelling the story of that harrowing Saturday morning adventure.

"Any whooo," retorted Darren good-naturedly while rolling his eyes and shaking his head at his equally sexy wife. They were definitely on the same wavelength in regards to kicking everyone out.

He had a delicious flashback of Amia in his lap on that same lounger weeks earlier. That vision required him to shift positions. He needed a distraction. She smelled too good and her easy beauty had him biting his lip as well.

"All I can say," Darren started, "is good riddance to An-Drewwww DeSimeon."

"Agreed. Adieu Andrewwww," Amia replied. This time, her French was spot on.

As the pair wrapped the evening stretched on their teal chaise lounger, Amia revisited the Andrew DeSimeon conversation.

"You know what's weird?" she asked. "When we said good riddance to Andrew DeSimeon, it reminded me of how Shamir said Simon's girlfriend said his name. I know there's no connection, but it just made me to think of that conversation with Shamir on the day mom and dad first saw him. Remember, Drewwww from Drubekistan?"

Maybe that's God's gentle nudge for you to find out about this person Marshon is talking about.

"I know you really don't want to see him."

"You're right, Babe. I really don't want to see him." Darren kissed Amia's crown as they spent a few moments watching television before turning in.

# Chapter 30

## *In a Word* – Emotions

Rhythmic tapping echoed throughout the seemingly never-ending corridor. Large gray cinderblocks peeked through years-old dingy paint. The peeling seafoam green coating wasn't the only thing in need of repair. In fact, the entire facility reeked of neglect.

Besides the occasional footsteps shuffling through intersecting hallways and the random dull buzzers admitting those with proper credentials, the only constant sound was the incessant tapping.

It was the byproduct of nervous energy flowing repeatedly down muscular thighs and calves, bouncing the owner's brown leather wing-tipped Oxfords. Never could a person have been so grateful for a decision to wear casual shoes.

If the rubber soles bouncing against the cold shiny concrete floors generated this much sound, the hard-bottomed alternatives would have surely rattled the rusting steel off the rafters.

Though he had been in these buildings to visit defendants hundreds of times throughout his career and had spent months confined in a similar institution in his youth, this visit was different.

This time, he wasn't looking for that one detail within the statement. He wasn't prepping a nervous defendant for trial or convincing a wrongfully convicted client to hold out hope for the upcoming appeal. Instead, he was futilely attempting to calm himself.

He was minutes away from confronting the bane of his existence. He knew it wasn't right to harbor hate, but he truly despised this man more than anything in the world. After all, for whatever reason, he still had power because he held an acceptance that was desperately craved.

"Darren Wilford," a stern voice called flatly.

Suddenly, hearing the name he'd been happily answering to since infancy, caused the blood to drain from his body. Darren's eyes widened as the dread heightened. His attention landed in the direction of the voice's owner.

The disinterested uniformed guard was standing with his back against the thick metal door. Darren had seen that unphased stance countless times over his career. He was accustomed to the lack of eye contact and unwelcomed greetings which ranged from empty to non-existent, but today was different. Everything now registered differently.

Darren's mouth opened for a second time since hearing his name. He was struggling to find his voice amidst the rising queasiness, but eventually heard Amia's encouragement in his ear. *'Your presence is enough. You've never needed Marshon. He needs you. Remember that.'*

"Yes, I'm Darren Wilford," he managed weakly, his mouth extra dry.

"Follow me. Down this hall and to the left."

One foot then another ushered Darren into and through the long corridor. The hall seemed to amplify the sounds of his soles connecting with the cold white surface. A minute later, Darren's feet directed him towards an open room with round cafeteria-style tables. The rapid heartbeat in his ears grew louder.

Black and white jumpsuit clad men were in different phases of their visits with guests. Darren had seen this hundreds of times as well. Inmates seeing friends and family, sometimes the only smiles they'd see for months.

The officer motioned to a table near the center of the room. Darren inhaled deeply, exhaling through clenched teeth. He willed Mia's words back to the forefront as his body somehow connected with the cold gray metal. The officer left without saying a word.

Darren swallowed hard. "*Damn it, Darren. Get it together*," he fussed beneath his breath.

Mia's words were back, *'You don't owe Marshon anything. He is your biological father, but your real dad is Gary Felding. You are not in Colorado because Marshon wants you to be there. You are there solely for him to answer your questions. You don't need anything else fr—.'*

Darren's thoughts were interrupted by the sounds of steel rubbing against steel as a gate buzzed open and footsteps could be heard coming into the space. Darren held his breath. He felt sick.

A few moments later, two individuals entered. Darren exhaled with relief. It was another inmate accompanied by an officer. The family who'd been waiting for thirty minutes greeted him with measured joy.

This process repeated itself seven or eight more times as other families greeted and bid farewell to their loved ones. By now, the overwhelming jitters were gone. Darren was actually starting to get annoyed and while it couldn't have been possible, he wondered if Marshon had orchestrated his seemingly excessive wait.

That tinge of frustration was exactly what Darren needed to get his mind right and reset. He decided to see Marshon not as the dad he desperately wanted, but as an unsuspecting opponent who is woefully underestimating his abilities. His nostrils flared and a hint of a smile crossed his face.

Darren was back in his element—the unflappable defense attorney taking on another pompous know-it-all.

"Game time, baby," he whispered to himself while clasping his hands together. Whenever he said that, it was about to go down.

Moments later, a new set of footsteps drew nearer following the now familiar rattling of the gray gate. This time, there were more than the usual two pairs. These sounds belonged to three security guards and one Marshon Wilford.

# Chapter 31

## *In a Word* – Callous

Darren took in the view of the man who attempted to frame him for murder. Ironically, it was the same man who'd taught him to ride a bike. He noted the now thinning hair accelerated by months of chemotherapy.

Young Darren recalled admiring the thick waves and the way his father would wink at him as he brushed his hair in the mornings. Though he couldn't remember the conversations, he had fond memories of getting ready for school while sharing the small sink and mirror with his father who would also be preparing for the day.

He remembered being bare chested standing in front of Marshon, comparing his preteen front double biceps to his father's then ample physique.

Darren almost felt a twinge of sorrow for the once strapping man whose dominating presence was all but gone, replaced by a frail shadow of the man who he'd witnessed brutally beating, stomping and even killing those who dared cross him. That remorse dissolved with the next sounds he heard.

"Took you long enough."

*That's it?* Darren thought in disbelief. He wasn't sure exactly what the first words he'd hear from his father in over thirty years would be, but these hadn't been on the radar.

*Thirty years and the first thing he says to me is 'Took you long enough,'* he fumed.

"*If that's how he's gonna play this. Let's get it,*" he thought to himself again.

"I'm here now, and so you know, I'm booked on the next flight out."

"Aww snap. I guess someone finally grew some chest hair—"

"Tick tock," Darren replied flatly.

"You haven't seen your old man in over thirty years and this is how you treat me, Mr. Attorney? That's cold."

Marshon paused. A lengthy coughing fit came from deep within. Darren noticed how long it took to get the cough under control.

"Are you ok? Do you need some water?"

"Oh, so now you care? Leaving me in here to rot and die. You're ungrateful, Son."

Summoning restraint, Darren leaned in a smidge, pacing his breathing before replying, "Ungrateful? Is that right? I'm an ungrateful son… Who knew?" Darren feigned a laugh to keep from flipping the table.

"Tell me, Marshon," he began. His eyes purposely locking onto his father's. "Which ungrateful son are you talking about? Is it the one who you planted cocaine on? Maybe it's the one you pinned two murders on and watched get handcuffed?

"Oh, I know. You're talking about the one you let sit in a juvenile detention center. Nah, better yet, I bet you're talking about the one who you so lovingly told he'd never amount to anything. Precisely *which ungrateful son* are you referring to?"

"You still holding onto that?" Marshon coughed again, though this one was much shorter than the first.

"Come on, Darren. I had your mom and the girls to think about. What did I look like going to jail and leaving everyone with nothing? You weren't going to be there for more than a year. You're trying to tell me you couldn't have done a year to keep your family together?"

Marshon paused to wait for Darren's apology. After all, in his mind, Darren's taking one for the family made complete sense.

*What the hell? Keep it together, Darren,* he thought, willing himself to stay focused.

"Did you just confess to framing me and imply that I should have been cool with it? I was fourteen." He somehow restrained his anger enough to push that statement out just above a whisper. "And, did you just say I was sacrificed for the good of the family...? Wasn't I supposed to be part of that family?" he managed through clenched teeth as his anger and hurt collided right there in the prison's common area.

"One little year was too much for you? After everything I did for you? All the protection I gave you while you were growing up? You had free reign in those streets. Nobody ever bothered you in school. All the other kids were getting bullied, getting beat up, getting shot... Not you, though. You were never touched—ever!"

By this point, Marshon was leaning forward, his eyes burrowing deep into Darren's. It was the same soul-stirring glare that Darren had seen Marson deliver to others and had himself received as a child.

"You're welcome," Marshon said as he eased back into the tan folding chair.

"If anything, you should be apologizing for what you did to our family, instead of whining about a little funky-ass year," Marshon managed after another short round of coughs, wiping his mouth on the dingy napkin he'd been holding.

Darren thought about Daniel and Christina and how much he loved them. *There is no way on Earth a man who loved his child could do what Marshon did to me and stand by it all these years later,"* he told himself.

Jamari was right. That father figure Darren spent years crafting in the workshop of his imagination didn't exist. He never did, and even after enduring thirty years of heartache, Darren's inner teenager still held out hope that they could make amends. Yet another defective dream conjured up in Darren's now fully demolished fantasy workshop.

Darren choked down the lump in his throat. He felt a ripping in his heart as it broke anew. This time though, he was prepared for it.

"The clock is still ticking," he gritted out, after a long pause to collect his emotions. He decided to switch directions in order to get what he came for.

"Marshon. No matter how this conversation goes, I'm leaving at the top of the hour. Now, I can spend the next fifty-three minutes getting what I came for, or I can bounce. It doesn't matter to me... Matter of fact... Guard? I'm done here."

Though Marshon would never flinch outwardly, inwardly he was wounded. True, time had passed, but Marshon had hoped to see the cute, awkward fourteen-year-old who used to idolize him. While angry when talking about Darren's ungratefulness, Marshon had been sincerely searching for that teenager while staring into his only son's eyes.

Darren hadn't been alone in spending anxious hours thinking about their first meeting. Just as the younger Wilford had been stung by the first words he'd heard from his father in thirty plus years, the elder Wilford was equally hurt.

Marshon wanted to hear Darren call him Dad one more time. Instead, his first born, whose cord he'd cut, was referring to him by first name. On top of that, Marshon had seen his son's face for a mere seven minutes after not having seen so much as a photo in over thirty years, and now he was threatening to leave.

"There's no need to be hostile. You're here. I'm here." Marshon said with the tone of a businessman. The father-son bonding that he'd secretly longed for wasn't going to happen, though there was nothing in the terminally ill man's letters, his greeting today, or his current disposition that provided Darren with any hint of interest.

Both hearts ached, but neither would allow the other to see it. Truth is, Darren's father was too much Marshon and Marshon's son was too much Wilford. Rather than risk the appearance of weakness, the pair buried their emotions.

Marshon's expertise at covering feelings went back fifty years. It was fine-tuned on the streets of Philly and mastered during his incarceration. On the other hand, Darren first learned the practice of burying feelings as a child while an understudy at the Marshon Wilford academy. He fined tuned the skill while confined in juvenile detention, ultimately perfecting it into an artform through his decades in the courtroom.

With neither man willing to bend, Marshon resumed his role as the cut-throat, alpha-mob boss who inspired legendary fear. His tablemate was no longer just his son. He was now sitting across from the unwavering, highly-regarded defense attorney who lived in prosecutor's nightmares.

"Let's get it," Marshon said.

Darren took notice. 'Let's get it.' That phrase was a regular in the rotation of Darren's vocabulary, but he wasn't sure exactly where it came from. In that moment, he realized it was one of Marshon's staples, said especially when conducting business with someone who was about to feel his wrath. Darren hadn't heard Marshon say it in eons.

"You gonna piss or get off the pot?" Marshon asked smugly."

Darren half smiled at another familiar phrase. This one though, was generally aimed at someone Marshon knew was afraid of him. That menacing, cat-that-ate-the-canary glare was back. This time though, Darren was prepared. No matter what, he would not be the first to blink.

"The new guy on your cell block. The one you've been talking about in your letters," Darren began as he sat back down. "Tell me about him."

# Chapter 32

## *In a Word* – Weighty

In the weeks since Darren's return from seeing Marshon, he'd been overly lenient with the kids, showering them with attention. He was always an attentive father, but Mia noted this was different. Darren seemed to almost be proving his love.

No, chocolate chip pancakes weren't over the top, but chocolate before school? Fine, staying up a bit late wasn't going to hurt anyone, but ten o'clock on a school night? Then, there was the new skateboard and sequined fabrics. Nothing wrong with that, except Christina's 'design studio' was already overrun with fabrics and Daniel had just scored a new skateboard on his birthday.

On the other hand, Amia noted that her loving husband was suddenly snippy and almost downright mean towards her. He shared some facts and details he'd learned from the conversation with Marshon, but he hadn't shared the intimate details; the ones that were responsible for his altered behavior.

Amia decided to distract Darren by donning a few of her latest pieces scored during an amazing eighty percent off sale. The cherry-red capris she was currently modeling showcased her curves nicely, though two sizes larger than she'd been wearing the last ten years. This latest spree was a result of Amia's inability to comfortably fit into her normally reliable power suits for her latest court appearances.

Though she could wear them, they were much too tight for her liking. The shopping outing was resignation and acknowledgement that most of her treasured items had been sliding farther back on the racks in her closet.

Amia sincerely hoped she could figure out the right concoction to get back into her favorite items. For now, though, the weight gain was here, and she needed to address it. Amia put on a brave face, though the reality of guaranteed unwanted pounds hurt. She couldn't work out the way she used to and her diet was already pretty good.

Still, with the goal of giving her distracted husband something else to ponder on, Amia donned her new navy suit jacket that complimented all the right angles and exited their spacious closet, opting to leave her bra and capris on the dresser. The sexy pose she'd struck and held against the opening for twenty seconds went unnoticed.

She let out a long sigh.

Amia reluctantly released her grip on the crown molding. Though she couldn't see herself, and she hadn't yet embraced the additional pounds, she was fond of her new D cups. For Amia, this was the only positive result of her weight gain thus far. She figured she must have looked amazing in that open jacket with just a cute pair of high cut, satin panties.

She paused and posed again, this time in front of their seven-foot mirror which leaned against a rear corner of their bedroom. She positioned herself so that Darren could see her coming while appreciating the way the purple undies hugged and nestled between her cheeks. Unfortunately, he never looked her way.

Another long, silent sigh followed.

"Babe, you've gotta talk about it. Come on. Get it off your chest," she urged, gently imploring him to release some of the thick steam clearly boiling just below the surface.

"I don't need to talk. I'm good, Amia." He continued staring out of their rear bedroom window.

"Babe, look at me," she continued, but her husband of fifteen years didn't budge. Amia could see his clenched jaw, but couldn't interpret the emotions behind it. Was it disappointment, anger, sadness or frustration? She didn't know what she was seeing. She just knew she needed to help.

"Darren, you haven't been yourself since you got back from Colorado. Babe, what's bothering you? Just tell me."

Finally, an exasperated Darren unloaded his feelings, but not in the way she expected.

"Damn it, Amia. I don't want to talk about it! Let it go for God's sake."

"Babe, it's me. I can see you're in pain. It's obvious. Talk to me, please... Let me carry some of the weight for you." Her voice was as soothing as it had ever been because every word she'd just uttered came from the bottom of her soul.

"Aren't you carrying enough extra weight already?" he snapped, immediately regretting those seven words that somehow found sound, traveled out of his throat, and landed in the center of their huge silver and white master bedroom.

Amia watched in slow motion as her husband rushed in her direction as if trying to beat the words before her brain interpreted and slammed the message into her heart at 300 miles per hour. She saw the muscular arms that she loved so much extending in her direction. They, along with every molecule in his body, were desperately trying to apologize.

The words hit exactly as he'd feared. Darren watched as his daggers stunned his beautiful, partially-naked queen into silence. The designer tag that had been casually swinging at the end of her larger coat sleeve seemed to have also been stunned into stillness.

"I'm so sorry. Amia... I didn't mean that... God knows, I didn't."

Darren knew that was a cheap shot, and the remorse was evident. He knew she was self-conscious about the new pounds that were, in his mind, wrapping perfectly around her hips, thighs and booty.

"Sweetheart? Amia?"

His heart sank as she left his presence to retrieve her aqua colored overnight bag from her closet. The same one she'd packed only two weeks earlier, just in case he'd changed his mind and agreed her accompanying him to USP Thomson penitentiary to confront Marshon.

"Amia. Please, stop. I'm sorry. Amia! Stop for a minute, please," he begged as she extracted articles from her dresser, stuffing them into the designer bag without missing a beat. Once full, she went back into their spacious walk in closet.

"Babe," he continued desperately trying to plead his case to his clearly heartbroken wife. Words hadn't come yet, but the tears were there.

"Amia, I didn't..."

His voice trailed off as she exited their closet with a medium sized duffle bag and began heading down the hallway towards the kids' rooms.

"No, Amia. Wait!" he yelled, urgently following her into Daniel's room. While those first seven words pierced her core, none of the ones he'd said since seemed to make a dent. She was another level of angry.

It was the kind of furor spawned from the hurt of having the only person she loved more than her children kick her dead in the gut. It was the pain of feeling the man who was supposed to love, honor and cherish her forever, jab a knife right between her ribs.

Seven words, which on any other day and in any other context could have been nothing, delivered a solid blow. They hurt infinitely more because they'd escaped Darren's lips; the same ones that so lovingly nibbled on her body day in and night out.

They were the same lips that lent to thousands of amazing conversations and countless hours of laughter. That jarring, soul-crushing comment came from the lips of her man—the master of words. The defense attorney whose jury-swaying summations were things of legend due to his careful selections.

It was hard to discern the cause of the most damage—what he actually said or the venom that propelled those thirteen syllables in her direction. Amia's heartache and rage continued spilling from her rims as she hastily withdrew T-shirts, shorts and undies from the drawers, slamming them into the leather bag.

"Amia, I—"

"You know, Jesus Christ himself could never have convinced me that you would ever be so disrespec— Don't! Touch! Me!"

Each word was accentuated with a sharp intentional pause as she recoiled from his touch, something in all their years, she'd never done. Darren let out a breath. Though she was clearly pissed, at least she spoke to him. There was a chance.

"You know, Darren. I have been sitting here day in and day out dealing with your snarky comments, letting 'em roll off my back because, I know you're going through." Amia took a breath to fight the heartache.

"I've even let you get yours multiple times, asking nothing in return, because I knew you were going through. I have tolerated you grabbing something to eat on your way home, even though you knew I cooked, just so you could avoid conversation. I never said anything, because I knew you were going—"

She stopped short, putting her hand in front of his face as he tried desperately to draw her near.

"No Sir," she said sharply while pulling out of his grasp.

"In all these years, no matter how angry I have been, I have never gone for the jugular, Darren. I couldn't dream of intentionally hurting you, because you're my person..."

Satisfied that she'd gotten enough outfits, she closed the last dresser drawer quickly and continued while wiping tears.

"Babe—"

"I can't believe you," she wept.

"I said, don't touch me," Amia screamed through her tears and evading his reach again. Anger returned as the dominating emotion as she headed to Christina's room to finish filling the other half of the bag.

# Chapter 33

## *In a Word* – Broken

"You lying, Bruh. Ain't no way. You did not say that to Amia."

Todd shook his head in disbelief. Up until Darren's revelation, he'd been providing counterweight as his bestie pounded the 200-pound punching bag. Darren dropped his head. He was still in disbelief himself.

"Dude, I love you. You know that, but you need your ass kicked for that."

"Get in line," Darren replied, burying his shaking head into his padded hands. "I been kicking my own ass for two days."

"What were you thinking?"

"I was just trying to get her to ease up off me. She kept coming at me trying to get me to talk about Marshon and what he said."

"What did he say?"

Darren sighed long and slow, dropping his head again.

"Nothing..."

"Nothing? Really...?" Todd hopped up, grabbing a swig of his water before pulling a black glove over his knuckles.

"I gotta tell ya, Dawg. I've seen a lot of shit in my life, but I ain't ever seen anyone with good sense risk losing their marriage over nothing."

Darren's misty eyes met Todd's squarely for the first time since opening the door thirty minutes earlier. It was the candidness of his college roommate that made all the difference. His heart sank for the hundredth time since the mudroom door closed behind Amia.

Darren grabbed a seat against the mirrored wall, absorbing the gravity of his situation. Todd eased down onto the matted floor next to Darren to comfort his best friend, who's hurt, anger, and fear finally came to a head. After a few moments, Todd surveyed the black and yellow man cave while reflecting.

"You know, the last time we hit bags down here was just after—"

"Weeboy," Darren recalled.

He lifted his head, resting it and all the weight he'd been carrying on the wall behind him. He looked at his best friend shaking his head before continuing, "Yeah. I was broken'. We went from enjoying our first newborn to Amia flatlining in the air flight on the way to the hospital. I've never been that terrified in my entire life. I remember begging the doctors not to tell her about the emergency hysterectomy."

"Cause you wanted to tell her," recalled Todd.

"I *needed* to be the one to tell her. I didn't think the doctors would have cared for her heart or chosen their words carefully enough because they were so used to delivering bad news."

"Speaking of bad news," Todd interjected, thinking this would be a good moment for a diversion.

"Remember the night my dad passed away?"

"For as long as I live," Darren replied.

Todd's father died the same night that he and his son TJ, then a toddler, were in a serious rollover car accident on I-20. Regina contacted Darren after being unable to get ahold of Todd. She shared the devastating news of Bill's death with Darren who, in turn, shared equally gut-wrenching information with her.

Darren had to tell his best friend's newly widowed mother that her only child had been rushed into emergency surgery to repair broken ribs, a fractured femur, and a punctured lung. That was followed by the revelation that her only grandchild had been rushed to Children's Hospital and was in intensive care. This was years before Darren met Amia. In fact, it was not long after the men walked the stage with college degrees in tow.

"It was right around the time," Todd started, "that I lost my entire savings in that dot.com startup. I was trying to hold onto a dead relationship with Rebecca, because I wanted TJ to grow up with his mom and dad in the same house, just like I did."

It was Todd's preoccupation and lack of focus that led to his excessive speed and the frightening collision with an eighteen-wheeler.

"D... I'll never forget how you stood in the gap for us, and I still don't know how you came up with the money to help me and mom get back on our feet, but thank you."

"It's all good. That was my second year at WW&M. I got my first-ever bonus. It came a couple days before everything went down with y'all. I didn't even know it was coming. Other than throwing some into equipment to start the camp, I didn't have any plans for that money, so it was yours."

"I still don't know what to say. I appreciate it. More than you know."

"Look, don't be getting all mushy on me, Dawg.

Todd smiled. "Darren, man... I was scared to death when you and Amia were in the hospital back then. Both of you were critical. I mean, literally touch and go for a while."

Now, it was Todd tilting is head towards the ceiling. His throat tightened at the thought of losing his brother. They'd been lock step since meeting on the first day of their Freshman year at Temple. Todd breathed a thankful sigh of relief.

"It wasn't our time, and I thank God every single day..." Darren took a long, deep breath leaning his head back against the wall. "You got any miracle advice tucked away in there," Darren asked, thinking about this disaster of his own making.

"I feel like God's not trying to hear from me right now. All I keep thinking about is how much I begged Him to let Amia live just for me to act like this... Dawg, I chose those words to get her to leave me alone... And she did. I just... I just need her to come back... God, I'm so sorry. Please, God. Please let her come back."

Todd wrapped an encouraging arm around Darren's neck as he soaked up the streaming tears with the towel he'd put over his face as the floodgates burst back open.

"She'll be back, D. You know I'm new to this Christian thing, but I'm pretty sure God's still listening. You've been too good a man for Him to stop taking your calls because you've been acting like an idiot lately.

"I think you're getting beat up by your conscience, and rightfully so. Janelle told me about it this morning. I couldn't—wouldn't—believe it. Dawg, you should be outside right now picking out your own switch.

"That's some dumb shit I'd expect from a low-life with no common sense or someone without any morals. Just straight up stupider than stupid, and it's all because you're letting Marshon Wilford live rent free inside your head.

"That woman is the best thing that's ever happened to you... Darren, Marshon has taken enough of your life. Don't you dare let him take your marriage, too."

Darren dabbed the final salty remnants before blowing his nose and tossing the towel in the direction of the laundry room.

“God, I still can’t believe I went there with Amia. T, that woman is everything I’ve ever wanted. She is every bit of perfect. I knew she was uncomfortable with the weight.” This was said with air quotes, because he didn’t see the pounds the way she did.

“She was just being the woman I fell in love with. She just wanted to help... She didn’t deserve that.”

“I know. You need to talk to her,” he encouraged.

“I want to, but she hasn’t spoken to me since she left on Friday. I’m going straight to voicemail,” Darren replied as he began pulling the gloves back onto his hands.

“And you said she went off? Like off off,” Todd asked?

“Yeah, Bruh. She went off off. You know Amia has never went there with anyone—like ever. She just doesn’t. In my seventeen years of knowing her, she’s never let it fly.

“T, when I tell you Amia Wilford exploded, I mean she snapped all the way off. Read my Black ass from cover to cover. She told me to be gone when she gets back here, put her hand up in my face, and slammed the door behind her... I didn’t know she had it in her,” he added with a disbelieving smile.

# Chapter 34

## *In a Word* – Unwind

A new cookbook joined the twelve others taking up residence on the short counter next to the white photo-adorned fridge. *Of course, there would be strawberries on the cover,* Amia thought to herself as she scanned the ceramic strawberries of all sizes hanging in various areas on the walls. They complimented the fruity curtains and strawberry-speckled throw rug in her parents' warm kitchen.

"I still don't understand why you and the kids came down without Darren." Ramon's comment was actually a question, though positioned as a thought.

"Dad, closing arguments start next week for this case he's working on. It doesn't look good, so he's buckling down on his summation."

That wasn't a complete lie. Darren was probably going to lose this case because his defendant got crossed up by the prosecutor and ended up perjuring himself twice on the stand. True, he was working extra hard on the wrap up, but that's not why he hadn't made the trek to Lancaster Friday evening.

"How did the visit with his father go?" Elaine asked. The word father was said in disdain with air quotes for emphasis.

"He's hurt and trying to figure out how to deal with it," replied Amia, sipping on a piping hot fresh cup of pressed Chamomile tea.

"Well," Elaine began, "my hat goes off to Darren and those girls for all they've done with their lives in spite of having those two as parents. Thank the Lord for keeping them and putting Mable and Gary in their lives. I still say, just because you can do something, doesn't mean you should. His parents," again accentuated with air quotes, "had no business with children."

"True, they weren't ideal, but they did give the world three pretty incredible human beings." Amia finished that thought with a tap of the photo taken at Daniel's birthday party which included the three siblings.

"I mean, one has a doctorate in neuro psychology. There's a travel nurse, and an attorney who's a partner at his law firm. Those genes combined into something pretty special."

"I know, and again, thank God for Gary and Mable. I still say it's a daggum shame that there aren't requirements for having kids. You've got to have credit to get a car, buy a house, and sometimes to get a job. You even have to get a license to drive. Hell, they want you to get a license to catch a flippin' fish, but a kid? Nah, you can leave the hospital with as many of those as you want. No qualifications required," she scoffed incredulously.

"Hang on there now, Mama. Not taking anything away from what you just said, but I think we might have failed a test or two back then." Ramon paused before adding, "Remember when I locked Amia in the car at the gas station?" Both parents began cracking up.

Of course, she heard the story multiple times through the years. Ramon left his wallet on the counter of the convenience store and hopped back out to retrieve it. Out of habit, he hit the door lock and hastily closed the door on the running vehicle with the then two-year-old in the back seat.

They erupted in laughter as Ramon recalled Amia gleefully waving at him with her little hands and pink and white sippy cup as he attempted to get her to unlock the sedan's door. The funniest part of that story was always when the police came and asked for Ramon's ID, but he couldn't give it to him because it was actually in his wallet; the contents of which were being strewn across the back seat after the amused toddler found it sitting on the seat next to her.

Amia loved hanging out with her parents. It was always the shot in the arm she needed. The harmony they exuded was manna to her soul. It explained their longevity. Amia noted that their love for each other was special. It was like Mable and Gary's, like Marty and Vicky's—like hers and Darren's.

"I'm gonna hit the road now. That'll put me home around six o'clock. We'll be back tomorrow."

"Still doesn't make sense to me, Amia. You came up Friday with the kids just to go back today and then you're both coming back again tomorrow? I dunno. That fish don't smell right," said Elaine, eyeing her daughter. Amia needed to think quick to throw her off because one thing's for sure, Elaine's intuition has never been wrong.

"Ma, everything's fine. Having us gone gives him two days of undivided attention and will allow him to focus. He won't have to compliment Barbie's latest outfit or check out the newest skateboard trick," she teased as the kids chased each other into the large red and white kitchen.

"Because we left Daddy alone for a couple of days, he'll actually get to enjoy the holiday tomorrow without having to think about work," she added, winking at the kids and hoping that was enough to throw Elaine off the scent.

"Bye Mom," rang out simultaneously as Daniel and Christina hugged Amia tightly.

"I love you guys. Be good for Grandma and Pop and Uncle Mir. See you tomorrow," she added with kisses for each youngster.

"Danny has been great for Shamir. Seeing them together again, warms my heart. Dan still thinks Shamir walks on water," Elaine smiled.

"Well, he did return from the dead, so it's gonna be hard to convince him otherwise," said Ramon. The family had been visiting Lancaster almost every weekend since Shamir's release from the hospital months earlier. At this point, Amia and Darren were comfortable with Shamir.

He still had a ways to go before being comfortable with public life and strangers and he was also still too afraid to be more than an arm's length away from his parents' protection. The Shamir they loved and knew was still in there, though. That gentle soul was no more a danger to their family than he was six years ago.

"See you guys tomorrow," added Amia, returning kisses and hugs from her parents and brother. "I'll call when I get in," she promised, waving as she pulled off and began her four-hour drive back to Pittsburgh.

As much as Amia wanted to tell her mom what was going on, she kept any negatives in her marriage away from the family. That was one piece of advice Mable imparted to her in the bride's room just before she and Darren walked down the aisle.

Mable wisely advised that the family will always remember that thing you were so angry or hurt about even after you have long forgotten and forgiven. She warned it would introduce an unnecessary bias that would be hard for Darren to overcome.

Mable instructed Mia to take it all to God instead. Of course, she advised Amia to always be candid and open with Darren and to trust themselves to work it out, but if there was something she needed to share, to do so with only one true friend. Amia smiled inwardly, recalling Darren's revelation of the same conversation with Gary.

While there were very few moments of real frustration or hurt in their fifteen-years of marriage, Amia took Mable's guidance to heart, never uttering so much as a gripe to her parents or family. She had taken this most recent trespass to God for almost an hour after leaving their home of thirteen years in tears.

As she merged onto I-76, heading back home to her husband, she smiled recalling her conversation with Janelle, the other keeper of her secrets. She'd asked her bestie to meet at the Coastal Sounds for a late lunch before the kids got out of school.

"Girl, I know good and well my big brother did not say what I think I heard you say. Has he lost his rabbit a— I mean, his rabbit mind? He knows better! Imma kick his a— behind."

Had it not been for the two older nuns enjoying soup and sandwiches across from them, Janelle's language would have been infinitely more colorful. Amia could almost hear the thee and four-letter medley. She also knew her spit-fire bestie well enough to know that Janelle would have had those white hooped earrings off by now to emphasize her point. Preacher's kid, yes. From 33rd Street and Harlem Ave, also yes.

"I handled it, J."

"What do you mean, you handled it? How? I know you didn't tell him to go straight to— take a long walk."

Amia was inwardly tickled at her friend's paused restraint as the sisters happily chatted within earshot.

"I did tell him to take a walk." She couldn't go into detail, so Amia provided the cliff notes version, which included packing a bag for her and the kids and an empty threat of breaking his fingers if he touched her again.

"I'm conflicted because I want to say good for you, Sis. I really do, but it's you and Darren. I don't want to say good for you, 'cause I wouldn't mean it. I don't know what to say, Amia."

Amia shook her head softly. She was still completely devastated and seething. Janelle covered her friend's rapidly tapping index finger to stop it from carving a crescent into the table's wooden surface. Moments later, they were saying goodbye to the nuns who'd finished their meals.

"I don't know what he's done, but you should forgive him, Honey," the older sister advised, leaning towards Amia and smiling.

Amia smiled back, misty eyed. "Thank you, Sister. God bless you."

"And great job controlling your language, young lady. But you really didn't have to hold your tongue for me. You'd be surprised at the stuff that comes out of this one's mouth."

The younger sister's instantly ashen face made the older nun's good-natured poke even funnier. With that, all four ladies bid farewell as the Sisters exited the café.

"Now, you know those two cut up in Mass *every Sunday*," Janelle commented. She and Amia were still smiling from their interaction with the fun-loving Catholics.

"Amia, Darren and I go back almost twenty-five years. I don't know what he was thinking, but I do know he's beside himself right now. He's not that guy and never has been," Janelle encouraged, gently holding Amia's hand after she forwarded a ninth call to voicemail.

"Ummm, so I've never met the pissed off Amia Wilford before, and I'm scared."

Amia's eyes stopped burning holes into the bistro's walls and met her friend's upon hearing Janelle's reference to being afraid.

"You're scared?"

"Yeah... I mean, part of me wishes this Amia had been at the Bearheart event. This woman right here might have snatched that dern lace front right off Asley Tesleep's bald head. That still burns me up. She's lucky I was busy begging God to send a legion of angels to carry me across the finish line, cause I'd have beat Ms. Thang with that wig and then wheeled her behind all the way into the maternity ward.

Amia shook her head at her friend, knowing full well, she and Jamari would have been watching videos of Janelle and Asley while practicing her summations weeks earlier. That said, she was still far too irritated to crack a smile.

"Imma say it again. This Amia scares me. I don't know who this lady is and, I don't have a clue what she's gonna do, but... could you please ask her not to kill Darren?"

"Kill Darren? What, J?"

"I mean it, Sis. You tell pissed off Amia that she'd better not touch one single, solitary hair on my brother's head. And don't look at me like that, either. I know he's bald."

Amia's eyebrow arched.

"Seriously, you know I stay watching Snapped, right?" Janelle didn't let Amia answer. It was a rhetorical question, after all. "It's always the nice ones. They don't know how to control their pissed-off-icity. And Sis, you've never been to this level of pissed-off-icty. I'm telling you right now, Amia Wilford," Janelle said, her hands clapping together with each word. "You better not hurt that man."

Janelle flipped her imaginary hair off her shoulders before taking a few elongated sips of her strawberry banana smoothie. With that, Amia let go, giving in to her trusty companion who'd been futilely trying to cheer her up.

"I cannot with you," she laughed.

"Listen, Sis," Janelle said, once the friends finished laughing at her antics. She gently held Amia's hand.

"We've all fallen short of God's glory. Me, you, your parents, my parents, Todd, and yes, even Darren. I'm not excusing or making excuses for him, 'cause he was dead wrong—full stop.

"I also know he's sick about this. That man will walk through Hell with gasoline drawls on for you. He messed up—no ifs, ands or buts. If you need to hang out with your parents to clear your head, go, and when you're done kickin' it with Mom and Dad, bring your little behind back home.

"And you've gotta figure out how to forgive him. I mean, there's at least one unforgivable thing that your man has forgiven you for, right Amia Wilford?"

She cringed knowing exactly what Janelle was about to say. She and Darren were preparing for their move to scenic Teeton Drive several years ago. The couple decided not to keep anything that would not be used in their new home. They'd taken car and truckloads of items to the Goodwill, Salvation Army, and local charity organizations in the weeks up to the move.

"I still can't believe I accidentally donated his high school letter jacket," Amia groaned behind the hands that covered her face as soon as Janelle referenced the unforgivable act.

"Oh my God..." Amia's eyes reappeared though her mouth was now covered as she relived her monumental blunder.

"J, I still have no idea how that jacket ended up in the donation bag. We didn't even know it was gone until we finished unpacking all of the miscellaneous bedroom boxes, and that was about two weeks after we moved in."

"Oh, best believe I remember, Amia Wilford! We must have hit up every donation center this side of Chicago trying to track that jacket down."

"Uggh. I know," she said still squirming at the thought. "But J, that was an accident. What Darren did was intentional. There's a difference."

"Mia, let's say you and Darren share a board. Darren intentionally puts a nail in it. Then you somehow accidentally put one in the board as well. At the end of the day, there are two holes in that board, regardless of how they got there... And you're each responsible for one of them.

"Listen, Sis. Forgiveness isn't tit for tat. You know that. I know you do. You're hurt and you should be, but dig deep, Amia. You love that man and he loves you. Find it in your heart to forgive him."

# Chapter 35

## *In a Word* – Reconcile

Amia lovingly cradled Darren's heaving head as he finally allowed himself to share the devastation which accompanied his confirmation that the man whose dimples adorn his face never really loved him.

Darren began divulging some of the lurid details about an hour before her Volvo made its way into their cul-de-sac and up their brick-paver driveway. He met his soulmate as she cut the engine. And though he'd said it dozens of times since answering her call a couple hours earlier, another apology was the first thing out of his mouth.

Amia didn't respond, at least not verbally. Instead, she wrapped her arms around her husband and held him tightly, feeling him melt into her embrace. Amia knew his heart. He hadn't been himself the past few weeks. What she knew for sure was this was Darren, her Darren. The man God created just for her.

He was in pain and lashed out. Sure, he was wrong, and yes, it hurt. In fact, it still hurt, but he didn't mean it. Amia knew that in her bones. She saw the horror in his eyes as the words escaped faster than he could pull them back.

In that moment, a heartache took over, directing her next steps. She was unprepared for her husband's angry snapback and instead of allowing her cooler head to prevail, responded with an equally knee-jerk reaction.

Moisture began penetrating her baby blue T-shirt as her powerful husband sobbed into her shoulder. It was a mixture of remorse, thanksgiving and anguish. He held Amia tightly as if trying to absorb her.

"I've got you, Babe. I will never think differently of you. Let it go. Let it out," she encouraged, while holding onto her man. Darren, eternally grateful for the gift of Amia's return, did just that.

He let that fourteen-year-old sob his heart out. He let the college kid who pretended his dad was watching his football games weep. Finally, Darren stopped shaming the forty-seven-year-old successful attorney for still longing for his birth father's approval.

Time froze as Amia held him, cradling his head and rubbing his back in response to his heart break. She did what God told her to do during their earlier chat and prayed for her husband. She prayed for his complete healing. She prayed for his mental freedom from Marshon. She held on tightly while covering him in prayers.

There were moments when her back hurt from supporting some of his 245 pounds, but she prayed that away too. Amia was not about to ask him to adjust or do anything to shift his focus. She was determined to stand in the gap for him—literally—for as long as she could because Darren, her Darren, needed her.

Around 8:30, the couple, stronger than ever, emerged from their bedroom in search of edible nourishment. The last couple hours had been spent making up. They started by washing away hurts under the heat of their oversized rainfall showerhead.

Then they unpacked baggage on the floor of their spacious walk in closet after Darren emptied Amia's overnight bag, vowing to never let it travel solo again. The pair finished by passionately reconnecting at every corner of their massive California king bed.

Back downstairs, the ravished twosome enjoyed ramen noodles with sriracha and veggies paired with a beer and a glass of wine.

"Did you hear about Marty's prank on Natalie on Friday evening?"

"With the tow truck driver," Amia replied laughing. "Yeah, I saw her post on Facebook. He is too much," she added.

*"So,"* Amia read from the Facebook post. *"I called my darling boss, Marty Worthy, from the Target parking lot to tell him I needed a tow truck because, I picked up a couple of nails and had two flat tires. Marty tells me that he knows a guy and will take care of it. The driver comes out. Now, imagine my surprise when he tells me it would cost $600 to hook up my car and tow it three miles.*

*"When I told him to forget it, he tells me that the cost just to come out was $550. As I'm about to cuss this man up one side and down the other, he gets a call from my darling boss and puts him on speaker. Do you know Marty proceeds to tell me not to worry about paying the full price because, he'd negotiated a special price for me, and I only needed to pay $549.99?"*

"Marty is out of control," they both laughed, also noting that he wrapped the trick up by paying for Natalie's tow to the tire store.

"Did you see, Trevaris made the All-City Team?"

"Um hum," Amia replied, pausing to fan the heat of the sriracha.

"That young man," Darren inhaled and exhaled with pride at Trevaris and his many achievements. "I'm so proud of him."

"Oh, oh, oh," Amia started excitedly while snapping her fingers. "Did you see the homecoming pictures, Babe? They are so cute."

Amia then retrieved her phone to share the photos his mother posted on Facebook. The couple took turns showing each other photos of Trevaris, Tori, and their little guy whose baby blue and white jumper matched his parents' homecoming outfits.

Darren placed a long kiss upon Amia's forehead, twirling a few sweat-strewn strands around his finger. Amia inhaled her husband's essence, allowing his sexy muskiness to seep into her senses.

He wasn't the only one who was grateful for this moment. She was equally thankful that he'd ignored her anger-infused command that he not be home when she returned. She was relieved when he answered on the first ring, though she'd sent twenty plus calls from him straight to voicemail.

"Babe, I'm sorry for the way I acted on Friday. You have to understand. I nev—"

"Listen," Darren whispered, his eyes searching hers. "I needed that, Amia. I'd been taking advantage of your good heart. You just let everything roll off your back, and you've done it for years. I was purposefully shutting you out, and you were rolling with it, still loving me and still being there. I was thinking about myself, not wanting to deal with those feelings, and I wasn't protecting you."

"You know, I love you, Darren."

"I know, but let me tell you something, Amia Jasmine Wilford. Watching you pack your bag and then pack our kids' bag shifted my entire existence. I mean, that reset button got smashed. I truly needed that wake-up call.

"The only thing I could think about was how badly I'd hurt you and how stupid I've been. I just begged God for one more chance. Amia, you not answering my calls... Sweet Jesus," he added, dropping his forkful of ramen and pulling her even tighter.

"As long as I live, I'm never going to forget the look on your face as words that came out of my mouth hurt you."

Darren then dutifully topped off Amia's glass of Moscato and tucked it back in between the other chilled bottles of bubbly. When he turned back to face his wife, Amia noted an interesting glimmer in his eyes.

"What?" Amia asked curiously as he leaned against the fridge, gazing at her with a smile. After a few more moments, Amia could see most of his endearing pearlies, but there was something else there. Amia eyed her handsome man trying to figure out what he was thinking. Finally, Darren let her in on his thoughts.

"That's exactly what I want Bean to do. She has to be strong enough to tell a Brotha to kick rocks if he ever comes incorrect. She needs to know her worth; to have the courage to demand better, even if it means walking away from her man or the life she loves."

He watched a few carbonated bubbles trace their way up the interior of the chilly green glass before looking back at his wife lovingly.

"I'm proud of you, Amia. I'm proud of you for putting your foot down. Now, don't get me wrong. That size ten red bottom is a beast. I ain't even gonna lie."

She smiled before releasing a long exhale. The agony she'd felt seeing her favorite piece of luggage plopped in her beige trunk for the first time ever without Darren's hammered leather tote next to it, was overshadowed only by the terror she felt watching the garage doors closing on her life through her rear-view mirror.

Before the pair began making up hours earlier, Amia reminded him that the one thing she would never tolerate was a man degrading her, no matter how much she loved him. After all, Amia's best friend at Carnegie Mellon, Renee, committed suicide after enduring years of mental abuse at the hands of her high school sweetheart.

Amia was fully aware of the destruction of confidence and self-worth that words from a loved one carry. While there was nothing in Darren that was even a micro fraction of Renee's then boyfriend, the culmination of his words following weeks of bad behavior struck a nerve. It's why his words landed so loudly in her soul. She'd even kept up with Renee's mother until her passing a few years earlier.

Darren's hands interlocked with hers. He kissed both, lingering on the three-and one-half carat diamond he'd lovingly placed on her finger seventeen years earlier.

"One thing's for sure, Christina Renee has an example of a fearless, strong, God-fearing woman." He emphasized her middle name lovingly as a nod to Amia's beloved friend.

"Babe, I thank God for you every single day. You are hardworking, kind, intelligent, classy, and full of grace. You truly are my treasure. You've gotta know you're everything I've ever wanted. Hear me when I say I love you more than anything in this world. I was a fool, Amia. You didn't deserve that, and it won't happen again."

"I know," she replied softly. They sat together in silence a few more moments leaning against each other, enjoying the intimacy of their bond before Darren changed the subject.

"Can I ask you a question?"

"Of course, Mr. Wilford," she responded, leaning curiously on her elbow and gazing into his deep eyes, still wondering how it was possible that he gets sexier every year.

"What was that little thing you did with your hips up there?"

"What thing? Ohhhh, this?" she added slyly, swiveling her hips and mimicking the earlier actions.

"You liked it?" she asked as he wrapped his arms around her waist drawing her near again. She smiled at his nonverbal response.

"Ummm, aren't you supposed to be using your words, Mr. Wilford?" she managed between the long, juicy kisses being planted on her full lips.

"I only have one, Dayum!"

Amia laughed, noting she would have to thank the hot yoga instructor for that little tip. Her additional sensual swaying aroused Darren's interest so much that he exchanged his half-eaten plate for another full serving of his wife.

The microwave beeped once more, signifying the rewarming of the previously microwaved noodles. The pair managed to finish their meals while Darren shared additional revelations from his time with Marshon.

# Chapter 36

## *In a Word* – Cupcakes

"I tell you what, y'all went off with this meal right here," exclaimed Ramon as he finished feeding one of the adorable twins the last bits of his mashed potatoes.

"Had to pull out all the stops for the first holiday meal with Shamir back," smiled Jordyn. She and Bria treated the extended Copeland clan to the spread which amassed the highest number of votes on their channel. The pair had asked their followers to share their favorite meals from *Broke & Eating Good* advising that the meal with the most votes was what they were making for their extra-special dinner.

While Jamari wrestled with the other adorable eleven-month-old over the last bite of Jordyn's extra thick Maryland style crab cake, Amia and Elaine began clearing the plates. Michele and Shamir polished off the baked mac and cheese and spicy potato salad. Shamir, sitting in his 'assigned' seat at the family's table, had difficulty remembering the last time he'd had a meal so amazing.

Amia returned with two bottles of wine and a couple of beers to pair with the long-awaited dessert. It was a special request from Darren. Due to the complexity and time commitment, this dessert only showed up on special occasions. Darren figured that the first holiday gathering at Elaine and Ramon's in celebration of Shamir's return would be worthy of the extra effort.

Finally, it was time. Bria happily sashayed into the dining room beaming with excitement. Her signature double decker cupcakes overflowing with crème cheese icing and strawberry filling were about to be the hottest things moving.

The anticipation was unmistakable. From the moment word got out about the cupcakes making an appearance, the entire family was on edge. Even Shamir, the only one who hadn't been fortunate enough to have partaken in the fares, was calling dibs. Ramon and Elaine had been the fortunate guinea pigs during Jordyn and Bria's early years and, as a result, had gotten to enjoy the evolution of Bria's award-winning dessert.

Oohs and ahhs filled the air as the tall, frosted dome lifted, revealing two dozen sugar sprinkled pieces of culinary mastery. The obligatory presentation photos were almost missed as the family eagerly dove in. Amia held her breath and waited as she watched for Shamir's reaction.

"This is your creation?" Shamir asked Bria with disbelief. "You thought of this?"

"Yep, I've been working on them for years," Bria beamed.

"She's been tweaking the recipe for a while and started racking up awards last year," chimed in Jordyn proudly supporting her older sister. Shamir stared at the delicious morsel and then at his sibling creator. The family waited with bated breath to hear which delicious adjectives he would use to describe the award-winning treat. They didn't have to wait much longer to hear what was on his mind.

"Simon's girlfriend brought cupcakes just like these a few times, usually around his birthday. Each year, it was a little different. I think the first one was lemon flavored. The last time I had it, there was a strawberry crème filling," he added, looking at the cupcakes with obvious confusion.

He was afraid to dive into the treat for fear that the familiar sweet ooze that filled his heart with hope during those dark years in captivity would spill out of the beautiful gems and onto the light green saucer before him.

Amia looked at Darren whose eyes were fixated on the serving tray. This was one of the things he revealed to her last night, so neither was surprised by Shamir's remarks. Marshon told him Shamir might recognize the pastries. Simon bragged about giving Shamir and Steven some of the foods and desserts created by his 'side piece,' co-creator of *Broke & Eating Good*.

Bria's brain was in overdrive as she tried to process what she was hearing. That was on pace with the minds of everyone else who'd squeezed around the table to ensure that one of the Rosé-infused cupcakes landed on their outstretched plates.

Amia squeezed Shamir's trembling hand, reassuring him that he was safe. Every eye in the house rested on Bria who was still absorbing the last sentence.

"Your boyfriend who never wanted to meet us, what was his name," asked Amia.

"Drew," whispered Bria almost inaudibly.

"This is crazy," said Jordyn. "Bree and I are always together. It's not possible... Is it Bree?"

"What is Drew's full name, Bria," asked Darren intently.

"Drew Simon," she whispered again in disbelief.

"Simon's girlfriend called him Drew," Shamir said as he proceeded to cut into the cupcake. Sure enough, the strawberry crème filling greeted his shaking fork. Every jaw in the beautiful two-story Victorian dropped followed immediately by questions and demands for answers.

Bria was beside herself. It was true. She had brought the cupcakes over to Drew's for special occasions. The first iteration of the famous recipe did have a lemon-inspired twist. Her eyes met Shamir's.

Her disbelief matched his. The pair had been best friends before the yacht's demise and Shamir's disappearance. How was it possible that she'd been to the home where he'd been held captive for years and never knew?

"I didn't know, Shamir. I promise. I never saw anyone there. I never heard anyone at the house," she said sobbing.

"I can't tell you how many times I told Steven that Simon's girlfriend sounded like you. Even though the voice was muffled through the walls, it just sounded like you. I couldn't wait for her to come over because I could hear something that sounded like home."

"Shamir, I didn't know."

"You couldn't have known, Bree. We wouldn't move at all when you came. If either me or Steven had, he'd have starved us. We learned that early on when we tried to get someone's attention by knocking on the pipes.

"It was exactly one week before we got food again, so we never made a move the whole time you would be there. What we did know is that we were going to have some good food for a few days because you always brought extra meals.

"Drew would ask me to bring a week's worth of meals so that he could have lunch and dinner after work. He was always working, so he'd ask me to make a lot. I just assumed he really liked my food." Horror stretched across Bria's body as the realization hit her. "He was giving it to you?"

Shamir just nodded. "Your voice and your food kept us going for the last couple of years."

The siblings met in the middle of the dining room hugging and sobbing into each other's arms. The family gathered around the hugging pair, adding their own tears to the mix.

"You know what's crazy," he asked after blowing his nose on one of the tissues that had been passed around. Shamir kept holding Bria as he continued. "Earlier this year, we listened helplessly as Simon beat his girlfriend—I mean you—down.

"She—I mean you—somehow broke free and started running away. We were never allowed to look out the windows, but Steven did. He knew he was dying, so to him it didn't matter.

"Steven said he saw Simon dragging you up the wall ledge. He saw you scratch his face and neck while trying to fight him off. He also saw Simon kick your right arm to get you to let go of the bush so he could pull you over."

Shamir found a spot on the ceiling to focus on, breathing through the frightening moment as it replayed in his head.

"The way you were screaming after the kick must have scared Simon because it was over almost immediately. We heard your car backing out of the driveway. Steven said he thought it was broken..." Shamir looked at his sister.

"My one regret was not being able to do anything. Not being able to help."

"You said this happened earlier this year?" asked Elaine. "Like, maybe in June?"

"Yeah. That's about right," replied Shamir, adding that it wasn't long after Memorial Day. Suddenly, thoughts flooded back to Daniel's thirteenth birthday party and Bria's injuries. Dots began connecting. Jamari and Ramon were beyond inflamed.

"That explains why there was no video of that fall in the Appalachians, right, Bria? Right, Jordyn?" Jamari quizzed with a no-nonsense tone. He absolutely did not play when it came to his sisters and to learn that one of them had been touched—no, beaten by a man—had him seeing red. The fact that this man was the same one who'd kidnapped his brother had him spitting fire.

"Everything about your lives is filmed for your channels, but y'all didn't video the hike through the *beautiful* Appalachian trails. That never made sense to me.

"The dead battery excuse didn't sit right either, because you had a power bank. Hell, you had *my* power bank," he scoffed. At this point, Jamari's demeanor told his sisters he had no patience for anything remotely resembling BS.

"Ok," confessed Jordyn. "Bree came over after it happened. It was a Saturday morning really early. We were supposed to leave for the cabin later that day. Drew was angry that she was going to be gone for two weeks. As usual, she didn't want to tell anyone, so we went to the cabin anyway."

"As usual?" That question rang out in unison. Bria was mortified.

"Jordyn?" Bria said, breaking quickly away from Shamir's embrace and almost begging her sister to stop talking. After all, Jordyn promised she wouldn't ever say anything. Undaunted, Jordyn continued.

"Have you ever wondered why Bree started wearing turtlenecks while filming *Broke & Eating Good* and *Broke with Reservations*?" The family paused, letting that question sink in.

"Jordie, please," Bria begged desperately. Her little sister continued, not missing a beat.

"No, Bree! I hated not being able to say anything. That man was beating on you, and you made me keep it a secret..." Jordyn cried. "Do you have any idea how I felt, Bree? You are my sister, and you wouldn't let me help. You kept showing up with bruises, and I had to pretend like everything was fine!" she screamed tearfully, releasing pent-up agony. "Did you ever think about how I felt not being able to help you?"

Jordyn sobbed into Ramon's arms, which he'd wrapped around her as soon as he heard the first crack in her voice. Jordyn wiped a few additional tears before continuing.

"Bree hasn't needed to wear the turtlenecks since Drew's been gone, but for the last couple of years, they hid bruises... Now, Bria wears them because they've become her signature."

Bria refused to make eye contact with anyone except Jordyn. She heard Jordyn's heartfelt confession, and even blinked back a few tears, but a promise was a promise—and Jordyn broke hers. She still extended an unmistakably disapproving glare in her younger sister's direction.

"Anyways," Jordyn sternly replied ignoring her sister's glare. "We ended up going to the hospital out in the mountains because her arm and ribs were hurting so badly. Thankfully, her ribs were just bruised, but her arm was fractured.

"We left before the two weeks were up, but did manage to film some videos. Normally, Bree and I both sign off with our big blowing kiss, but if you go back and look at those four episodes, the plates were propped up near her face. She kept her sunglasses on, and just did the duck lips."

"Where is Drew now?" asked a newer voice from the corner of the room. It belonged to Braedon, the same Braedon who Bria hadn't bothered to give the time of day in years past. For the last several months though, she and the 'skinny White guy' as she'd called him previously, had been dating and were now completely inseparable.

The normally easy going and mild-mannered young man's blood was boiling right along with all the men in the home, if not more, after hearing the story. After all, he'd lived in the flat across the hall from Jordyn and Bria at the time.

Braedon was finishing a run with his shepherd mix as Jordyn and Bria pulled in following their return from the mountains. He'd helped the injured girl of his dreams up the steps.

# Chapter 37

## *In a Word* – Simmering

Dish after dish clanged in the background as warm, soapy water washed away the remnants of an incredible meal. While the crumbs, gravies and icing dissolved into the deep farmhouse sink, there was still a bunch of cleaning left—literally and figuratively.

Amia, always the coolest head in the room, decided to press pause. She couldn't actually see the infernos, but could literally feel the temperature rising within her parents' home. She knew a break was needed and suggested clearing the table as a diffuser.

Amia pulled Jamari aside asking him to check in on Shamir, then Ramon, then Elaine. Her strategy was twofold.

First, it would quell Jamari's rage by having him channel his psychological expertise. In order to be of service to the mental health of his family, Jamari needed to recenter. This would cause him to refocus, resulting in his calming down—which was goal number two.

He smiled at his big sister, resting his head on her shoulder while squeezing her tightly. Amia was without a doubt the family's angel. While no one wanted to concede to the change of pace, everyone knew she was right. Her level-headed, easy-going nature was the manna to this family's fiery soul.

Jamari took another moment to love on his sister, thanking her for all the guidance and reassurance through the years. True, Amia grounded this entire family, but she was Jamari's anchor. The pair shared an unbreakable bond since she'd rescued him from himself at age thirteen.

She took the then misguided, angry teen in, snatching him from the life he was trying to live, but wasn't supposed to have. Though fresh out of college and only twenty-six at the time, Amia convinced her parents to let him move in with her. Decades later, the charismatic professor still treasured his sister's ability to understand him better than anyone.

"I'm good, Sis," he assured her moments later, smiling as his eyes found hers. Amia exhaled, her hand resting on his heart.

"Good. We need you, Mar."

She kissed his cheek just as Michele turned the corner in search of her handsome husband.

The lingering pieces of anger disappeared as soon as Michele and her thick chestnut brown curls entered the hallway.

Amia noted it was impossible to scowl when that cutie and her sparkly personality showed up. Her heart smiled as she watched the pair disappear down the hall, her mind drifting back to the couple's journey the last few years.

"Are you sure there's no other way, Jamari?" asked a concerned Amia upon learning that Michele had volunteered for the international endeavor.

"She can get engineering experience right here in the US. Why go out of the country? You two have only been married for a few years," she'd stated back then. "Are you sure?"

"Yes, Mia," Jamari responded. "She wants to move up in the organization and to do that, she needs more engineering experience. There are people who need bridges built to make survival easier. With this fellowship, she gets to merge her desire to make a difference with her need to learn how to construct bridges. She'll gain wider design and anchoring knowledge, which will give her an edge."

What Jamari hadn't shared with his adoring older sister and family was that Michele had done the internship years earlier when she was fresh out of college. It was a perfect cover for what was really happening. Because she had already had the experience, Michele was able to feed stories to Jamari that he could then relay to his inquisitive family.

The truth was Michele hadn't been out of the country. She was actually pregnant. Instead of sharing what should be the most exciting news ever, the young couple concocted the story.

Jamari and Michele suffered a heartbreaking miscarriage while twenty weeks pregnant during their first year of marriage. In their second year, the pair endured the unspeakable devastation of a stillborn.

In addition to their unimaginable personal losses, their families also suffered through each heartbreak. Both grandmas were shopping for baby clothes, toys, and gifts with each pregnancy.

After Jasper's tragic birth, the pair immediately moved out of their previous apartment because they couldn't bear walking past the baby blue nursery that would never be home to the precious newborn who they'd loved more than life.

They just couldn't bear the thought of having another unsuccessful public pregnancy. This story allowed Michele to be excused from the non-stop birthday parties, engagements, graduations, and other occasions which are the DNA of large families.

It also allowed them to conceal the growing belly that they wanted to love on more than anything, but were terrified to fall in love with. Jamari would go to work and show his face at random events before ducking back home to care for Michele.

Though lying to the family was hard and Michele's missing out on the birth of her niece was painful, the pair had no intentions of revealing Michele's pregnancy until the babies were here.

Jamari trusted God, but his faith had been rattled. He knew God was faithful and he'd obviously seen the Lord's hand moving on his behalf. Jamari went from dealing drugs and probation to approving graduate students for graduation. Michele also knew the Lord, but her faith wasn't as solid and with their past two tragedies, it was shaky—at best.

It was Michele's plea to not tell the families and while deep down, he did not want to hide the pregnancy, Jamari fully understood. He would never forget the horror on her face as the OB GYN commanded her to stop pushing. He watched anxiously as the doctor unwrapped the cord which had been wrapped around the tiny infant's neck several times.

Jamari still remembered the screaming that rang throughout the small white delivery room as the shattered grandparents were rushed out while the medical staff worked unsuccessfully to usher life back into their seven-pound three-ounce infant whose once strong heartbeat had disappeared from the fetal monitor.

Ramon, in an effort to help his son and daughter-in-law in some way, took their keys and removed the meticulously positioned car seat from the brown and black back seat of their newly purchased Camry. His heart broke again noticing the newly affixed 'Baby on Board' sign in the rear window.

Following that devastating late morning, their relationships with the families were forever changed. Everyone handled Jamari and Michele with kid gloves because the loss had been so traumatic.

People were hesitant to share the joyful news of another surprise pregnancy. Coworkers who'd thrown baby showers, felt baby bumps and ribbed the dad to be, were understandably awkward. Even friends and relatives were afraid to invite the pair to baby showers, fearing that they could be seen as insensitive.

Thankfully though, that tiny tan car seat with its brown and blue teddy bears remained in Ramon and Elaine's basement until they received a predawn call from a happily sobbing Jamari last October. His almost incoherent voice informed them that they were now grandparents to a healthy baby boy and girl.

Because everyone thought Michele was out of the country and no one knew she was pregnant, there had been no baby showers. There were also no cribs, no bottles, no onesies and no baby blankets other than the multicolored pastel ones the loving nurses had swaddled the four-pound cuties in.

Once everyone recovered from the shockwave of surprise newborns and bodies were again moving in response to signals from perplexed but overjoyed brains, the young Copeland home was flooded by friends and family.

Before Jamari escorted Michele and their extremely precious cargo home from the hospital, the converted reading room of their tiny two-bedroom red bricked home had been returned to its original intention. It was now a warm, cozy space featuring pink and blue striped walls with cutesy baby décor.

Newly assembled cribs were dressed in pink and blue linen by both grandmothers. They set up nursing pillows next to the quaint brown rocking chair and changing table donated by Amia and Darren.

Diapers, gifts, toys and all the necessities required to welcome babies found homes in crevices of newly erected bookshelves. Amia's heart was smiling at the remembrance of meeting those babies and squeezing her brother as a first-time dad.

One of the impromptu gifts was a blue jean diaper bag which Michele bumped playfully against Jamari, causing him to bump against the wall. She wrapped her arm around her husband's as they turned the corner of their parents' home, disappearing from Amia's view.

# Chapter 38

## *In a Word* – Connections

With the kitchen cleaned, food put away, babies down with bottles and kids happily engrossed with the electronics of their choice, the family gathered again, this time in the den which had been the backdrop for game nights, movie nights and countless other family activities experienced in their childhood home. Tonight's assembly would be like none before.

"So, Bria," Ramon began, opening the highly anticipated conversation. "There wasn't any indication that this Drew or Simon had Shamir or Steven at his home?"

"No. There wasn't. I promise, I never heard anything. He never let on that there was any unusual activity. Like I said, he always asked me to make a bunch of whatever I was making because he'd take it for lunch throughout the week. I never thought anything of it.

"I've been in that pantry hundreds of times. All four walls had shelving. I didn't see a knob or anything that told me there was a door." Bria paused to regain her composure. "Please believe me, I didn't know."

Braedon pulled her into his chest, swallowing Bria up in his arms.

"What happened the morning of your trip to the mountains, Bree?" asked Elaine as she handed Braedon a few tissues which he gently used to dab Bria's cheeks. Elaine then squeezed into the loveseat with the pair coaxing Bria from his loving arms into hers.

"I hit him back," she whispered.

"What Jordyn said is true. It happened a lot. Most times, it was because I said something he didn't like, or I didn't do what he wanted. Towards the end, it felt like he was hitting me because there was one too many clouds in the sky."

Bria then turned towards Jordyn.

"I'm sorry, Jordie. I never thought about your feelings. I didn't know I was hurting you... Friends?" Bria asked. She eased off the couch, stepping around the decade's old coffee table to meet her sister.

"Forever," Jordyn replied as she also stepped around the rectangular mahogany centerpiece for a long embrace with Bria.

"Bree," Elaine began, "why would you be with a man who puts his hands on you?"

"Why wouldn't you say anything?" asked Ramon. His hurt and rage began to bubble again.

"Bree, you have three million followers. You are the "Eating Good" of *Broke & Eating Good*. Why would you stay with him?" Jamari asked with pained curiosity.

Bria nervously looked at Braedon. His warm blue eyes lovingly encouraged her from behind brown square frames as his head nodded in support. She then found Jordyn who'd returned to her seat across the room. Her little sister's eyes were equally supportive, but insistent that her older sister and best friend come completely clean.

Bria took a deep breath and closed her eyes tightly. She had no idea how the family would react, but the truth is, she was just as tired of holding onto this secret as Jordyn had been in keeping hers. She felt Braedon's fingers easing between her manicured digits, wrapping around them securely. She leaned her head to meet the encouraging kiss he'd planted on her cheek.

"Drew isn't broke or struggling. He never has been. He's a very successful Pharmacist who graduated top of his class at UNC's school of Pharmacy. He also wasn't married." Bria released a long exhale.

"I made up the whole thing about him being broke and embarrassed to meet you... The truth is Drew hated Amia and Darren, and I was trying to protect them."

As the disbelief and confusion rose to a crescendo and as all mouths cracked to ask why, Bria opened the purse that Braedon had gently slid onto her lap. She unzipped a compartment and extracted a long, tattered gray envelope.

# Chapter 39

## *In a Word* – Coaxed

"Good morning," a soft, firm voice managed while watching a male nurse lock the large gray wheels in place. The next words were held until the young man ensured the patient's air tubes were positioned properly and without obstruction before leaving the pair alone with the prison guard who'd positioned himself in the opening of the scuffed up, off-white entry door.

"So, you're the famous Amia Wilford. I see why that boy ain't got no damn sense. You sure are easy to look at."

She half smiled and lightly scratched an area at her upper breast which had been irritated since she left home with Janelle heading for the airport. She noticed the elderly man's gaze lingering at her V-neck and adjusted the material against her caramel complexion.

"And you are the infamous Marshon Wilford," Amia replied politely without acknowledging his gaze.

"I see you're still calling the shots," she added with a half-smile referencing his swatting the LPN's hands and shooing him away.

Amia could see her recognition of his control had landed well. She'd been rehearsing Jamari's notes and fine-tuning her speaking points throughout the almost three-hour flight. Amia represented and cross examined enough narcissists to know that nothing gets them to engage more than stroking their ego. She engaged in friendly banter with him for a few moments until Marshon apologized for not having another son who was stronger than Darren.

Amia bit her tongue.

*Focus, girl. Don't respond. Stay the course.*

Her game face was intact, but her flesh was getting hot, causing her skin to itch again. She tried her best to scratch it without drawing unwanted attention. Because Amia needed answers from Marshon, confronting him about that last remark would have to wait. She remembered the mission and employed a different tactic.

"Marshon," she started with an earnest, soothing tone.

"You were a legend in your day. Darren, is also a legend."

She persisted, undeterred by his obvious disbelief.

"Darren Wilford has sent hundreds of kids to college on full scholarships, gotten thousands of kids money towards education, and created constant jobs through his camps. He's even mentored others who've gone on to open their own camps nationwide. Darren has saved countless lives who surely would have been lost to the streets.

"He did all that with the killer instinct he got from you. Marshon, Darren is always the smartest man in the room. He got that from you. Listen, your son didn't live the life you lived. Truth be told, only you could have done that. You had a command out there that people had to respect.

"Darren, has mastered that command. He was a monster on the field. I wish you could have seen him play. He's a master in the courtroom. I wish you could see him at work. Darren walks up in that bad boy like he owns the place."

Amia paused, making eye contact with her husband's father. No doubt, there is a confidence that speaks when Darren walks. While it's partially due to his unfailing commitment to the craft, it's Darren's talks with God on behalf of his clients that seal the deal.

Amia wanted Marshon to see his son in the same light that she and everyone else saw her husband. According to Jamari, to do that, she needed Marshon to feel that he contributed to Darren's success, whether he was there or not.

"Camille even says that Darren walks like you..."

*I think I'm getting through.* Amia thought to herself as she saw him fighting a smile that threatened to pull at his lips' corners.

"I know one thing. You must have been something else in your heyday Marshon, because that walk that Darren has... Honey, that right there is a beast."

The battle against the grin was lost. Though Marshon's pearlies were yellowed from decades of smoking and months of chemotherapy, she could clearly see the origins of Darren's amazing smile. She matched his beam with one of her own.

The lonely hospice space became a little warmer as the now familiar strangers connected. Amia's soothing voice, and warm, Holy Ghost sponsored smile had earned her yet another friend. She no longer needed Jamari's notes.

"Mr. Marshon, Sir," she smiled again, watching his cheeks constrict in response.

"Darren didn't follow in your footsteps on the streets. That was all you, and from what I hear, no one has come close to you since. I need you to know your son, Darren Jamison Wilford, is almost as powerful as you in our world.

"Oooh, and let me tell you," Amia slid her chair closer to him, as if about to impart some juicy gossip.

"Check this out. Prosecutors don't want to face Darren in court. They offer plea deals off the jump to ensure they don't have to go up against him. And not just average plea bargains, I mean really good plea bargains. That's how much they fear him.

"Not only that, your son is a really good man, Marshon. He's an incredible father to your grandkids. I wish you could see him. He still looks out for his sisters, just like he did when they were kids. You'd be so proud. Darren has been the best man at weddings of kids whose lives were changed after he took them under his wing. That's who your son is.

"Earlier, you said you were sorry you didn't have another son. Honestly, Sir, I'm sorry you didn't have another one, too. The world really could use a lot more Darren Wilfords."

Amia watched moisture trail down the sides of his face dropping onto the white patterned medical gown. She covered his shaking hand. As bad and misguided as this man had been, those remorseful tears were real.

He'd spent thirty plus years angry and embarrassed at his son's 'lack of courage.' He'd spent the last few weeks secretly upset at the missed opportunity to bond with Darren, and had Amia not insisted on visiting Marshon alone after Bria handed them that letter days earlier, he would have died with that burden.

"I did see him," he whispered.

"You did see him? What do you mean? Marshon, what are you talk—"

"He played for Temple in the Big East. I caught a couple games when I was at Sing Sing. I tell you what..." Marshon paused, allowing the oxygen to refill his lungs.

"There was no offensive running game up the middle when my son was on the field." Marshon was brimming with pride.

"I should have told him. I wanted to," he added as more tears followed. Amia took that moment to let Marshon know about his son's pain and struggles. She told him how Darren's one prayer was to hear his dad say he was proud of him.

"That was my hope all these years, too. I wanted to tell him I loved him and I was proud of him when he came to see me but, I couldn't. My pride wouldn't..."

Amia handed him a tissue to capture the streams flowing along his face. She couldn't believe it. Darren returned from USP Thomson devastated by Marshon's uncaring indifference.

"When he was leaving, I told him that I never loved him... That he was only here because the condom broke... I told him that I never wanted him and that he was an embarrassment..." Marshon wept.

Amia dabbed her eyes. Those gut-wrenching words were what led to her husband's altered behavior and him ultimately lashing out at her. Her heart hurt.

"I didn't mean any of it," he managed. "Look at this."

Amia's eyes drifted to his right arm bearing a faded prison tattoo. She cried as she read the inscription inside and around the clenched fist.

"My son," Marshon began, quoting the message. "The man I never deserved... Could you tell Darren I'm proud of him, Amia?"

She wiped the tears that were trickling down her face. One salty drop managed to roll off her chin, landing on the itchy area of her breast. Amia had been suppressing the urge to scratch to avoid interrupting the moment, but she couldn't bear it any longer. Properly scratching the itch meant Marshon would see cleavage, but at this point, Amia didn't care. She had to address it. As suspected, his eyes were fixated on her exposed skin.

She angled her body away from Marshon, and away from the security guard to get the final good scratch in. With the itch soothed momentarily, she turned again to face the now wide-eyed father of her husband. Her lips moved a few times, but no words escaped.

"Marshon, my sister, Bria Copeland, had a letter from you that she received from her boyfriend, Drew Simon. He's the same man who kidnapped Camille's husband and my brother, both of whom Darren loved very much."

Marshon grimaced as the morphine was beginning to wear off.

"Do you need me to call the nurse."

The callous youthful Marshon who still lived in her husband's nightmares, wouldn't have deserved any leniency, but the ailing, gentle man sitting across from her, did.

"I'll manage," he answered, shaking his head from right to left.

"I don't have a lot of time left... Andrew DeSimeon," he whispered.

The confusion was evident. Amia was trying to understand how that name found its way into this conversation.

"Your sister's boyfriend," he added. "His name isn't Drew Simon. His name is Andrew DeSimeon."

# Chapter 40

## *In a Word* – Realizations

If Amia's gasp had been audible, its echoes would have vibrated off every cement wall in the entire facility. Her mind raced. Goosebumps emerged as the fine hairs on her arms rose in response.

She stood for the first time since entering the cool gray hospice space. Her itchy breast was now accompanied by unsteady legs and a queasy stomach as she tried to ingest what she'd heard.

"Bree said Drew just disappeared one day, never answering her calls again."

She remembered Shamir talking about the day Simon left and never returned. According to her brother, Simon was chipper that morning, looking forward to an extra-special sexual rendezvous.

"Oh my God," she whispered as she recalled the long scars on Andrew DeSimeon's face and neck as she sat across from his that Saturday morning months earlier. She thought about Shamir's revelation that Bree had scratched Simon during their fight.

She recalled Andrew DeSimeon leering at her across the table, fully intending to sleep with her in exchange for some sort of proof he claimed to have on Darren regarding his camp's financing.

"Drew Simon... Andrew DeSimeon."

Amia was muttering in disbelief.

Andrew was arrested on the spot and held without bond. He's been in prison ever since. Amia's hand covered her mouth upon realizing she was the 'Fine Honey' that Shamir said Andrew had planned to 'dip into'.

"Oh, Jesus."

Amia's shaky legs found her chair before making eye contact with Marshon again. He was fading, but acutely aware of his deathbed bombshell.

"Marshon? Why us? Please tell me why Andrew hates us?"

He was increasingly uncomfortable. His breath was becoming labored. He waved off the LPNs who'd rushed in due to the increasing alarms, signaling unstable vitals.

They repositioned his nose tubes, insisting he accept a little morphine to make him more comfortable. Wanting to keep his bearings, Marshon refused, weakly raising his index finger to request an additional moment. Seeing his fight, Amia advocated for Marshon, ensuring the nurses abided by his wishes.

She then continued quickly, "Marshon, I know you love Darren and your girls. Camille has a PhD and Adrienne is a nurse. They are everything you could have ever hoped for," Amia assured him. She needed him to hear that, hoping it would help him hold on a little longer.

Speaking very quickly, Amia added, "Marshon, Steven O'Tannen was Camille's husband. He was a college track coach and mentor who was changing lives. Andrew let that good man, your daughter's husband, rot from the inside out. He died a slow, painful death in Andrew's basement. You have prostate cancer, Marshon.

"Can you imagine living the rest of your life without anything to help manage this pain?" Amia swiveled to find his eyes which had looked towards the wall with that question. One thing was for certain, Marshon understood Steven's suffering.

Today's agony would be short lived because the morphine was coming. The thought of enduring this level of pain day in and day out without any ability to escape it was unimaginable. Amia scratched her itchy breast again, locking onto his teary eyes once more before continuing.

"Andrew wants to inflict that kind of pain on your son. Why, Marshon?" she pressed again.

"Your daughter's husband is dead. Andrew is coming after Darren. If you don't help me, guess what? Adrienne, your baby girl, is next. Please Marshon. Give me something."

Marshon's head lifted at the thought of any harm coming to his baby girl. In his mind, she was still seven. Perfect and innocent. She saw a fire reenter his exhausted eyes. If he never did another thing in the few days he had left, Marshon would ensure Adrienne was safe from the sociopath who'd been transferred to cell block A upon his arrival at the Colorado penitentiary only seven weeks earlier.

"Andrew's grandmother's home was broken into almost sixteen years ago. The cops had suspects in custody and were about to close the case. His sister was a suspect, but they didn't have anything on her.

Because she wanted a Brotha representing her granddaughter, Andrew's grandma mortgaged her home. He said a couple weeks after getting the money, Darren dropped his sister's case over some pictures and a video that he said you tampered with.

"His grandmother lost the house and died right after Andrew's sister was convicted. His sister was beaten to death six months into her sentence. That's w-" Marshon paused, allowing air to cycle in and out. "...That's why he hates you both."

Amia's mind rapidly filtered through hundreds of cases before stopping suddenly at one in particular which was tried during her second year at the firm.

"I remember that case. Audrey something." Amia's fingers massaged her forehead as if willing Audrey's last name forward.

"I can't remember her last name right now, but she was involved in that robbery. Audrey told everyone that she'd left her grandma's house to get some medicine to help with severe food poisoning.

"She said she almost crashed the car a couple of times because she was throwing up so much. Her story was that she'd bought the medicine at the convenience store before heading back to her grandmother's home.

"The video I found was of her walking into the police station that night to give her statement. She wasn't having any symptoms, but the bottle of Pepto that she was on camera purchasing to help with the food poisoning was never opened. It was still in her purse with the wrapper intact.

"Marshon, Darren stopped representing her only after she confessed to being involved with an organized burglary ring that targeted the elderly. And even after he removed himself from the case, your son, the class act that he is, still helped her.

"It was Darren, not Audrey's attorney, who convinced her to cooperate with the State and got her sentence reduced from thirty-three years to twenty-two. He couldn't represent her because of who the ring targeted, but he did use his influence to give her a chance at a life when she got out.

"Andrew can hate me for finding that video and producing those photos which led to his sister's confession. He can hate me because the inmates targeted the woman who preyed on their grandparents. There's no revenge to be gotten against Darren. He did right by Audrey.

"Marshon," Amia began again, picking up the pace.

"Andrew said he had copies of something that would prove Darren used illegal funds to start the Will Forward football camp. Darren used a bonus he received during his third year at the firm. Did Andrew ever say anything about that?"

Amia didn't expect an answer to this question. Marshon was now barely managing due to the pain. She sat next to him speaking quietly while covering his hand as he hung on. Amia admired his willingness to stay lucid, so that he could finish talking and help his kids.

There was no denying Darren got that quality from his father. She wished her husband was here, but she was confident that if he'd come, the walls would have been up. Marshon would have never have shown this level of vulnerability.

"Amia... Thank you."

"You are very welcome."

"Tell Adrienne and Camille that I love them and always have. I might not have been there, but they were always with me," he added before wailing in pain.

Amia stepped aside allowing the staff to tend to Marshon and ease his pain. They parted allowing the pair to say a final goodbye while a male RN flushed saline into the IV before pushing the long-overdue relief into his system.

"Goodbye, Amia," he whispered.

"I'll see you later... Dad," she replied, wiping the new tears that began falling. Amia recalled a revelation during their earlier conversation. Marshon shared that his one wish was to hear his kids call him Dad one last time.

While Amia couldn't grant that particular wish, she was Marshon's daughter-in-law. *I can call him dad,* she thought to herself—and so she did. Marshon began to cry, but suppressed it, due to the strain sobbing would have on his lungs.

Instead, the tears fell as he locked onto Amia's eyes. One weak hand reached out for hers while the other covered the deep, sweet ache in his heart.

"See you later."

"Wait, Amia," he yelled weakly as the nurse pushed the first milliliters into the port.

"Paul Bradley."

Those were the last words before he broke into a fit of coughs. The tall, prison officer who'd been standing guard in the hospice room throughout Amia's visit led her out of the room. She leaned against the wall to collect herself.

"Please Ma'am. I have to ask you to keep moving," the officer said. Amia couldn't speak. She just nodded and continued following the guard, noting he must have gotten something in his eyes because he kept rubbing them. He opened the door, handing her off to another officer.

"Ma'am," was all Officer Eric could muster. Moved by the early-morning emotions, he'd been silently shedding tears of his own.

# Chapter 41

## *In a Word* – Torn

All eyes focused on the handsome, disgraced former prosecutor as the special prosecutor pressed pause, freezing Marshon Wilford's gaunt face on the forty-two inch flat screen.

"I'm going to give you an opportunity to tell your side of the story before I press play again," the tall, heavy set man said matter-of-factly as he twisted the end of his upturned mustache. His offer was met by silence.

"Frank, I'm offering your client a one-time deal," he added as he slid the leather portfolio towards Paul Bradley's attorney.

"Felony blackmail, perjury, racketeering, forgery and-" He extracted a navy-blue Montblanc from his brown tweed blazer's interior pocket. "... Because I'm feeling generous, and Paul was an attorney, and we attorneys look out for each other, I'm willing to offer just four years and eleven months for perjury."

"Five years is the maximum for perjury, Lionel," replied Franklin Steepleton, Paul Bradley's attorney.

"I'm aware," Lionel Hampton replied flatly.

"Your client took an oath to conduct himself with integrity and civility. He swore to protect the Constitution and The People. Need I remind you that your client exercised the power of that office to railroad a child. It's a disgrace, Franklin. My offer is thirty years. Take it or leave it."

The stocky special prosecutor then clicked the gold cap of the Montblac pen, retracting its bald point before tucking it back into the jacket pocket.

"Come on, Lionel. That's preposterous," exclaimed Frank.

"Thirty years is the offer. It's good for twenty-three hours and... Let's see..." He paused, bending his elbow to glance at the blue leather strap wrapped around his thick wrist.

The impressive blue and silver Omega's face told him everything he needed to know. "It's good for twenty-three hours, fifty-nine minutes and forty-one seconds," he stated with force before pressing play and exiting.

Darren sat quietly on the edge of his large brown desk, peering out into the city. The familiar skyline glowed in varying hues of yellow and white from the lights of the staggered office buildings. Their nine to five occupants had long since sent their last emails and wrapped their final conference calls. He followed the lights of a tiny tug boat making its way down the jet-black river.

"Are you gonna hang out in here all night?" asked a warm, friendly voice whose owner had just entered his office. Darren turned to acknowledge the visitor, but did not respond.

"Amia is something special. I knew that the moment she walked into my office for her interview all those years ago."

Darren nodded, but still didn't reply. Martin "Marty" Worthy, the founding partner of WW&M who'd hired Darren and Amia when they were both fresh out of college, joined him behind the desk, opting to perch on the window ledge.

"How's her rash doing?" he asked with a smile. Darren laughed, shaking his head at his wife's penny-pinching, and its consequences.

"Much better. It'll be completely gone in another day or so."

"The men chuckled again remembering Amia's obvious discomfort though her back was facing the camera. They could see her scratching. Marty shook his head at the notion of Amia flashing Marshon when the irritation became unbearable. Darren joined his old friend and mentor in chuckling at her antics. He needed the distraction. This had been a tough five days.

"Now we know why that body spray was marked down." Darren added.

"You still haven't told her that you both make decent money?" Marty said, referencing Amia's well-known reputation for thriftiness.

"She handles the finances!" Darren replied. "But, I can assure you she paid full price for the alcohol pads."

They both laughed again before returning to the contents of the video which was turned over to the authorities after Marshon dropped the dime on Paul Bradley. He revealed that the former prosecutor was conspiring with Andrew DeSimeon and that the pair were blackmailing Amia's sister, Bria.

Amia was fully aware that all visits were recorded, even for those in hospice care at the prison. She'd banked on a remorseful Marshon, though Darren and Jamari advised her not to hold her breath.

It was after Marshon revealed that he'd seen Darren play football and asked her to relay a message to his son that she leaned in, advising him that Darren would see the video if he gave her anything useful. Her prayer was that Marshon would provide answers that could help her husband and sister.

Anything material that he shared would have been subpoenaed as evidence, and she knew the video would find its way to Darren soon enough. Throughout the visit, Amia adhered to Jamari's rules of engagement, flattery, praise, and reverence—wash, rinse, and repeat.

She did that while leaning on God for the extra heaping of patience and guidance which helped tremendously. His grace enhanced her tongue's restraint, allowing the words to fall in line, leading to the revealing recorded conversation.

"I spoke with Amia after she got back from USP Thomson," Marty started after Darren flipped him the championship football he'd been fidgeting with since the day ended.

"She told me that she hoped you'd get some closure with Marshon... I don't know if what I'm seeing looks like closure," he finished, returning the treasure back to its owner.

"How do you feel?"

"I don't know, Marty. Remember I told you a while back that I made my peace and closed that door? Honestly, Marshon could have died without ever having said another thing to me, and I'd have been good."

There was no wiggle in his voice. No doubt, or shred of hurt. Darren's eyes rested on the championship bowl ball which still bore the signatures of his college teammates and coaches. He slipped his fingers between the laces, inhaling deeply and exhaling slowly.

His attention traveled to an obscure white box resting on the brown curio cabinet's middle shelf. Marty's eyes followed suit, noticing the cube for the first time.

"He had himself shipped here."

Darren produced a final grey envelope. This one, however, wasn't weathered from processing. There was no metered stamp ushering aches into his heart. It was just an envelope. Folded neatly inside was Marshon's final letter to his son, written after Amia's visit.

*I was never the man I should have been. I knew how to be better. Your grandfather, my father, died when Desiree was pregnant with you. He was the best man and father I could have asked for. I hear you're just like him. I'm proud of you, Son. I wish I would have been the dad to you that mine was to me.*

*I hope you can find it in your heart to forgive me. I hope there's at least one good memory of me that you can share with Daniel and Christina. Amia showed me pictures. Danny looks like your granddad and Christina reminds me of Adrienne. Please keep looking after your sisters for me.*

*Amia asked me if I knew Jesus and prayed with me before she left. I don't know if I'll actually get through the gates, but she seemed pretty sure I would. I know why you love her so much, Son.*

*She's a good woman. Your mom was too. I pray I get to see her in heaven. It's been a few years since she left, and I miss her every day. I love you, Darren. I'm proud of you, and I'm sorry for the pain I caused. Love, Dad.*

Both men futilely blinked back tears as Marty tucked the letter back into the now-sacred envelope.

"I can't help but wonder if I hadn't shredded all those letters and gone to see him earlier, maybe we could have had a relationship before he pas—"

"Oh, that's what we're not gonna do," replied Marty, resting a firm hand on Darren's knee, dabbing the moisture on his cheek.

"Look at me, Son."

Darren's heart swelled. He recalled the conversations with Todd and Jamari and always noted that he'd been blessed enough to have two fathers, but the truth is, Darren had three.

Marty always loved and doted on that man. Darren was the son the father of three girls never had. In fact, Marty happily spent the better of two decades mentoring and guiding him.

Marty waited patiently as the man he'd befriended as a terrified teenager in an impossible situation lifted his eyes off the white leather between his hands to meet his.

"We talked about this after you opened the second letter almost two ago now. As a matter of fact, we sat right here, in this same spot late one night. Remember that?"

"Yeah, I remember. It was raining cats and dogs. We hung out until it let up and ended up putting a small dent in that Cognac."

"Wait now. That was more you than me," Marty recalled, smiling.

The elder partner stood to peer out over the blackened city. His slender hands resting in either pocket of his black slacks. "Come stand next to me."

The men stood in silence staring into the darkness.

"There's a mom out there wishing her love was enough to get her daughter to put those drugs down. There's a shy kid down there who's ready to lay it on the line and ask the popular girl to homecoming. A family over there is learning that the organ they've been praying for is now available.

"All of those are real situations. I know you wanted things to be different, but that's not what was written into your life story. God knew what Marshon's life was going to be. He also knew how it would end.

"Did you have a relationship with Marshon? No, and God's not surprised by that. Will you get to see him again? Yeah. I truly believe you will. Amia made sure of it—and God's not surprised by that either.

"You listen to me, Darren Wilford." Marty draped a slender hand around the solid shoulder of his friend, business partner, and son.

"Stop taking time away from your family by fantasizing about something that was never gonna happen. God has written some truly incredible experiences into your life, but there was never a relationship with Marshon Wilford added to the book of Darren. If it had been, you wouldn't be standing here talking about what ifs."

Marty pulled him in for a long side hug.

"I want you to take that imaginary chapter you keep trying to force into your life's story, put it in that white box over there on the shelf, and release every one of those pages when you scatter your father's ashes.

"He was far from perfect, but he gave us you, and for that, I'll be forever grateful to Marshon Wilford. You're an honorable man and a good son. That man died proud of you. Scatter his ashes somewhere nice and tell him all about your life while you're at it."

Darren's bald head snapped back as he turned towards Marty. An incredulous chuckle escaped his throat. Darren squeezed Marty tightly.

"Cards on the table?"

"Of course," Marty replied.

"I was angry when the warden's office called saying that Marshon wanted me to have his ashes. I initially told them no. Then, I agreed to take them. Thought I'd drop him off at the landfill. Then, the box showed up… I couldn't do it. Then I was pissed again.

"Now, I'm standing here with you, smiling, because I get to scatter his ashes.

"Wow…" he said, pausing to reflect. "Before you walked in here this evening, this wasn't a gift. It was a burden… Thank you, Marty—for everything. I love you, man."

Marty waited while Darren returned the football to its holder behind the corner curios' glass doors. The white box now sat next to the ball. It was nestled between a family photo, a snapshot of he and Danny's first 5K, and an undersized birthday bracelet made by Christina. He then collected his briefcase and other items.

"I saw that trick you pulled on Tyree about his BAR exam results today. I can't believe you got Judge Emmerson in on it. You're something else, Marty."

"He is one of the last ones. I had to get him," Marty added with a laugh. The duo continued chatting until exiting the elevators and pausing in the foyer.

"We should probably have those duffle bags vacuumed. I'm sure there's a gang of spiders and old fossils taking up residence in them," Darren said of the thirty-year-old green bags which had been staples of WW&M's history. The photo of the bags' owner was perched on the glass shelf above the luggage. With the hustle and bustle of life, they were rarely noticed anymore.

Darren's newly grateful state allowed him to pause and pay attention. He looked around the space, admiring the firm's trademark water fountain. That five-foot beauty had been the backdrop for everything from job offers to bar exam results to wedding proposals. A trend Darren started seventeen years ago when he proposed to Amia.

Darren's happy heart recalled that beautiful moment. He could still see her happy feet, could still hear her scream. He could see himself spinning her around in a circle in front of that fountain after she made him the happiest man on earth.

"Night, Marty. Drive safely. Give Vicky a kiss for me."

The unspeakable joy in Darren's heart emerged as a constant praise accompanying his return to Teeton Drive. It continued as he entered his blessed home, embracing the kids while drawing Amia into his complete wholeness—for the first time in years.

# Chapter 42

## *In a Word* – Breather

"They're back here!" yelled Daniel excitedly as he led Amia and Darren into Ramon and Elaine's new, cozy and well-shaded backyard. Jamari and Michele, now thirty-four weeks pregnant, were corralling energetic toddlers who were forever on the move.

Today they were celebrating Shamir's triumphant return to the track two years after returning home. Amia's heart smiled, thinking of all the times she'd told the slender, athletic cutie that he should be in pictures. Having survived the unimaginable, new-found celebrity status meant his lightly freckled face and thick waves were now everywhere.

While he hadn't taken the top spot on the podium, the now twenty-eight-year-old was on top of the world. He was once again a college student, weaving in and out of classes and embracing the hallowed orange and blue spirit that he'd longed for.

Though Andrew DeSimeon's plea deal forever relieved Shamir's worry of facing him again, a lasting side-effect of his ordeal was anxiety; specifically, fear for his safety.

His parents' cozy, brick split-level offered the perfect opportunity to rebuild his life while living comfortably off campus. The quaint home, nestled in a quiet, gated Baltimore suburb allowed him to unplug and almost disappear.

With Shamir being arguably one of the most famous people on the planet, security had become a constant presence, aiding in his peace of mind. Their continuous proximity helped him focus and not worry about being grabbed while switching classes or navigating across campus.

A constant reality for him now, Shamir was still getting used to crowds. Today's packed-out stadium was the largest to date. The standing ovation and extended applause as he stood on the infield for the first time in eight years was eclipsed only by the thunderous applause that accompanied his hard-fought third-place photo finish.

Shamir managed to close a fifteen-yard gap between himself and first place which resulted in all three front-runners leaning in at the final inches. The world watched as an obviously emotional Shamir was surrounded and hugged by overcome teammates and equally moved competitors.

As confidence boosting as the support he'd received today was, Shamir was thankful this afternoon's gathering was limited to familiar faces. Darren sought out his lovely wife, joining her on the patio to watch the endearing spectacle unfolding below.

Daniel, in none other than that orange and white striped cap, was glued next to his favorite uncle, showing him the finish-line photo, which was sure to become one of the most iconic signs of triumph ever. Elaine was brushing non-existent wrinkles out of the orange tablecloth while Ramon snapped photos.

Bria and Jordyn, both with sky high puffy ponytails boasting beads by Christina Bean Studios, were flanked by their respective beaus, alternating between content photos for their channels and posing for family mementos.

Amia leaned her head back into Darren's firm chest, inhaling the mixture of her man and the late spring breeze. Her extended exhale was in gratefulness for some calm in the midst of the family's seemingly endless ordeals. Shamir was back in his element.

The investigation into Bria finally concluded with her complete exoneration following Paul Bradley's confession. He'd eventually take a plea which essentially iced the cake on Andrew DeSimeon.

Once the dots connected confirming Drew Simon and Andrew DeSimeon were indeed the same person, the home which had held the youngest Copeland son captive for years was located. Scores of agencies converged on the property, finding the dungeon cleverly hidden at the back of the pantry.

Steven's remains were found buried in a shallow grave at the edge of the estate, confirming Shamir's suspicions that Simon had not taken Steven to the hospital in search of help.

Weeks later, forensics confirmed Steven O'Tannen's cause of death was a broken neck and suffocation. The report also indicated late-stage stomach cancer, explaining the pain, excessive weight loss and bleeding Shamir described.

The Coroner's report was damning, instantly adding capital murder and felony neglect to the myriad of charges facing Andrew DeSimeon.

Quoting the lead detective on Shamir's investigation, "While it was possible that Andrew DeSimeon attempted to kill Steven O'Tannen quickly by breaking his neck, the traces of dirt found in his lungs indicated that Steven did not die immediately."

Camille, Steven's widow, and his family properly laid him to rest with a second funeral. This time, it was with even more backing of his beloved Morgan State University, the NCAA, and political figures who were all as outraged as the world upon confirmation that the friendly, difference-making crusader had indeed suffered as gruesomely as Shamir described.

A few weeks after Steven's funeral, international news organizations broadcasted the family's in-person reactions to the demolition of the formerly pristine three-acre estate which had stood at the northwestern banks of the Chesapeake for almost seventy years.

Paul Bradley's confession corroborated Bria's revelation that she had paid the courier to drop the envelope off at the

Coastal Sounds two years earlier while the sisters were enjoying brunch. It explained how someone would have known Amia would be at the café that morning to receive the parcel.

The former prosecutor testified that he'd been blackmailing Bria for years, ever since convincing her that Darren had illegally started the Will Forward football camp with dirty money.

His well-spun story concluded with her big sister, the kindest heart Bria knew, serving years in prison and her precious Daniel and Christina growing up without their parents. Paul initially assured Bria that he wasn't planning to go to the police. Later though, the demands began.

"It started off small," Paul said in his recorded confession.

"I made Bria pretend to be interested in Amia and Darren's cases so she could share information with me to strengthen my cases. Then, I made her swipe Amia's keys or her wallet so she'd be late for court."

Paul also confessed to making Bria his personal transport, requiring that she deliver an assortment of documents, including the one she had dropped off at the Coastal Sounds Cafe that morning. He then confirmed Bria's claim that at some point, she refused to participate in sabotaging her family for the sake of saving them. She'd planned to come clean and tell Amia and Darren about Paul's 'evidence.'

"It was right around that time," Paul said, "that Bria Copeland began seeing Andrew DeSimeon. I mean, it couldn't have been more perfect. Andrew was a murderer who'd gotten off on a technicality. I no longer needed the original ruse.

"All I had to do was let the courts know that she, the sister and sister-in-law of two of the brightest attorneys in the Mid-Atlantic, was dating a cold-blooded killer."

The skilled prosecutor laid the demise of Amia and Darren's careers, their families, and WW&M out so well that Bria's only option was to remain complicit. After all, at the beginning of their relationship, Andrew appeared to be a wonderful guy.

Bria wholeheartedly bought the handsome charismatic sociopath's story about being framed by the police. He'd used the well-documented botched confession as proof supporting his sob story. Andrew played on her emotions, pretending to be devastated that law enforcement and the media still portrayed him as guilty.

While well-dressed and good looking, Bria's attraction and willingness to overlook Andrew's red flags were linked solely to her previously incredibly low self-esteem, of which the family only learned the depths of, at Daniel's birthday party.

Amia smiled as she watched her younger sisters continuously dazzle the man of the hour with each new uncovered dish. It made her think about another surprise the pair uncovered years earlier. Darren almost felt the grin stretching across her face, as he pulled her into him a little tighter.

"Babe," she whispered as he pecked her forehead, "I was just thinking about the day Trevaris' DNA test results showed up. Remember that?" she asked.

"Yep," he replied. A matching grin stretched across his face. The pair waved at Jordyn and Bria whose eyes had wandered in their direction at that very moment.

Years earlier, Paul Bradley sat in his large office surrounded by thousands of legal decisions encased within a hundred brown and blue leather-backed volumes aligning multiple bookshelves. He leaned back in his oversized arm chair reveling in the genius of his most recent agreement.

"This new catering contract with *Broke & Eating Good* is multipurpose. First, I earn more community favor by supporting a Black-owned minority business. Next, I'll be seen as a bridge-builder because that same minority business is owned by women who happened to be related to opposing counsel. It's a win, win for me," He said.

"This new relationship gives me unfettered access to Bria Copeland. She'll deliver any news and documents I want—whenever I want," he gloated.

"And the best part is no one will ever question why the sister and sister-in-law of two very prominent defense attorneys spends so much time visiting the prosecution's office," he added with a laugh as he touted the benefits of the flawless masterplan with Andrew DeSimeon, Paul's then partner in crime.

Andrew had been occupying one of Paul's two blue leather client chairs. Because they each had grievances with Amia and Darren, the pair crafted the plan together. Andrew "Simon" would convince Bria to approach Paul with a catering offer. Paul would, of course, accept their offer.

What Paul hadn't factored was Tori—his daughter, a huge fan of Bria and Jordyn's—reaching out to them. Tori knew of the sister's relationships to Amia and Darren through hundreds of *Broke & Eating Good* and *Broke With Reservations* posts featuring the family. Jordyn learned of the DNA results and Trevaris' plight during her week to review and respond to inbox messages.

Though Paul calculated the strategic partnership, he was woefully unaware that Amia would not only share advice and tidbits on her cases when asked by Bria, she'd also provide a few investigative secrets and tricks of the trade with her sisters. Amia was, of course, unaware of the ploy. Her reason for dropping the knowledge was in hopes it might inspire either of her younger sisters to lend their powerful voices to the field.

With Tori's email, Jordyn had something against Paul that she could use to pry her sister from under the prosecutor's thumb. Jordyn leveraged her relationship with Paul's then new clerk, who'd confirmed hearing his boss' expletive-laden outbursts aimed in Bria's direction. The former District Attorney hadn't counted on his love-struck intern sacrificing his dream job by fishing that folder out of his trash and turning it over to Jordyn.

“Paul Bradley is trying his grandson’s father for murder,” Jordyn said as she sat in a mom-and-pop coffee shop with Alex scanning the pages. “Is that legal?”

“I don’t think so,” Alex replied with sadness in his voice. “Jordyn, I’ve wanted this job since Paul was a guest speaker in one of my pre-law classes several years ago.” Alex shook his head, inhaling and exhaling slowly. “I wanted to be just like him...” He took a few additional drawn-out breaths. “He can’t get away with this, Jordie. Please show Darren and Amia immediately.”

“I will. Thank you, Alejandro,” Jordyn said as she quickly and tightly hugged the cute aspiring attorney. Jordyn dropped the envelope into the front seat of Amia’s Volvo using the key Bria swiped at Paul’s direction.

# Chapter 43

##  – Exhale

The family waved Amia and Darren over to the picnic tables. "Alright. We're coming," the pair replied in unison.

Amia slid in next to Elaine, blowing a loving kiss to Jordyn and Paul's former intern, now fiancée Alex, as he patted her there-but-barely belly. Braedon, another avid distance runner, bonded with Shamir almost instantly. They were undoubtedly breaking down today's soul-stirring two-mile event quarter by quarter.

The family enjoyed the festivities, good food, and each other's company well into the evening. As had become the norm, a new carton of cards, letters and gifts were ushered into the family's den for Shamir's eventual review.

"Do you really read all of these?" Jamari asked in awe at the volume that had arrived since yesterday's visit to the post office.

"Yeah," replied Shamir, equally surprised by the number of assorted envelopes.

"I mean... It's crazy. I was once an unknown twenty-year-old without a care in the world. Now, there are photographers climbing over each other to get a picture. The security team caught one guy in the neighbor's tree the other day.

"There are people willing to pay millions of dollars just to meet me... I don't know what to do with that," he added while patting a stylish brand-new pair of blue and orange Brooks which comfortably supported his slender, but proportioned frame. This was just one of thousands of gifts he'd received since the story of his remarkable return.

Scores of unrelenting media were clamoring for an exclusive interview which had been granted only two weeks before today's track meet.

Prior to her stunt at the Bear Heart event, and subsequently contacting the national news, Asley Tesleep would have been shoe in for the exclusive. Instead, Skylar Banks, another Will Forward alum and beat reporter at a well-known Georgia television station, was elevated to national attention. Ten years after taking his last snap as a camper, Skyler remained connected to Amia and Darren, sharing milestones, births and

Christmas photos, even asking for career advice after landing his dream job only two years earlier.

The Copeland family and WW&M attorneys agreed to Shamir sitting down with Skylar for an hour-long conversation. It was this interview which led to a lifetime supply of Brooks sneakers as these were the brand Shamir had been running in for the past several years.

"Welp," said Jamari, "with Elaine Copeland as your agent, publicist, and manager, you don't have to worry about any of that... You ain't talking to none of them." Laughter broke into the space as everyone acknowledged the amount of truth contained in that statement.

"I can only imagine what next week's mail drop is gonna look like," remarked Darren.

"Especially after today. Next week is gonna be insane. You gotta send me a video of that, Uncle Mir," Daniel said.

Eventually, trash talking—the tell-tale sign of Bid Whist—filled one outdoor picnic table. Darren and Elaine were in the midst of an epic Boston with Alex and Braedon as their latest victims. The other table was being 'monopolized' by Amia and Jamari, who were again emptying bank accounts and creating housing shortages.

Ramon surrendered the last of his earnings after his most recent release from jail and was now enjoying a cigar on the patio. While the well-placed outdoor lighting clearly illuminated cards and boards alike, they did not highlight the solemn, grateful tear he'd shed as he drank in the interactions.

The Copeland patriarch laughed as Darren slapped a deuce on the table, erasing the latest hopefuls, Bria and Shamir's, last hopes of making board. The artfulness of the card's spin paled in comparison to the coordinated robotic dances of the winners. Though a staple of the family gatherings, the full-throated laughter was a clear indicator that their celebration never got old.

Amia drank it all in, also shaking her head as she admired the antics. If Shamir had any lingering reservations about being welcomed back into the fold, Amia figured they were surely erased this evening. After all, only the most beloved family and friends were treated to this level of gloating.

Grateful smiles stretched across their faces as they nodded lovingly in the other's direction. The family fun stretched well into the wee hours, enjoying every moment before returning to their respective lives and upcoming festivities.

# Chapter 44

## *In a Word* – Confession

The WW&M staff sat in utter silence, some with mouths gaping open, others with hands partially covering dropped jaws. Other than a frequent crackle of wood popping in the roaring fireplace, the only other audible sounds in the massive living room were gasps.

They were gathered at Weeboy Manor, the impressive three-story log cabin on the banks of the Ohio River, owned by Marty Worthy. This beloved home had been in his family for generations, ever since his great-grandfather, Weeboy Worthy, settled into Pittsburgh well over a century earlier.

Marty and his wife, Vicky, hosted countless WW&M events here throughout the last forty years, sharing the home's beauty with his second family. This afternoon's event at

Weeboy Manor teemed with happiness and excitement but was also bittersweet as it was the backdrop for Marty's retirement.

Forty-two years after starting the now nationally acclaimed law firm with his dearly departed friend, Geoff Washington, Marty, was ready to exchange the courtrooms and trial dates in Pittsburgh for catamarans and bistros in Morocco.

The collective gasps hadn't been due to an unexpected retirement announcement. No, those sharp inhales and collective pouts came months earlier when Marty wrapped an all-staff meeting with that Earth-shifting revelation.

By now, everyone was fully prepared to say their goodbyes. They'd gotten in the last lunches and leaned in for the expert advice that would no longer bellow through the halls of the grand Victorian office. They'd gotten the signoffs and approvals. All that was left was to see one of their treasured cornerstones off.

The firm and their families were gathered, excited to share in one last toast. They were thrilled to share the tan and white electric bikes purchased with pooled funds which would surely lend to amazing memories for Marty and Vicky while enjoying holidays in the hills and valleys of Morocco.

The WW&M firm stared at the television screen trying to process what they were hearing and seeing. More silent questions began swirling as the families were asked to leave the sunken, ambient space for one final all-staff meeting. It was odd enough that Marty and Mike hadn't shown up for the retirement party. On top of that, they were kicking off the event with a meeting, and it was a Saturday.

Amia and Darren were as confused as everyone else. Though Darren was also a partner, he seemed to be the odd man out on the day's agenda. Amia knew Vicky and Sabrina, Mike's wife, would not be here. They'd been in Seattle for a conference and their flights were delayed due to storms in the Pacific Northeast.

She couldn't understand why the women were still so insistent that the retirement party carry on without them. This was Marty's retirement party, after all. It wasn't like they were going to have another one. Sure, Marty technically still owned WW&M, so he could have had another retirement party, but it was definitely odd.

Once he could no longer see children or non-staff members in Weeboy's spacious living room, Marty repositioned his telephone for the virtual conference. The collective gasps were in response to seeing Mike, Sabrina, and Vicky in the small, white room with him.

"As you know, I've never been one for parties thrown in my honor," started Marty. "I keep telling you all that and for some reason, you keep doing things like this," he said with a half-hearted laugh. It was met with an equally partial laugh.

"I'll get to the point, because you deserve to hear this from me."

"Actually," interrupted Mike Meyers, the M of the WW&M Law Firm.

"You should hear it from me... About thirty-five years ago, I brought a case to Marty and Geoff. The defendant, Mark Vittini, was a gangster. Marty knew it, but couldn't prove it.

Geoff and I reviewed his paperwork and we did our research on him. Everything checked out.

"Against Marty's better judgment, we stayed on retainer for Mark for years. He funneled tons of business our way. Again, all the paperwork checked out. Though Mark owned several bars and a couple of gas stations, Marty always thought there was something else to it, but we couldn't ever find anything.

"In our tenth year in business, we moved into the first floor of WW&M. We purchased the entire building in our thirteenth year. Right after that, Mark came in with two duffle bags full of cash. He also had deeds of sale for each of his six business that had been sold. Mark told me there was no one he trusted more than Worthy, Washington & Meyers to hold onto the money.

"Mark Vittini? His photo and duffle bags are in the foyer by the fountain. Marty, you've never said you were suspicious of the funds," remarked Darren. Marty remained silent.

"Again, to me and Geoff, everything looked legit," continued Mike.

"Marty didn't buy it. In fact, he wanted us to drop the bags off at the police department. Geoff told Marty that we would hold onto it for a week which is exactly how much time Mark needed to wrap up his affairs and return. We agreed if he wasn't back, we'd turn it in."

"Two weeks later..." Vicky began. "He hadn't returned. Instead, we received a certified letter from him telling us to keep it."

Vicky paused, taking a breath before continuing, "I convinced Marty to do good with the money. He wasn't certain where it came from, but we'd done our due diligence. There was a paper trail and it looked good," she explained.

"As the firm's accountant, I weaved the money into salary increases for the staff. We donated tons of money all over the country. We sponsored scholarships, and even used some of the money to renovate. Those of you who've been with us for a while remember us having to heat up food on that tiny white microwave while the kitchen was renovated."

Several members chuckled warmly recalling the month-long kitchen renovation and the minor inconvenience it caused.

"Darren," called Marty. Amia had begun making her way over to her husband as soon as Mike mentioned Marty's reservations about that particular client's finances. She knew exactly where this was going and by Darren's interlaced fingers on top of his head, she knew her husband was tracking the path as well.

"Darren," called Marty again.

He pulled his disbelieving eyes from the long dark ebony beam spanning the length of the space below the vaulted ceiling. Darren's heart sank and his temperature rose, cooling a bit as he felt Amia's loving hand rest on his shoulder.

"You're the only partner in this room. We need you," she whispered, almost sensing Darren's desire to walk out.

"The camp financing?" Darren asked hoarsely.

"Hang on a second," Amia challenged looking at the four beloved 'family members' huddled together in the small white room.

"What's with the unmarked room? Are all of you in Seattle? Why couldn't you tell us this in person?" she added, addressing the ten-thousand-pound, neon-green elephant in the room.

Just then, a blinking red dot appeared on the seventy-two-inch television screen. Immediately below it, was a message: 'Meeting Recording in Progress.'

# Chapter 45

## *In a Word* – Jarring

Another round of collective breaths, murmurs and muffled expletives preceded the departures of several more stunned WW&M associates. There was a pregnant pause as the foursome on the screen watched their treasured mentees and understudies quickly collecting their respective family members and leaving in disbelief.

"Jesus," murmured Darren as he turned back to the screen. Marty, Mike, Vivian, and Sabrina were still connected thanks to Amia. She'd grabbed the remote a smidge before Darren's thick angry fingers found the power button.

Marty and Vicky's youngest daughter, Trinity, saw the few remaining perplexed members of the staff out before returning to the awkwardly silent space.

"For some reason, I've lived the past ten years actually thinking I was a partner at this firm. Can you believe that?"

Darren asked the question sarcastically as he popped a handful of olives. Under normal circumstances, they would have been swirling along the bottoms of dirty martinis.

Unfortunately, the salty green treats had only made it into one triangular glass prior to the start of this strange afternoon meeting.

"Darren, Amia?" called Trinity as she reentered the room. Amia's eyebrow arched at the sight of the tall, stocky man who'd followed Trinity back in. His presence dominated the space just as it had the last time she'd seen him.

"Lionel?" asked Darren, his scowl instantly transitioning from angry to curious. His eyes met Amia's after venturing back to the screen. The pair noted that the quad in the nondescript white room were unsurprised by Lionel Hampton's presence. The Special Prosecutor firmly shook the confused couple's hands before perching on the oversized end chair.

"Well, damn," said Darren flatly. "Let's get it," he added, inviting the disclosures to begin while chasing the final olive with a club soda.

"Pause the recording, Mike," commanded Lionel calmly, his luxury leather oxfords waving casually from his outstretched legs.

"Everything should be on record," countered Marty.

Amia's breath caught in her throat as she swallowed. Everything on record was Marty's mantra when it came to practicing law, but was explicitly stated when the cases were explosive. Whatever was coming was about to shift the Earth's axis.

"Alright, everything on record," Mike said with a solemn nod. The blinking record light reappeared, almost seeming to do so in slow motion.

"Darren, during your initial interview," Mike started. "You told us about your dream of starting the camp. Geoff asked Vicky that day to figure out how we could help you get it off the ground.

"We understood what you wanted to do. We just wanted to ensure you could do it. We'd offered you cash and even tried to partially finance the camp to get it off the ground, but you, being you, refused to take anything. That was the year of the first bonus. We said that all attorneys received a bonus that year, but it was only you."

"Stop!" Darren commanded, his heart aching.

"You're telling me, it's true? Will Forwards' funding started with dirty money?"

"Son, we watched you draw up the plans. We watched you chase that dream, picking up footballs here, cleats and jerseys there," Marty added.

"Darren," tried Vicky.

"If we had known Will Forward would be the success it is today, we'd have never used any of that money. We just wanted to support your vision," she added with a strained voice.

"Marty," Amia snapped carefully. She loved and respected him and could see the pain on everyone's face on the screen, so she knew they understood the gravity. Amia also wanted to measure her temper as she did not want to fuel the inferno that was already boiling inside of Darren.

"And that's not all," added Mike solemnly.

"We purchased our current office with proceeds from the rest of that money we invested. The IRS is currently investigating that..." Mike dropped his head as the confession left his lips.

"Darren, I resigned this morning," he added with another pained breath.

"With Marty's retirement, you and I would have been the cornerstones, but with my lapses in judgment, I'm afraid I'd ruin the reputation you, Marty, and our beloved brother, Geoff created."

Amia swallowed hard at the realization that Darren would be the sole remaining partner. He was ready for co-partnership. She'd seen the plans that he and Mike drew up. She looked at her husband who was listening to the ongoing revelations in pure disbelief.

"Darren, that's why Lionel's here," chimed Marty. "He's obviously got enough experience to advise you until you find replacements for us."

"Advise me? What the Hell are you talking about, Marty? Where are you?"

"Marty, Morocco doesn't have an extradition treaty. Is that why you're retiring there?" Amia asked. Her voice teamed with fear and confusion. "Are you and Mike running? Is that why you're not physically here?"

"It's complicated," replied Vicky.

"It's complic— Where's the complexity? It's an easy yes or no..." exclaimed Amia, as aggravation appeared to finally grab the coolest head in the room.

"I'm sorry," Amia interjected.

"Marty, this reminds me of the evening you sat in our living room fifteen years ago and told me that your brother was actually my father. You and Vicky held onto that secret for almost thirty years. I thought we decided there'd be no more secrets?"

"We did," Darren cut in.

"Surely you remember that. Amia almost bled to death right there in that kitchen with our newborn next to her," he shouted angrily. The next sound was Darren's glass shattering after being launched in the kitchen's direction.

He was breathing fire at the memory of being shot by Marty's brother, Max, and the irony that it had happened here at Weeboy Manor, where yet another bombshell was launched into the atmosphere of the gated community. The fact was, Darren could still see the distressed, oak slats of the wrap-around porch's ceiling as he laid on his back, critically wounded.

Though fighting for his life, he could still remember Elaine emerging from inside Weeboy holding their newborn while covered in Amia's blood and screaming for Mable's help. Darren would forever remember begging his horrified mother to leave his side to care for his wife instead.

He vividly recalled the anguish on Mable's face as the retired ER nurse pressed Elaine's hands into his wound, commanding that she hold the pressure and keep him talking before retreating into the home to care for Amia.

Helplessness and terror were not feelings welcomed by anyone, especially Darren. His life-long immediate response to both was action and aggression. The latter of which explained the glass's impromptu collision with the brown fieldstone wall.

"Oh, for the love of God," bellowed Lionel, who'd been watching the emotional scene unfold.

"Ladies, could you escort your husbands in here before this ruse goes too far sideways," he added, smiling at the folks on the screen.

# Chapter 46

## *In a Word* – Speechless

Voices and footsteps began wafting back into the living room as the 'astonished' staff and their families who'd 'left' earlier began emerging from various hallways and corridors. They were all in on the once-in-a-lifetime hoax.

Marty, Mike, and their spouses reentered the living room, each pointing at Amia and Darren whose mouths were still gaping. Amia's hand was affixed to her mouth as the realization they'd been the unwitting victims of Marty's most elaborate prank ever, hit her.

The pair was speechless, though Darren, a bit more than Amia. In his twenty plus years at the firm, Marty had never been able to pull one over on him. Darren recounted the numerous attempts, all of which had been thwarted. He thought of all the heavy hitters Marty called in for his previously failed plots.

Darren knew the story of Mark Jorgenson and the bundles of cash. That was legend, but it was Mike tying his bonus to dirty money that set the hook. After all, this was the same bonus that Paul Bradley repeatedly proclaimed never existed.

Amia playfully pushed Marty and Mike's extended arms away, refusing to hug the prankster partners. Her mouth was still gaping, but bore a huge incredulous smile. She could not believe it. Amia then turned to all of the WW&M staff, throwing evil laughing eyes at them for being complicit.

"Imma pay for that glass," Darren said as he hugged Marty, lifting him off the floor while congratulating the soon-to-be retiree for finally getting him. Mike, on the other hand, was immediately informed that his day was coming. The pair laughed and hugged, with Darren still shaking his head.

"I finally, finally get to retire!" Marty said. "I was ready to go ten years ago, but there was no way I could have retired in peace without getting you," goaded Marty as he nonchalantly stirred the olive in his dirty martini.

"How did you-" Amia's words stopped short as she was still completely flabbergasted.

"Remember during Paul's confession when he told the detectives they should look into Darren because there was no bonus?"

"Yeah," she replied, accepting a kiss on the forehead from her husband who was slowly collecting himself. Marty winked at Darren as he continued.

"When Paul said there was no bonus, he was wrong. There was a bonus. He didn't get one that year, because we paid for his Continuing Education classes and Errors & Omission insurance.

"Yeah," added Mike who'd just joined the trio at the bar.

"I remember that nonsense. Paul Bradley was always something else. I wasn't feeling him at all, but you know, he and Geoff were Frat brothers, so we gave him a shot."

"Honestly, he's lucky I didn't fire him on the spot for not completing the recertifications and letting his insurance lapse, but I was always trying to help you young attorneys get your footing. We actually cut Paul loose not long after that. One complaint was enough, but after a second complaint of him being abusive towards our staff, he had to go.

"Getting back to the bonus though. Besides me, Mike, and Geoff, you and Paul were the only other attorneys at WW&M at that time.

"The three of us decided to pool our cuts of the bonus and added it to what we'd planned to give you. We figured it would be enough to get Will Forward off the ground and leave some spare change," Marty said.

Amia's heart swelled in unison with Darren's. They choked back tears as the partners embraced yet again.

"Darren, remember the night we talked about you spreading Marshon's ashes? Well, you mentioned Mark Vittini's duffle bags being dusty. I'd honestly forgotten all about them, but that's when I got the idea to tie them together."

"God, Marty. You got me so good," Darren replied, his hand slapping his chest. "I still can't believe this."

Marty tipped his glass, winking at Darren. His smile would not leave his face. The satisfaction of getting the one person who was unfoolable was too gratifying. He took a moment to allow that to sit in, before letting them in on another tidbit of information. Why not, right?

"There were actually only two times that the three of us pooled funds rather than using them individually. I just told you about the first. The other time was when we hired Amia."

Amia tilted her head in response, trying to figure out what he meant.

"Do you remember what you requested as a starting salary?"

"Probably not since that was a loonnng time ago," Mike added teasingly.

"You know what, Mike Meyers?" Amia replied. Darren pretended to hold his wife back as she threw up the dukes. Marty took a sip of his merlot before continuing.

"Your interview was the week before we paid the bonuses out. When I went back to Geoff and Mike, I asked them if they would chip a portion of their bonus towards your salary. I couldn't put my finger on it... I didn't know who you were or anything about you, but I told them that I thought you could be a game changer for WW&M."

Mike nodded in response, before adding, "We've obviously seen our share of outstanding candidates through the years, but there has only been one who Marty was that confident about. He kept saying, 'There's something about her. I can't put my finger on it, but she's special. We have to make an offer she can't refuse.'"

"We three chipped in our funds and that's how you got $15,000 more than your asking salary," Marty concluded.

"I remember that..." Amia said as she began connecting the dots. She was excited but wondered what she was getting herself into with that significant of a pay increase. She remembered the call with Elaine and Ramon, sharing her concerns with her parents. Ramon reminded Amia of WW&M's prestige; assuring her that they knew talent when they saw it.

Her jaw was again open though completely deprived of words. Instead, another round of hugs abounded as glasses clinked. The amount of love that spilled from that corner of real estate was indescribable, and a decades-long bond somehow grew stronger.

Amia always admired the integrity and heart of her beloved WW&M. She'd wanted to be a part of this incredible conglomerate since hearing about them while in college and applied, hoping for the best. Twenty years later, she was still in love with the firm and in awe of its leadership.

"God is good," she said simply.

"All the time!" they replied.

The conversation paused as Marty's phone rang and chatted warmly with the caller. Shortly thereafter, he was back.

"That was Jamari wishing me a happy retirement. He couldn't make it because Michele's got those third-trimester aches and can't get comfortable. Man, I remember those days," he laughed. "He's on back rub and foot massage duty while entertaining the twins this evening."

"Only four weeks to go," Amia said excitedly of her new niece or nephew's arrival. "We cannot wait to meet him or her."

"That young man still inspires me every day. What he has done with his life… It's remarkable." Marty looked away as a mist began filling his eyes. After all, he'd also had a front-row seat to Jamari's evolution from a wayward, rebellious teen.

Amia smiled fondly at her boss and mentor. It was going to be weird walking the halls of WW&M and not seeing him. They were going to miss the quiet steady power that defined his presence. Amia wondered how incredible Marty must feel seeing all the fruits of his life's work continuing on without him.

As that final thought crossed her mind, Vicky returned, retrieving her husband, the man of the hour. Marty gave a moving speech to the staff, thanking them for their commitment to justice and community service. He thanked his partners, Mike and Geoff, for believing in his vision of a barrier-breaking law firm that would be a beacon and pillar of excellence.

Marty credited his extreme patience and knack for trust-building to a meeting with a fourteen-year-old at a juvenile detention center over thirty years earlier. Marty told the staff that he didn't sleep for weeks because "that stubborn kid named Darren Wilford refused to talk."

He thanked Darren for changing his life, ending with, "I love you, Son."

"Here, here," was the resounding response as everyone lifted their glass in honor of the Lion of WW&M. Before setting down the mic for the last time, Marty acknowledged Amia, thanking her research and intuition for giving WW&M its staunch reputation for uncovering the truth.

He cited her hunch less than six months into the job which led to a shocking acquittal in an embezzlement case. Marty confessed that WW&M had only taken the case as a favor and they knew it was a loser, but the case was high profile. He knew that, win or lose, they'd have a national footprint as a result.

Darren proudly hugged his wife while listening to Marty pour on the praise. He recalled the instant attraction as he watched her follow Janelle to a small desk on the opposite side of the office just over nineteen years earlier.

He remembered Amia timidly knocking on his door to get his opinion about her hunch. Being new, she didn't want to go to the partners with something that may have been nothing, so chose to bounce her thoughts off Darren. He smiled, recalling his gripping a stress ball to make himself focus on the words and not on the easy beauty who had just illuminated his doorway.

"Amia, thank you for being you," Marty continued. "Thank you for being the big sister to my and Vicky's girls. I'll never forget you coming to Geoff, Mike and me to ask, correction, to tell us that you were taking in your brother, Jamari, and that you needed to move some things around. I remember you had an idea of how it would work. No... Actually, that's not right either," he smiled.

"Let me tell y'all... This Sista right here told us exactly how things were gonna work and exactly when they were gonna happen. Didn't she, Mike?"

"Hashtag, truth. I was scurred," Mike replied, faking a shiver. Marty paused, allowing the laughter to die down. He was absolutely going to miss that wit.

"Mike, how about you fly in on Fridays for comedy hour?" he said, as Mike raised his glass to his long-time friend. "Sabrina, I promise to send him back every Sunday.

"But seriously, Amia. We understood what you were doing, and we were one hundred percent there for it. As a twenty-six-year-old young lady, you had more guts than most of us then forty and fifty-year-old men... Honey, you taught every single one of us what courage and bravery meant, and you still teach us that to this day. A rousing, "Here, Here," preceded a long round of applause.

"I'll close with this, Amia Wilford. One W in WW&M is retiring... You have a W, and when you're ready, we would love to see Worthy, Wilford & Meyers become Wilford, Wilford & Meyers."

"Yeah, that was one of the things we talked about while we were in Morocco a few minutes ago," added Mike.

# Chapter 47

## *In a Word* – Partners

The applause had long since died down. Staff and family members had electric slid, cupid shuffled, wobbled, and twerked well into the evening. Photos with Marty had been taken, stories of lives changed because of him had been told.

The remaining attendees gathered on the back terrace for drinks and small talk with Marty one last time. Trinity, Weeboy's new owner along with sisters Faith and Hope, were chatting on the west side with Shamir and Jordyn's fiancée, Alex. He'd just celebrated his one-year anniversary at WW&M and had to be there for the legend's sendoff. Amia smiled as she watched Shamir engaging with the young women.

*Crazy how time flies,* she thought. When she met the girls, they were eleven, ten, and eight. Now, Trinity was in her thirties with the younger two knocking on club thirty's door.

Amia then turned to Elaine and Ramon who were conversing with Marty and Vicky. Marty and Elaine, forever bonded by a horrific night in California forty-plus years ago, were saying their goodbyes.

He hugged her and Ramon knowingly. Though assured and reassured that he was not responsible for Elaine's assault at the hands of his brother, Max, Marty still needlessly bore some of the burden. No doubt, these extended hugs and final goodbyes between Marty, Elaine, Ramon, and Vicky included one final heartfelt apology. It would undoubtedly have been countered by an equally final thank you to Marty for his role in sending his serial rapist brother to prison.

"Babe," asked Amia who'd returned from seeing her parents and Shamir out. They'd decided to turn in, staying at Amia and Darren's for the night. There was no way they'd miss Marty's retirement and seeing him and Vicky off.

"Did Marty really suggest that I could be a partner? There's Gerard, Malcolm, Saritha and Eddie; all of them are amazing attorneys, and I know they've expressed an interest. I've never even thought of it. Why would he and Mike think of me for that? I'm flattered obviously, but it's crazy."

"Crazy, why? Sure, they are all beasts in the court and could be partner, but you shadowed Marty for years and you're my wife. You've got insight that none of them have."

"I guess. it's just weird that he'd say it here in front of everyone. I've literally never said anything."

Darren gazed into his wife's eyes. Her coils softly reflecting the direction of the night's breeze.

"I asked them to consider you because, in my opinion, you're the best person for the job, and no. I'm not saying that because you're my wife.

"You are gifted, Babe. The firm respects you. Hell, the entire Legal community respects you. You know the corporate side and you drop deuces in the courtroom," he added, once again thanking God for allowing him to be in this amazing woman's life.

Amia's heart raced, her jugular thumping in response. She was confident in her abilities. She knew she was a skilled attorney. Her service leadership approach meant she had an unending amount of favor from her peers. It's just that she'd never considered herself for the role. In fact, she was content and fulfilled in her current role.

Her entire being went giddy as the notion sunk in. She wrapped her long arms around her soulmate who held onto her tightly. Darren recognized her abilities so much that he recommended her for partner. Amia's lips found his in the moonlight. An eightieth dimension of love opened between the pair on that terrace.

"Thank you," she managed, hoarsely.

"For what?" he responded. "The fact that you're the only one on the list is all you're doing."

Amia tilted her head again, not understanding why the attorneys she'd just named were not on the table.

"Why are they not considering others?"

"Mike and I decided that he and I would be the only partners at WW&M… that is, unless and until you said yes," he added with those beautiful dimples adorning that incredible smile.

"I love you."

"Annnd, we're outta here," Darren announced following her suggestive strokes of his palm. They'd been left alone on the expansive space as Mike, Marty, and Marty's college roommate and best friend Lionel, enjoyed one final night cap in front of the fire.

The pair caught the tail end of Marty ribbing Lionel for his endless appetite of high-end goods. This came as he admired the silver Cartier timepiece decorating his old friend's wrist.

"Well, I've paid my dues. I've paid my tithes, and I've even paid my taxes," he bellowed under his breath.

"Plus, it's my understanding that I can't take it with me," he added, pausing to rub a smudge from a lens of his woodgrain finish Burberry eyeglasses. Lionel's tone reminded Amia of a late-night R&B disk jockey.

The pair collected their sleeping youngsters from the extra comfy sofas of Weeboy Manor's sunken living room, stealing one additional ogle of Lionel's wide-faced platinum ticker. The stately manor appeared even more grand as they took it all in, understanding this era was ending.

Amia reveled in the nostalgia, grateful for the memories this place lent to their lives. Though still in the Worthy family, the number of events at Weeboy would decrease dramatically with Marty and Vicky's departure. Everyone accepted that reality.

The final hugs ensued. They exited the three-story log cabin's eight foot wooden and glass double doors, stepping into the next phase of WW&M. Amia turned to her mentor whose arm was around his better half's waist.

"I accept your offer, with one condition."

Intrigue stretched across each partners' face.

"Do tell," replied Marty.

"Alright, Counselor. State your terms," Darren said.

"Oh, Lordt hammercy," Mike groaned.

Amia waited until all the patio occupants regained their composure.

"I want to expand WW&M Pro Bono. We could get admin assistance from undergrads and paralegal assistance from grad students. It would be the perfect internship. We could scale the business model."

"The Pro Bono division is here because you and Janelle had an idea ten years ago," Marty began. "We've done a ton of good with that division. The Trevaris Reynold's case came to us from the Pro Bono wing, if I remember correctly," Marty said.

"It did," Amia replied.

"I was at the Pro Bono office a couple years ago meeting with one of the clients and overheard a few of our paralegals talking about his case."

"That is right," Mike said. "I remember you "politely" taking over one of the staff meetings and arguing that his case should be taken by one of us. You didn't think his case should have been handled by our newer attorneys. I think you actually followed us to our cars that night."

Amia smiled. Her mild-tempered reputation was matched only by her unyielding persistence. If she believed in something, she wasn't letting go. With the Partners reserved parking spots being right next to each other, she chose to hang out at work until they were ready to leave.

Amia met them as they were heading out, talking up the case and its inconsistencies in the hallway, onto the elevator, through the foyer and into the well-lit parking lot. Once the partners agreed they should review the case, it came down to capacity. Neither of them had room.

Marty was advising on a high-profile politician's case in Washington, DC. Mike was busy with his ailing parents who'd recently moved in, and Darren was buried in a stack of cases as well as his camp responsibilities.

"You should take Trevaris' case, Amia," Darren suggested back then. "You're just as good—if not better than me, Mike and Marty—and deep down you know it."

She knew her track record. She knew she was good, but she felt that case needed a bulldog—someone who wasn't afraid to speak their mind. Ultimately, Darren took the case, but only after Amia offered to sit second chair.

"Sounds like WW&M Pro Bono is expanding," Marty said. "I love it."

"Agreed. We'll draw it up," Darren promised, smiling through swelling emotions.

"Done," said Mike. "All jokes aside, Amia. If Darren hadn't beaten me to the punch, I would have put your name in the hat for Partner. I play around and love to have fun, but hear me loud and clear, because I'm dead serious right now. We know some incredible attorneys—near and far. All of them agree that there's not a better pick than you for the role.

Amia's eyes traveled to Marty and Vicky, then Mike and Sabrina, all of whose smiles widened as Amia realized they'd been touting their next choice for Partner to industry peers. She then connected with the loving eyes that had been proudly gazing down at her all evening.

"Oh, so y'all are just full of surprises, huh?"

Amia's nodding smile said it all, though she still made it official.

"I would be honored to partner with you at WW&M."

Marty and his niece shared an extended hug. He was her second father, and Amia was going to miss him. True, Marty and Vicky would be in town for another month, but it still felt like goodbye. "I love you, Marty. Thank you for everything."

"I love you too, Amia Wilford. And, I'm going to miss you, but I'll enjoy retirement so much more knowing you'll be there, keeping these two in check."

Amia squeezed him tighter.

"We'll visit."

"You'd better," he replied, kissing her cheek. "Go be great, Amia Wilford. I'm so godly proud of you."

Amia couldn't speak. She just squeezed him once again before moving on to hug Vicky tightly. It was now Darren's turn to embrace his dear friend. He thanked Marty again for believing in him and changing his life.

"I believed in you, but me changing your life? No, Sir. I didn't, and won't take any credit. You changed your own life, Son... Mine too... I thank God more times than you know for writing you into my life's story. I am a better man because of you."

This time, it was Marty from whom words escaped. The friends and partners shared an equally extended embrace as Amia turned to hug Mike and Sabrina after promising Vicky that she'd keep an eye on the girls.

"See you Monday, Partner," she said contently.

Darren pulled their new gray Audi SUV back into the finished garage. Each parent extracted an exhausted youngster, ushering them up the carpeted stairs and into their respective rooms. Christina quickly went to the restroom, slipped on PJs and crawled into her princess canopy bed.

Amia then snuck back downstairs to check on her parents and Shamir, who were all sound asleep. She returned to Daniel's room to bear witness to the fun. As expected, Daniel, an exceptionally hard sleeper, had to be stripped, redressed, then positioned into the lower-level of his. charcoal bunkbed.

Amia smiled, watching her husband wrestle with his limp, flopping body, laughing inwardly as Darren declared Daniel would be sleeping in whatever he was wearing when he fell asleep from here on out.

Her heart was full. Amia began to thank God for his goodness. Her arms stretched to the heavens as she kneeled on the beige carpeting. She was clear on God's unyielding favor and the endless blessings that He heaped upon her family.

Amia said another prayer of thanksgiving for her parents, sisters, their partners, and her brother. She thanked God for Janelle and Todd and the health of their family. She prayed for traveling mercy for everyone on the road.

Finally, Amia said a grateful prayer for her husband, the man who was everything her heart desired. Darren peered out at his beautiful wife, literally his partner in life, on her knees in the hallway. Daniel's room fell dark as he switched the soccer-inspired table lamp off to join her, closing the door behind.

The couple held each other and gave thanks, praising God for his goodness and mercy. Eventually, their lips touched. The fitted polo was hoisted from that one pair of jeans that Amia absolutely loved. Darren stood, lifting his wife with him. Her eyes never left his as the black and green checkered garment stretched over his bald head, leaving a chiseled masterpiece in its wake.

"Why are you so fine, though?" Amia whispered as the chocolate specimen—her chocolate specimen—stood bare chested before her. Darren didn't reply, at least, not audibly. Instead, he began eating her alive with his eyes. That seductive leer was intensified by an incessantly slow, unconscious licking of his lips.

The raw intensity was causing Amia to fumble with the last button of her one-shouldered blouse. He licked his lips again as he recalled observing her smooth skin disappearing behind each button and loop closure as she got dressed hours earlier. His mouth watered at the visual of her thighs lending their amazing curves to those cherry red capris which had been distracting him all night.

Though he could have happily spent a couple of forevers watching Amia undress, Darren had waited long enough. His strong hands drew her body into his as their tongues engaged in a delicious battle. The asymmetrical top hit the carpet within seconds. Amia's hands began undoing his belt as she was urged backward towards their bedroom.

"Stay right there," he commanded with a wanton gaze and raspy tone. He bounded softly down the stairs and into the kitchen, returning with his blazer which he'd dropped while attempting to steady Daniel. That was in one hand. In the other was an open jar of delicious Coastal Sounds peach jam.

Darren traced some of that sweet goodness along Amia's neck, quickly following it with his tongue. Amia took the opportunity to lap and suck the remnants from around and between his thick fingers as she continued her backwards motion. Darren retrieved his polo and Amia's blouse before the thick, frosted bedroom doors locked behind them.

"Babe," she said with a seriousness that pulled his attention away from the lovely globes which he'd just freed from the strapless bra's enclosure. His eyes connected with hers and his heart sank, knowing the conversation that had been looming on the horizon had finally arrived. He held her tightly before motioning Amia to join him on the bed.

"We do so much good with Pro Bono. With an expansion, we're going to have even more new attorneys and more demanding cases."

Darren swallowed past the lump in his throat. He knew his wife and was fully aware of Amia's undying passion for WW&M Pro Bono. She'd done amazing work with this division. He just didn't want to envision a world without-

"That's gonna need a leadership presence almost daily," Amia continued, taking a deep pained breath because, while excited, she was also struggling.

"Amia," Darren began. The emotions that began rising when she mentioned wanting to expand the Pro Bono wing had returned. "I knew when I put your name in as Partner that there was a chance you'd trade our office for that one."

He squeezed her again trying to ease the ache of change. For twenty years, the pair had eaten lunch in each other's offices, flirted in the breakroom, and even tag-teamed WW&M staff meetings in matching outfits.

"Pro Bono is as successful as it is because of you," he said bravely while dabbing his wife's conflicted tears. "You're supposed to be there," he managed.

"I'm so sorry, Darren. That means we won't see each other as much... I'm throwing a wrench in the Partner plan. I know you and Mike-"

"Hold up, Mia. Pro Bono has been calling you for years. Don't apologize for answering. God laid that on your heart and look what has happened with you just being there once a week."

Darren paused. The crushing sadness that accompanied his being unable to drop off a two cream, three sugar laden cup of Joe at Amia's desk every morning had almost disappeared. In its place was joy and pride. He'd gotten to bring his wife coffee every morning for years and bounce ideas off of her at the office. Now, this woman who'd put everyone's cares above hers, was getting ready to walk into her purpose.

"You listen to me, Amia Wilford," he said wrapping his strong hands around hers. "All Mike, Marty and I wanted was for you to be a Partner at WW&M. You are now a Partner. Sweetheart, whether you're physically in our downtown office or based at Pro Bono, doesn't matter. You're our Partner," he added with a gleaming smile, before adding. "Do you know what's gonna happen when you're over there with Janelle devoting full-time attention?"

Amia smiled. She was fully aware of the impending impact and was grateful for the opportunity. As a bonus, she'd get to spend more time with bestie, Janelle, who'd been serving as office administrator since its launch ten years earlier. The move would also allow their husbands and best friends, Darren and Todd, to see more of each other since Darren would undoubtedly be popping into Pro Bono regularly.

She dipped a slender finger into the peachy deliciousness that had been set on the nightstand when she settled onto the bed next to her soulmate. Soon enough, Amia Wilford would begin an amazing journey, approaching the bench as the newest partner of the prestigious WW&M law firm and head of their highly-regarded flagship initiative. These adventures were sure to bring their shares of twists and turns. For now, the briefcases and posturing would have to wait. Darren's raspy breaths danced in her ear as she slowly licked the jam from his shoulder.

"I hope you didn't plan on getting any sleep tonight, Partner," Darren whispered.

"Mmmm, haven't you heard, Partner?" Amia replied slyly. "Sleep's overrated." Her short, French-manicured nails began leaving trails of flavored yumminess across his thick lips.

"Hold that thought," she said as she grabbed her vibrating phone from the sleek nightstand. Under normal circumstances, the new messages would have waited, but in this instance, Amia and Darren's phones simultaneously registered the late-night back-to-back notifications.

"Oh my God!" Amia screamed turning her phone towards Darren and scooting quickly back off their bed. "I guess we know why Michele couldn't get comfortable," she said of Jamari's reason for missing Marty's retirement party.

"Look at that," Darren's wide grin outshined hers in the darkness as he also reversed course on their king-sized bed. Just then, Amia heard Elaine and Ramon urgently calling her name. Their phones had also received the new group messages.

"It's a boy," Amia cried happily as she glanced back at the photo showing her brother, Michele, and their healthy newborn who'd decided to move his scheduled arrival up by four weeks.

"I got Chrissy. You've got Dan," she joked as she raced her husband in getting dressed. She hopped into a pair of joggers, dragging a T-shirt over her head which would be used as the excuse for her wild, stretched strands.  Amia excitedly opened their door followed closely by Darren as they met her overjoyed parents and Shamir.

## *In Two Words* – The End

# About the Author

Shamicka C. Toney loves to write entertaining Christian stories featuring real-world, relatable issues that anyone can identify with. Imperfect characters with rich backstories and believable flaws only make her books more engaging. She finds other perspectives deeply fascinating and wishes to expand her understating of the world to help her write even richer stories.

Shamicka has been married to her wonderful husband for nineteen years and is a mother to three incredible, upstanding young men in their twenties. When she's not writing, she loves painting, spending time with her family, meeting new people, and experiencing all life has to offer. She loves to laugh, learn new things, and hone her skills. Shamicka hopes that all people — religious and not — will enjoy her heartwarming stories of love, family values, and courage.

Hi there,

I truly hope you've enjoyed reading Approaching the Bench and would love to hear your thoughts! Please consider leaving a review. You can visit my website at www.shamickatoney.com or simply scan the below QRC:

Click SHOP and on the image for Approaching the Bench. Scroll to the Write a Review link and click that to leave your feedback.

You may also click the Contact Us tab to send a message or leave a review. Hit subscribe and stay up-to-date on events and get previews of merchandise and future novels.

Thank you, again! Blessings.

–